. Ouida

Held in bondage or Granville de Vigne

. Ouida

Held in bondage or Granville de Vigne

ISBN/EAN: 9783742889812

Manufactured in Europe, USA, Canada, Australia, Japa

Cover: Foto ©Andreas Hilbeck / pixelio.de

Manufactured and distributed by brebook publishing software
(www.brebook.com)

. Ouida

Held in bondage or Granville de Vigne

"HELD IN BONDAGE;"

OR

GRANVILLE DE VIGNE.

𝔄 𝔗𝔞𝔩𝔢 𝔬𝔣 𝔱𝔥𝔢 𝔇𝔞𝔶.

By OUIDA.

"A young man married is a man that's marred."—SHAKESPEARE.

IN THREE VOLUMES.
VOL. II.

LONDON: TINSLEY, BROTHERS,
18, CATHERINE STREET STRAND.
1863.

CONTENTS OF VOL. II.

"HELD IN BONDAGE;"

OR,

GRANVILLE DE VIGNE.

CHAPTER I.

" L'AMITIÉ EST L'AMOUR SANS AILES."

SCARCELY anyone was in town except a few very
early birds, heralds of the coming season, and
the Members, victims to an unpitying nation;
but there were still some people one knew dotted
about in Belgravia and Park Lane, others in
jointure-houses or villas up 'Tamese Ripe,' among
them a very pretty widow, Leila Lady Puffdoff,
who dwelt in the retirement of her dower-house
at Twickenham, and enlivened the latter portion
of her veuvage by *matinées musicales*, breakfasts,
and luncheons for some of those dear friends who
had been the detestation of *le feu* Puffdoff. To
a combination of all three, Sabretasche, De Vigne,
Curly, a man called Monckton, and myself, drove

in De Vigne's drag a day or two after our ren-
contre with little Alma Tressillian.

'An amateur affair, isn't it ?' asked De Vigne.
'Artistes' morning concerts are bad enough, where
Italian singers barbarize "Annie Laurie" into an
allegro movement with shakes and aspeggios, and
English singers scream Italian with vile British
o's and a's; but amateur *matinées musicales*, where
highly-finished young beauties in becoming morning toilettes excruciate one's ears, whether they
have melody in their voices or no, just because
they have been taught by Garcia or Gardoni, are
absolutely unbearable. Don't you think so, you
worshipper of harmony?'

' I ? Certainly,' responded Sabretasche. 'As
a' rule, I shun all amateur things. Where professional people, who have applied sixteen hours
a day, all their energies, and all their capabilities,
to one subject, even then rarely succeed, how is it
possible but that the performances of those who
take up the study as a pastime must be a mise-
rable failure, or at best but second-rate? Occasionally, however (indeed, *whenever* you see it,
but the sight is so rare !), talent will do for you
without study more than study ever will—'

'As you will show us in your songs this morning, I suppose ?' laughed Monckton.

'If I sang ill I should never sing at all,' replied Sabretasche, carelessly, with that consciousness of power which true talent is as sure to have, as it is sure *not* to have undue self-appreciation. 'I mean, however, in Miss Molyneux's Aria; even you will admire that, De Vigne.'

'Violet?' said Monckton. 'She does sing tolerably; but I can't say I like that girl—so much too satirical for a woman.'

'I dare say you may find her so. I know popular preachers who consider Thackeray too satirical as an author, because he drew the portrait of Charles Honeymann,' said Sabretasche, quietly.

'Something new to hear the Colonel defending a woman's character,' whispered the injured Monckton to me on the back seat. 'He generally is more the cause of blackening 'em, eh?'

Sabretasche was quite right; it was a treat to hear Violet Molyneux's rich, passionate, bell-like voice. We, just at that time barren of Prime donne, had heard nothing like it of late; and Violet's voice was really one which, as a professional, would have ranked her very high. Besides, there was a tone in it, a certain freshness and gladness, mingled with a strange pathos and passion, which moved even those among her auditors

most blasés, most fastidious, and most ready to
sneer, into silence and admiration.

'That is music,' said De Vigne, in the door of
the music-room. 'If she would sing at morning
concerts I would forswear them no longer. Look
at that fellow; if he be ever really caught at all,
it will be by her voice.'

I looked at 'that fellow,' being Sabretasche,
who leaned against the organ, close to Violet
Molyneux; his face was calm and impassive as
ever, but his melancholy eyes were fixed upon her
with such intense earnestness, that Violet, glancing
up at him as she sang, coloured, despite all her
self-possession, and her voice was unsteady for
half a note. Lauzun though the Colonel was, I
believe Violet's voice pleased him still more than
her beauty. The latter beguiled the senses, as
many others had before; the former beguiled the
soul, a far rarer charm!

'You came late; half our concert was over?'
said Violet to him, after luncheon, as they stood
talking in a winter-garden, one of the whims—
and a very charming whim, too—of the Puffdoff's.

'I came in time to sing what I had promised,
and to hear what I desired, your—'

'You did like it?'

'Too well to compliment you on it. I "liked" it as I liked, or rather I *felt* it—as I have felt, occasionally, the tender and holy beauty of Raphael, the hushed glories of a summer night, the mystical chimes of a starlit sea. Your voice did me good, as those things did, until the feverish fret and noise of practical life wore off their influence again.'

Violet gave a deep sigh of delight.

'You make me so happy! I often think that the doctrine of immortality has no better plea than the vague yearning for something unseen and unconceived, the unuttered desire which rises in us, at the sound of true music. I have heard music at which I could have shed more bitter tears than any I have known, for I have had no sorrow, and which answered the restless passions of my heart better than any human mind that ever wrote.'

'Quite true; and that is why, to me, music is one of the strangest gifts to men. Painting creates, but creates by imitation. If a man imagine an angel, he must paint from the woman's face that he loves best—the Fornarina sat for the Madonna. If he paint a god, he must take a man for model; anything different from man would be grotesque· We never see a Jupiter, or a Christ that is anything more than a fiercely-handsome, or a sadly-handsome man. Music, on the contrary, creates from a spirit-world of its own: the fable of Orpheus and its lyre is not wholly a fable. In the passionate crash and tumult of an overture, in the tender pathos of one low tenor note, in the full swell of a Magnificat, in the low sigh of a Miserere, the human heart throws off the frippery and worry of the world, the nobler impulses, the softer charity, the unuttered aspirations, that are buried, yet still live, beneath so much that is garish and contemptible, wake up; and a man remembers all he is and all he might have been, and grieves, as the dwellers in Arcadia grieved over their exile, over his better nature lost.'

' Ah,' answered Violet, her gay spirits saddened by the tone in which Sabretasche, ordinarily so careless, light, nonchalant, and unruffled, spoke, ' if we were always what we are in such moments, how different would the world be! If human nature lasted what it is in its best moments, poets would have no need to fable of an Eden.'

Sabretasche looked down on her long and earnestly.

' Do you know that you are to me something as music is to you? When I am with you I am

' What curse have you on you'?' she said, involuntarily.

Sabretasche turned his eyes on her filled with
unutterable sadness.

' Do not rouse my demon; let him sleep while
he can! But, Violet, when you hear about in the
world of which you and I are both votaries—
as hear you have done and will do—many tales of
my past and my present, many reports and scandals circulated by my friends, believe them or not
as you like by what you know of me; but believe,
at the least, that I am neither so light-hearted
nor so hard-hearted as they consider me. You are
kind enough to honour me with your—your interest; you will never guess how dearly I prize
it; but there are things in my career which I
cannot reveal to you, and against interest in me
and my fate I warn you; it can bring you no
happiness, for it can never go *beyond* friendship ! '

It was a strange speech from a man to
a woman; especially from a man famous for
his conquests, to a woman famous for her
beauty!

He saw a shiver pass over Violet's form,
and the delicate rose hue of her cheeks
faded utterly. He sighed bitterly as he added,

the blue veins rising in his calm white fore-head:

'None to love me have I; I never had, I never may have!'

Great tears gathered slowly in Violet's eyes, and despite all her self-control, fell down on the glowing petals of the West Indian flowers.

'But you will let me know more of you than anyone else does?' she said, in a hurried, broken voice. 'You will not at least forbid me your friendship?'

'Friendship — friendship!' repeated Sabre-tasche, with a strange smile. 'You do not know what an idle word, what a treacherous salve, what a vain impossibility is friendship between men and women! Yet if you are willing to give me yours, I will do my best to merit it, and to keep myself to it. Now let us go. I like too well to be with you to dare be with you long.'

'What does Sabretasche mean with Moly-neux's daughter?' said De Vigne to me in a *cabinet de peinture*, De Vigne having only just escaped from the harpy's clutch of the little Countess's fairy fingers.

'How should I tell? He's a confounded in-constant fellow, you know. He's always flirting with some woman or other.'

' Flirtation doesn't make men look as he looked
while he listened to her. Flirtation amuses. Sabretasche is not amused here, but rather, I should
say, intensely worried.'

' What should worry him ? He could marry
the girl if he wished.'

' How can you tell ? '

' Well, I suppose so. The Molyneux would let
him have her fast enough. Her mother wants
to get her off; she don't like two milliners' bills
in Regent Street and the Palais-Royal. But *you*
interesting yourself in a love affair ! What a Saul
among the prophets ! '

' Spare your wit, Arthur. I never meddle with
such tinder, I assure you. I am not overfond of
my fellow-creatures, but I don't hate them intensely enough to help them to marry. I say,
have you not been sufficiently bored here? The
concert is over. Let us go, shall we ? '

' With pleasure. I say you have not paid your
promised visit to little Tressillian. 'Tisn't far;
we might walk over, eh ? '

' So we will. Are you after poor Alma's *chevelure dorée* already ? ' laughed De Vigne. ' Make
her mistress of Longholme, Chevasney, and I'll
give her away to you with pleasure. I won't be
a party to other conditions, for her grandfather's

sake—her guardian's sake, rather. By the way,
I must make out whether she knows or not that
the relationship was a myth.'

'Thank you. I have no private reason for pro-
posing the call, except the always good and excel-
lent one of passing the time and seeing a pretty
woman. There is the Puffdoff coming after you
again. Let's get away while we can.'

We were soon out of that little bijou of a
dower-house that shrined the weeds and wiles of
the late Puffdoff's handsome Countess, and smoking our cigars, as we walked across to Richmond.

Alma was sitting at her easel, with her back to
the door, painting earnestly, with little Sylvo at
her side. She was dressed prettily, inexpensively,
I have no doubt, but somehow more picturesquely
than many of the women in hundred guinea
dresses and point worth a dowry—the picturesqueness of artistic taste, and innate refinement, which
gave her the brilliance and grace of a picture.
She turned rapidly at the closing of the door,
sprang up, and ran towards De Vigne with that
impulsiveness which always made her seem much
younger than she was.

'Ah! you *have* come at last! I began to think
you would cheat me as you cheated me of the

yachting trip to Lorave ; and yet I thought you
would not disappoint me.'

'No, but I shall scold you,' said De Vigne, 'for
sitting there, wearing your eyes out—as Mrs. Lee
phrases it—over your easel. Why do you do it ?'

'It is my only companion," pleaded Alma.
'With my brush I can escape away into an ideal
world, and shut out the real and actual, with all
its harshness, trials, and privations. You know
the sun shines only for me upon canvas; and besides,' she added, with a gay smile, 'to take a
practical view of it, I must make what talent I
have into gold.'

'Poor little thing!' exclaimed De Vigne.' It
struck him, who had flung about thousands at his
pleasure ever since he was a boy, as singular, and
as somehow unjust, that this girl, young as she
was, should have to labour for her living with the
genius with which nature had endowed her so
royally—genius the divine, the god-given, the
signet-seal, so rare, so priceless, with which nature
marks the few who are to ennoble and sanctify
the mass !

'Ah ! I *am* a poor little thing !' repeated Alma,
with a *moue mutine* indicative of supreme self-pity
and indignation at her fate. 'I should love society ;
I see nothing but nurse and Sylvo. I love fun ; I

have nobody to talk to but the goldfinch. I
hate solitude, and I am always alone. I should
like beautiful music, beautiful pictures, gardens,
statues, conservatories, luxuries. This quiet life
is not at all my *rôle* ; I vegetate in it.'

'More honour to you to bear it so well, Miss
Tressillian,' said I.

'Oh, I don't bear it well,' interrupted Alma.
'I sometimes get as impatient as a bird beating its
wings against a cage; I grow as restless in its
monotony as you can fancy. I am not a philosopher, and never shall be.'

'Life will make you one in spite of yourself,'
said De Vigne.

'Never! If I ever come to rose-leaves, I will
lie down on them *coûte qui coûte*. As long as I
can only get a straw mattress, there is not much
virtue in renunciation.'

'But there are cankerous worms in rose-leaves,'
smiled De Vigne.

'But who would ever enjoy the roses if they
were always remembering that? Where is the
good?'

'You little epicurean!' laughed De Vigne,
looking at her amusedly. His remembrance of
her as a child made him treat her with a certain gentle familiarity. 'You would have a brief

summer, like the butterflies. That sort of summer costs dear, when the butterfly lies dying on the brown autumn leaves, and envies the bee housed safely at home.'

'*N'importe!*' cried the little lady, recklessly. 'The butterfly, at least, has enjoyed life, and the bee, I would bet, goes on humming and bustling all the year round, never knowing whether the fuchsias are red or white, as long as there is honey in them; only looking in orchises with an eye to business, and never giving a minute in his breathless toil to scent the heliotropes, or kiss the blue-bells, for their beauty's sake!'

'Possibly not; but when the fuchsias and orchises, blue-bells and heliotropes, are withered and dried, and raked away by ruhless gardeners for the unpoetic destiny of making leaf mould; and the ground is frozen, and the trees are bare, and the wind whistles over the snow—how then? Which is the best off, butterfly or bee?'

'Hold your tongue!' laughed Alma. 'You put me in mind of those horrible moral apologues, and that detestable incitement to supreme selfishness, "*La cigale ayant chanté tout l'été*," where the ant is made out a most praiseworthy person, but appears to me simply cruel and mean. But to answer you is easy enough. What good does the bee get from his hard work? Has his honey taken away from him for other people's eating, and is smoked out of his house, poor little thing, by human monsters, whom, if he knew his power, he could sting to death! The butterfly, on the contrary, enjoys himself to the last, dies in the course of nature, and leaves others to enjoy themselves after him.'

'You did not lose your tongue in Lorave, Alma?' said De Vigne, with a grave air of solicitous interest.

With the little Tressillian he had a little of his old fun, something of his old laugh.

'No, indeed; and I should be very sorry if I had, for I love talking.'

'You need not tell us that,' smiled De Vigne.

'I will never talk to you again,' cried Alma, with supreme dignity: 'or, rather, I never would if I were not too magnanimous to avenge an insult by such enormous punishment.'

'To yourself. Just so. You are quite right,' said De Vigne, with an amused smile. 'What are you painting now, Alma? May we see?'

'I was drawing you,' she answered, turning the easel towards him. It was a really wonderful portrait from memory, done in pastels.

'My likeness? By Jove!' cried De Vigne,

'What on earth put it into your head, *petite*, to do that?'

'I knew you would make a splendid picture—your face is beautiful,' answered Alma, tranquilly.'

Whereon De Vigne went into a fit of laughter, the first real laughter that I had heard since his marriage-day.

'Why do you laugh?' asked Alma; 'I only tell you the truth?'

At which gratifying assurance De Vigne laughed still more. The girl amused him, as Richelieu's and Montaigne's little cats amused them when they laid down the sceptre and the pen, and tied the string to their kittens' corks. And thinking of her still merely as Tressillian's little granddaughter, he was not on his guard with her as with other women, and treated her with cordiality and freedom.

'Well, Alma, I am extremely obliged to you. You have made a much handsomer fellow of me than Maclise would have done, I am afraid,' said he, smiling; 'and if ever my picture is wanted side by side with Wellington's, I hope, for the sake of creating an impression on posterity, that you will be kind enough to paint it for me.'

'It is not more handsome than you,' said Alma.

resolutely. 'It is too bad of you to laugh so, but that is like men's ingratitude.'

'Don't abuse us,' said De Vigne; 'that is so stale a stage-trick! Women are eternally running after us, and eternally vowing that they would not stir a step for any of us. They spend their whole existence in trying to catch us, but their whole breath reiterating that they only take us out of compassion. If I hear a lady abuse or find fault with us, I know that her grapes " *sont trop verts, et bons pour des goujats.*"'

Alma laughed:

'Very probably. But I don't abuse you. I prefer yours to my own sex. Your code of honour is far better than ours.'

'The generality of women have no notion of honour at all!' said De Vigne; 'they tell falsehoods and circulate scandals without being called to account for it, and the laxity of honour in trifles that they learn in the nursery and schoolrooms corrodes their sense of right towards others in all their after-life. A boy at school is soon taught that, however lax he may be in other things, it is "sneaky" to peach, and learns a rough sort of Spartan honour; a girl, on the contrary, tells tales of her sisters unreproved, and hears mamma in her drawing-room take away the

character of a "dearest friend" whom she sees
her meet the next moment with a caress and an
endearment. But modern society is too "reli-
gious" to remember to be honourable ; and is too
occupied with proclaiming its "morality" to have
any time to give to common honesty.'

' As Sir John Lacquers taught us!'

'Lacquers and scores like him, whose slips are
passed over because their scrip is inscribed with a
large text, and pilgrim's purse full of Almighty
Dollars. I think of publishing a "Manual of
Early Lessons for Eminent Christians:" I. Do
good so that not only your right hand knows it,
but all your neighbourhood likewise. II. Give as
it is likely to be given unto you. III. Strain
very hard at a sin the size of a gnat if it be your
poor relation's, and swallow one the size of a
camel if it be your patron's. IV. Never pray in
your closet, as no one will be the wiser, but go as
high as you can on the housetop, that society
may think you the holiest man in Israel. V.
Borrow of your friend without paying him, because he will not harm you, but give good interest
to strangers, because they may have the law on
you. VI. Judge severely, that gaining applause
for your condemnation of others you may contrive
to hide your own shortcomings. VII. Eat *pâtés*

de foie gras in secresy, but have *jours maigres* in public, that men who cannot see you in secret may reward you openly! I could write a whole Paraphrase of the Gospel as used and translated by the " Church of England" and other elect of the kingdom of Heaven; an election, by the way, exceedingly like that of Themistocles, where every man writes down his own name first, entirely regardless of lack of right or qualification for the honour!'

'But different in this respect,' said Alma, 'that there the generals *did* remember to put Themistocles after them; whereas the shining lights of the different creeds are a great deal too occupied with securing their own future comfort to think of drawing any of their brothers up with them. The churches all take a cross for their symbol; they would be nearer the truth if they took the beam without the transverse; for egotism is more their point than self-sacrifice! But will you look at my pet-picture?'

The picture she spoke of stood with its face to the wall. As she turned it round, De Vigne and I gave an involuntary exclamation of surprise, it so far surpassed anything we should have fancied a girl of her age could have accomplished. The picture was one not possible to criticize chilly by

exacting rules of art and of perspective. One
looked at it as Murillo looked at the first Madonna
of his wonderful mulatto, not to discuss critically,
but to admire the genius stamped upon it, to
admire the vivid breathing vitality, the delicate
grace, and wonderful power marked upon its
canvas.

De Vigne looked at it silently while Alma
spoke; he continued silent some minutes after
she had ceased; then he turned suddenly:

' Alma, if you choose, you can be as great a
woman as Elizabeth Sirani—a greater than Rosa
Bonheur, because what she gives to horses and
cows, you will give to human nature. Be content.
Whatever sorrows or privations come to you, you
will have God's best gift, which no man can take
away, the greatest prize in life—genius!'

Alma looked up at him, her eyes brilliant as
diamonds, her whole face flushed, her lips trembling.

' You think so? Thank God! I would have
died to hear you say that.'

' Better live to prove it!' said De Vigne, mourn-
fully. ' Your picture is both well conceived and
well carried out: it tells its own story; the imagin-
ing of it is poetic, the treatment artistic. There
are faults, no doubt, but I like it too well to look

out for them. Will you let me have it at my
house a little while? I have some friends who
are artists, others who are cognoscenti, and I should
like to hear their opinion on it.'

'Will you keep it?' asked Alma, with the first
shyness I had seen in her. 'If you would hang
it anywhere in your house, and just look at it now
and then, I should be so glad. Will you?'

'I will keep it with pleasure, my dear child;
but I will keep it as I would Landseer's, or Mul-
ready's, by being allowed the pleasure of adding it
to my collection. Your picture is worth—'

'Oh, don't talk of "worth!"' cried Alma, vehemently. 'Take it—take it, as I give it you, with
all my heart! I am so glad to give you anything,
you were so kind to *him!*' Did he say anything
in his letter to you that I might hear?'

De Vigne turned quickly:

'Did you not read it? It was unsealed.'

'Read it? No! You could not think for a
moment that another person's letter was less sacred
to me because it happened to be unsealed! That
is not your own code, I should say. What right
have you to suppose me more dishonourable than
yourself?'

Her eyes sparkled dangerously, the colour was
hot in her cheeks, the imputation had roused her

spirit, and her fiery indignation was as becoming as it was amusing.

'I beg your pardon. I was wrong,' said De Vigne. 'You have a man's sense of honour, not a woman's; I am glad of it. Your grandpapa says very little. It was merely to ask me if I met you, to be your friend. It is little enough I can ever aid you in, and my friendship will be of little use to you, but, such as it is, it will be yours, if you like to take it.'

She held her hand out to him by way of answer! There were too many tears in her voice for her to trust herself to say anything.

'You do not remember your parents at all?' asked De Vigne.

She shook her head:

'I remember no home but Weive Hurst. Nurse told me both died when I was a baby, and that grandpapa could never bear me to mention them to him: I don't know why. How happy I was at Weive Hurst! I wonder if I shall ever be again?'

'To be sure you will,' said De Vigne, kindly. 'You have a capacity for happiness, and are gay under heavy clouds; at eighteen no one has said good-by to all the sunshine of life. Well, you have read Monte Christo! You must remember his last words.'

'"*Attendre et espérer*"? repeated Alma. 'To
me they are the saddest words in human language.
They are so seldom the joy-bells to herald a new
future—they are so often the death-knell to a
past wasted in futile striving and disappointed
desire. "*Attendre et espérer!*" How many golden
days pass in trusting to those words; and when
their trust be at last recompensed, how often the
fulfilment comes too late to be enjoyed. "*Attendre
et espérer!*" Ah! that is all very well for those
who have some fixed goal in view—some aim
which they will attain if they have but energy
and patience enough to go steadily on to the end;
but only to wait for an indefinite better fate,
which year after year retreats still farther—only
to hope against hope for what never comes, and in
all probability will never come—*that* is not quite
so easy.'

'If not, it is the lot of all. I agree with you,
nothing chafes and frets one more than waiting;
it wears all the bloom off the fruit to waste all our
golden hours gazing at it afar off, and longing for
it with Tantalus thirst. It has never suited me.
I have too often brushed the bloom off mine
plucking them too soon. I agree with you, to
wait for happiness is a living death, to hope for it
is a dreamer's phantasy; but it is not like *your*

usual doctrine, you little enthusiast, who are still
such a child that you believe in the possible realization of all your fond ideals? What were you
saying to me the other day at Strawberry Hill
about Chatterton, that if the poor boy had only
had the courage to wait and hope, he might have
reaped long years of honour and fame?'

'But Chatterton had an aim; and he had more;
he had genius. I know he was goaded to madness by poverty. I know how bitter must have
been the weary fret of thinking what he should
eat, and wherewithal he should be clothed, the jar
and grind of every-day wants, of petty, inexorable
cares. At the same time, I wonder that he did not
live for his works; that for their sake he did not
suffer and endure; that he did not live to make
the world acknowledge all that marked him out
from the common herd. I know how he wearied
of life; yet I wished he had conquered it. Genius
should ever be stronger than its detractors.
" What is the use of my writing poetry that no
one reads?" asked Shelley. Yet he knew that
the time would come when it would be read by
men wiser than those of his generation, and he
wrote on, following the inspiration of his own
divine gift. Men know and acknowledge now
how divine a gift it was.'

'True,' answered De Vigne; 'wrestle with fate, and it will bless you, is a wise and a right counsel; still here and there in that wrestling-match it is possible to get a *croc en jambe*, which leaves us at the mercy of Fate, do what we may to resist her. Men of genius have very rarely been appreciated in their own time. Too often nations spend wealth upon a monument to him whom they let die for want of a shilling. Too many, like Cervantes, have lacked bread while they penned what served to make their country honoured and illustrious. They could write of him:

> " Porque se digva qua uno mano herida
> Pudo dar à su dueño eterna vida; "

but they could leave him to poverty for all that. A prophet has no honour in his own country, still less in his own time; but if the prophets be true and wise men they will not look for honour, but follow Philip Sydney's counsel, look in their own hearts and write, and leave the seed in their brain as ploughmen the corn in the furrows—content that it will bring forth a harvest at the last, if it be ripe, good wheat.'

'Yet it is sad if they are forced to see only the dark and barren earth, and the golden harvest only rise to wave over their tomb?'

'It is; but, petite, there are few things *not* sad

in life, and one of the saddest of them is, as Emerson
says, "the madness with which the passing age mis-
chooses the object on which all candles shine, and
all eyes are turned." The populace who crowded to look at Charles and Louise de Kerroualle
coming to Hampton never knew or thought of
Cromwell's Latin secretary, dictating in his study,
old, blind, and poor. Well, it only shows us what
fools men are, either to court the world or care
for it! A propos of *célèbres*, Alma, you, vowed as
you are to historic associations, should never be
dull here, with all the souvenirs that are round
Richmond and Twickenham?'

'Ah!' said Alma turning her bright beaming
face on him, 'how often I think of them all!—of
the talk round that little deal table in the Grotto;
of Swift, with his brilliant azure eyes, and his
wonderful satire, and his exigeant selfish loves;
of Mrs. Clive, with her humorous stories; and
Harry Fielding, laughing as he wrote his scenes,
and packing away his papers to eat his scrag of
mutton as gleefully as if it were an entremêt; and
Walpole, fitting up a Gothic chapel and writing
for a Paris suit, publishing " Otranto," and talking,
scandales in Boodle's—how often I think of them!'

'You need not tell me that,' laughed De Vigne.
'With your historic passion, you live in the past.

Well! it is safer and less deceptive, if not less
visionary, than living in the future.'

'Perhaps I do both; yet I have little to hope
from the future.'

'Why?' said De Vigne, kindly. 'Who knows
but what one of your old favourites, the fairies,
may bring good gifts to their little queen? We
will hope so, at least.'

Alma shook her head. 'I am afraid not. The
only fairy that has any power now is Money; and
the good gifts the gods give us now-a-days, only
go to those who have golden coffers to put them
in!'

The morning after, while De Vigne was break-
fasting, the cart that brought in Mrs. Lee's home-
made bread to town left at his house Alma's picture; she had looked, I suppose, for his address in
the Court Guide, and rememembered her promise,
though I am afraid the recipient of her gift had
forgotten the subject altogether.

When it came, however, he hung it in a good
light, and pointed it out to Sabretasche, who
dined with him that night, to meet a mutual
Paris friend.

'What do you think of that picture, Colonel?'
he said, as we came into the drawing-room for a
rubber. Whist was no great favourite with De

Vigne; he preferred the rapidity and exciting whirl of loo or lansquenet; but he played it well, and Sabretasche and De Cassagnac were especially fond of it. It suited the Colonel to lean back in a soft chair, and make those calm, subtle combinations. He said the game was so deliciously tranquil and silent!

Sabretasche set down his coffee-cup, put his glass in his eye, and lounged up to it.

'Of this water-colour? I like it exceedingly. Where did you get it? It is not the style of any one I know; it is more like one of your countrymen's, Cassagnac, eh? It wants toning down; the light through that stained window is a trifle too bright, but the boy's face is perfect I would give something to have idealized it; and the hair is as soft as silk. I like it extremely, De Vigne. Where did you get it?'

'I picked it up by accident. It pleased my eye, and I wanted to know if my eye led me right. I know you are a great connoisseur.'

'There is true power in it, and an exquisite delicacy of touch. The artist is young, isn't he? Do you know him?'

'Slightly. He works for his livelihood, and is only eighteen.'

'Eighteen? By Jove! if the boy go on as he

has begun he will beat Maclise and Ingress.   Has
he ever tried his hand at oils?'

'I don't know, I'm sure.'

'It's a pity he shouldn't.   He works for his livelihood, you say?   If he will do me a picture as
good as this, leaving the subject to himself, I will
give him fifty guineas for it, if he think that sufficient.   Some day, when we have nothing better
to do, you will take me to his studio—a garret in
Poland Street, probably, is it not?   Those poor
wretches!   How they live on bread-and-cheese
and a pipe of bird's-eye, I cannot conceive!   If the
time ever come when I have my turbot and hock
no longer, I shall resort to an overdose of morphia.
What is the value of life when life is no longer
enjoyment?'

'Yet,' suggested De Vigne,' 'if only those were
alive who enjoyed living, the earth would be barren very speedily, I fancy.'

'That depends on how you read enjoyment,'
said De Cassagnac.

'Enjoyment is easily enough defined—taking
pleasure in things, and having things in which to
take pleasure!   Some men have the power to enjoy, and not the opportunity; others the opportunity, and not the power; the combination of
both makes the enjoyment, I take it.'

'But enjoyment is a very different thing to different men. Enjoyment, for Sabretasche, lies in *soirées*, like the Gore House, or Madame de Sablé's, wine as good as your claret, women as pretty as La Dorah, good music, good painting, and immeasurable dolce. Enjoyment lies, for Professor Owen, in the fossil tooth of an ichthyosaurus ; for an Italian lazzarone, in sun, dirt, and maccaroni ; for a woman, in dress, conquests, and tall footmen ; for the Tipton Slasher, in the belt, undisputed : enjoyments are as myriad as the stars.'

'I know what you mean, my dear fellow,' said Sabretasche, dropping his eye-glass, and taking up his cup again. ' You mean that Hodge, the bricklayer, goes home covered with whitewash, sits down to Dutch cheese, with the brats screaming about, with the same relish as I sit down to my very best-served dinner. It is true, so far, that I should rather be in purgatory than in whitewash, should turn sick at the cheese, murder the children and kill my own self afterwards ; and that Hodge, by dint of habit and blunted senses, can support life where I should end it in pure self-defence. But I do not believe that Hodge enjoys himself—how should he, poor wretch ! with not a single *agrément* of life ? He does not

know all he misses, and he is not much better
than the beast of the field; but at the same time
he only endures life, he can't be said to enjoy it.
I agree with De Vigne, that there is but one
definition of enjoyment, and the "two handfuls,
with quiet and contentment of spirit," is a poetic
myth, for poverty and enjoyment can by no means
run in tandem.'

'And contentment is another myth,' added De
Vigne. 'If a man has all he wants, he is contented, because he has no wish beyond, and is a
happy man; if he has not what he wants, and is
conscious of something lacking, he cannot be
called contented, for he is not so.'

'Precisely! I don't look to be contented, that is
not in the lot of man; all I ask are the *agréments*
and refinements of life, and without them life is a
curse. Neither Diogenes, limiting himself to cab-
bages and water, nor Alexander, drunk with the
conquest of the empires, was one bit more contented at heart than the other. Discontent
prompted the one to quit mankind and cast off
wealth, the other to rule mankind and amass
wealth.'

'And, after all, there is no virtue in contentment, since contentment is satisfaction in one's
lot; there is far more virtue in endurance—

strong, manful, steady, endurance—of a fate that
is adverse, and which one admits to be such, but
against which one still fights hard.   Patience is
all very well, but pluck is better,' said De Vigne.
The tables are set.   Shall we cut for partners?
You and Cassagnac!   Chevasney and I may give
ourselves up for lost!'

CHAPTER II.

THE FAWN ROBIN HOOD WAS TO SPARE.

DE VIGNE never did anything by halves, to use a sufficiently expressive, if not over, elegant, colloquialism. He hated and mistrusted women, not individually, but sweepingly, en masse. At the same time, there were in him, naturally, too much chivalry and generosity not to make him pity the 'Little Tressillian,' and show her kindness to the best of his power. In the first place, the girl was alone, and had no money ;—in the second, he had known her as a child, still held her as such, indeed, and never thought of classing her among his detested '*beau sexe* ;' in the third, the letter of Boughton Tressillian had in a way recommended her to his care, and, though De Vigne would have been the first to laugh at another man who had taken up a girl of eighteen as a *protégée*, and made sure no harm could come of it, he really looked on Alma as a child, though a very attractive and interesting child it is true, and would have stared at you if you had made his kindness to her the subject of one of those jests customary on the acquaintance of a man about town and an unprotected girl. As he had promised, he picked out some of the choicest books of his library,—not such as young ladies read generally, but such as it might be better if they did—and sent them to her, with the reviews and periodicals of the month. He sent her, too, one of his parrots, for her to teach, he said, she being such an admirable adept in the locutory art, and ordered her a cartload of flowers, to put her in mind of Weive Hurst.

'Her room looked so pitifully dull, poor child!' said he, one morning, when I was lunching with him. 'Those flowers will brighten it up a little. Raymond, did you send Robert down with those things to Richmond?'

'Yes, Major.'

I chanced to look at the man as he spoke ; he was the new valet, a smooth, fair-faced fellow, really gentlemanlike to look at, not, *ça va sans dire*, the 'gentlemanism' of high breeding, but the gentlemanlyism of many an oily parson or sleek parvenu. There was a sly twinkle in his light eyes, and a quick, fox-like glance as he answered his master, which looked as if he at least attached some amusement to the Major's acquaintance with the pretty artiste.

De Vigne, unhappily, never remembered the presence of servants; he thought they had no more eyes or ears than the chairs or tables around him. They served him as the plates or the glasses did, and they were no more than those to him; though more mischief, reports, and *embrouillements* have come from the prying eyes, coarse tongues, and second-hand slanders of those ' necessary evils ' than we ever dream of, for the buzz of the servants' hall is often as poisonous as the subdued murmur of the scandal-retailing boudoir above stairs.

How it came about, I don't know, but Alma, some way or other, was not long kept *in petto*. Some three weeks after Sabretasche, Curly, Severn, Castleton, and one or two other men, were at De Vigne's house. We had been playing Baccarat, his favourite game, and were now supping, between three and four, chatting of two-year-olds and Derby prophecies, of bon mots and beauties, of how Mademoiselle Fifine had fleeced little Pulteney, and Bob Green's roan mare won a handicap for 200 sovs., of Lilla Dorah's last extravagance in the ' shady groves of the Evangelist,' and of the decidedly bad ankles now displayed to

us at Her Majesty's; with similiar floating topics
of the town.

It was curious to see the difference between
men's outer and inner lives. There was Sabretasche lying back in the very easiest chair in the
room, witty, charming, urbane, with not a trace on
his calm delicate features of the care within him
that he had bade Violet Molyneux not tempt him
to unveil. There was Tom Severn, of the Queen's
Bays, with twenty '*in re's*' hanging over his head,
and a hundred 'little bills' on his mind, going to
the dogs by express train, who had been playing
away as if he had had Coutts' to back him. There
was Wyndham, with as dark and melancholy a past
as ever pursued a man, a past of which I know he
repented, not in ostentatious sackcloth and ashes,
but bitterly and unfeignedly in silence and humility,
tossing down Moet's with a gay laugh and a ready
jest, as agreeable in the card-room as he was eloquent in the Lower House. There was Charlie
Fitzhardinge, who, ten years ago, had accidentally
killed his youngest brother, a Benjamin tenderly
and deeply loved by him, and had never ceased to
be haunted by that fair distorted face, laughing
and chatting as if he had never had a care on his
shoulders. There was Vane Castleton, the worst,
as I have told you, of all Tiara's sons; with his

low voice, his fair smooth brow, his engaging address, whom nobody would have thought would
have hurt a fly, yet whom we called 'Butcher,'
because, in his petty malignity, he had hamstrung
a luckless mare of his for not winning a Sweep-
stakes, and had shot dead the brother of a girl
whom he had eloped with, and left three weeks
after without a shilling to help herself, for trying,
poor boy! to revenge his sister; there was De
Vigne—yet no! De Vigne's face was no mask, but
was the type true enough of his character and
wore the truce of an unquiet fate.

'Halloa, De Vigne,' began Tom Severn, 'a
pretty story this is about you, you sly dog! So
this painter of yours we were all called in to
admire, a little time ago, is a little concealed
Venus, eh?'

De Vigne looked up from helping me to some
mayonnaise.

'Explain yourself, Tom; I don't understand you.'

'*Won't* understand, you mean. You know
you've a little beauty locked up all to yourself at
Richmond, and never have told it to your bosom
friends. Shockingly shabby of you, De Vigne, to
show us that water-colour and let us believe it
was done by a young fellow in Poland Street!
However, I suppose you don't want any rivals

poaching on your manor, and the girl *is* stunning, the blokes say, so we must forgive you.'

De Vigne looked supremely disdainful and a little annoyed.

'Pray, my dear Severn, may I ask where you picked up this cock-and-bull story?'

'Oh, yes. Winters, and Egerton, and Steele were making chaff about it in the Army and Navy this morning, saying Hercules had found his Omphale, and they were glad of it, for Dejanira was a devil!'

The blood flushed over De Vigne's white forehead as Severn, in the thoughtlessness of his heart, spoke what *he* meant as good nature; even yet he could not hear unmoved, the slightest allusion to the Trefusis, the one disgrace upon his life, the one stain upon his name.

'How *they* heard it I can't tell you,' said Severn; 'you must ask 'em. Somebody saw the girl looking after you at the gate, I believe. She's a deuced pretty thing—trust you for that, though. But what do you call it a cock-and-bull story for? It's too likely a one for you to deny it with any chance of our believing you, and Heaven knows why you should try. You may hate women now, but everybody knows you never forswore them. We are all shepherds here, as Robin Hood says.'

De Vigne was annoyed : in the first place, that this report, which could but be detrimental to her, should, in so brief a time, already have circulated about himself and Alma; in the second, any interference with him or his pursuits or plans always irritated him exceedingly; in the third, he knew that if he ever disabused their minds of his having any connection with Alma, to know that a pretty woman was living alone and unprotected was for these fellows to ferret her out immediately, to which her *métier* of professional artist would give them the means at once. He was exceedingly annoyed; but he was too wise a man not to know that manifestation of his annoyance would be the surest way to confirm the gossip that had got about concerning them, which for himself, of course, didn't matter two straws.

He laughed slightly. 'We are, it is true, Tom; nevertheless, there is a fawn here and there that it is the duty of all of us, Robin Hoods though we be, to spare; don't you know that? I assure you that the gossip you have heard *is* pure gossip, but gossip which annoys me, for this reason, that the lady who is the innocent subject of it is the granddaughter of a late friend of mine, Tressillian, of Weive Hurst, whom I met accidentally a few weeks ago. Her picture hangs in my room because she wished

to have Sabretasche's judgment upon it, as a
dilettante. Beyond, I have no interest in her, nor
she in me, and for the sake of my dead friend, any
insult to her name I shall certainly consider as one
to my own.'

He spoke quietly and carelessly, but his words
had weight. De Vigne had never been known to
condescend to a lie, not even to a subterfuge or a
prevarication, and there was a haughty *noli me
tangere* air about him.

'All right, old boy,' said Tom. '*I* didn't know,
you see; fellows will talk.'

'Of course they will,' said De Vigne, eating his
marinade leisurely; 'and in nine times out of ten
they would have been right. I never set up to be
a pharisee, God knows! However, I have no
temptation now, for love affairs are no longer to
my taste. I leave them to Corydons like Curly.'

' But, hang it ! De Vigne,' said Vane Castleton,
'Tom's description of this little Trevelyan, Trevanion—what is it?—is so delightful, if you don't
care for her yourself, you might let your friends.
Introduce us all, do.'

'Thank you, Castleton,' said De Vigne, drily.
'Though you *are* a Duke's son, I must say I don't
think you a very desirable addition to a lady's
acquaintance.'

He cordially detested Castleton, than who a vainer or more intensely selfish fellow never curled his whiskers nor befooled women, and he had only invited him because he had been arm-in-arm with Severn when De Vigne had asked Tom that morning in Regent Street.

Lord Vane pushed his fine fair curls off his forehead—an habitual trick of his; his brow was very low, and his blond hair, of which he took immense care, was everlastingly falling across his eyes. 'Jealous, after all! A trifle of the dog in the manger, eh? with all your philosophy and a—a—what do you call it, chivalry?' he said, with a supercilious smile.

I knew De Vigne was growing impatient; his eyes brightened, his mouth grew set, and he pulled his left wristband over his wrist with a jerk. I think that left arm felt an intense longing in its muscles and sinews to 'straighten from the shoulder;' with him, as with David, it was a great difficulty to keep the fire from 'kindling.' But he spoke quietly, very quietly for him; more so than he would have done if no other name than his own had been implicated in it; for he knew the world too well not to know, also, that to make a woman the subject of a dispute or a brawl is to do her the worst service you can.

'I shall not take your speech as it might be
taken, Castleton,' he said, gravely, with a haughty
smile upon his lips. 'My *friends* accept my word,
and understand my meaning; what *you* may think
of me or not is really of so little consequence that
I do not care to inquire your opinion.'

Castleton's eyes scintillated with that cold un-
pleasant glare with which light eyes sometimes
kindle when angry. If he had been an Eton or
Rugby boy, one would have called him 'sulky;'
for a man of rank and fashion the word would have
been too small. A scene might have ensued, but
Sabretasche—most inimitable tactician—broke
the silence with his soft low voice:

'De Vigne, do you know that Harvey Good-
win's steel greys are going for an old song in the
Yard? I fancy I shall buy them.'

So the conversation was turned, and Alma's
name was dropped. Curly, however, half out of
méchanceté, half because he never heard of a pretty
woman without making a point of seeing her,
never let De Vigne alone till he had promised to
introduce him to her.

'Do, old fellow,' urged Curly, 'because you
know I remember her at Weive Hurst, and she
had such deuced lovely eyes then. Do! I promise you to treat her as if she were the richest

heiress in the kingdom and hedged round with
a perfect abatis of chaperones. I can't say
more!'

So De Vigne took him down, being quite sure
that if he did not show him the way Curly would
find it for himself, and knowing, too, that Curly,
though he was a 'little wild,' as good natured-
ladies phrase it, was a true gentleman; and when
a man is that, you may trust him, where his
honour is touched or his generosity concerned, to
break through his outer shell of fashion, ennui, or
dissipation, and 'come out strong.'

So De Vigne, as I say, took him down one
morning, when we had nothing to do, to St. Crucis.
It was a queer idea, as conventionalities go, for a
young girl to receive our visits without any chape-
rone to protect her and play propriety; but the
little lady was one out of a thousand; she could
do things that no other woman could, and she
welcomed us with such a mixture of frank and
child-like simplicity, with the self-possession, wit,
and ease of a woman accustomed to society, that it
was very pretty to see her. And we should have
known but a very trifle of life if we had not felt
how utterly distant from boldness of any kind was
our Little Tressillian's charming vivacity and candour—a vivacity that can only come from an un-

burdened mind, a candour that can only spring
from a heart that thinks no ill because it means
none. 'To the pure all things are pure.' True
words! Many a spotless rain-drop gleams unsoiled
on a filthy and betrodden *trottoir*; many a worm
grovels in native mud beneath an unspotted and
virgin covering of fairest snow.

It was really pretty to see Alma entertain her
callers. She was perfectly natural, because she
never thought about herself. She was delighted
to see De Vigne, and happy to see us as he had
brought us—not quite as flattering a reason for
our welcome as Curly and I were accustomed to
receive.

'Have you walked every day, Alma, as I told
you?' said De Vigne.

'Not every day,' said Alma, penitentially. 'I
will when the summer comes, but the eternal spring
upon my canvas is much dearer and more tempting to me than your chill and changeable English
spring.'

'You are very naughty, then,' said De Vigne;
'you will be sorry ten years hence for having
wasted your health. What is your aim in working eternally like this?'

'To make money to buy my shoes, and my
gloves, and my dresses. I have nobody to buy

them for me; that is aim practical enough to please you, is it not?'

'But that is not your only one, I fancy?' smiled Curly. 'Miss Tressillian scarcely looks like the expounder of prosaic doctrine.'

'No; not my only one,' answered Alma, quickly, her dark blue eyes lighting up under their silky and upcurled lashes. 'They say there is no love more tender than the love of an artist for his work, whether he is author, painter, or musician; and I believe it For the fruit of your talent you bear a love that no one, save those who feel it, can ever attempt to understand. You long to strengthen your wings, to exert your strength, to cultivate your powers, till you can make them such as must command applause; and when I see a masterpiece, of whatever *genre*, I feel as if I should never rest, till I, too, had laid some worthy offering upon the altar of Art.'

Ideal and enthusiastic as the words may seem, coldly considered; as she spoke them, with her eloquent voice and gesticulation, and her whole face beaming with the earnestness of her own belief, we, quickest of all mortals to sneer at 'sentiment,' felt no inclination to ridicule here, but rather a sad regret for the cold winds that we knew would soon break and scatter the warm

petals of this bright, joyous, Southern flower,
and gave a wistful backward glance to the time
when we, too, had like thoughts—we, too, like
fervour !

De Vigne felt it; but, as his wont was, turned
it with a laugh :

'Curly, you need not have started that young
lady ! In that fertile brain I ought to have warned
you there is a powder-magazine of enthusiasm
ready to explode at the mere hint of a firebrand,
which one ought not to approach within a mile at
the least.   It will blow itself up some day in its
own excessive energy, and get quenched in the
world's cold water !'

'Heaven forefend !' cried Curly.   'The enthusiasm, which you so irreverently compare to gun-
powder, is too rare and too precious not to be
taken all the care of that one can.   If the ladies of
the world had a little of such fire, we, their sons,
or lovers, or brothers, might be a trifle less useless, vapid, and wearied.'

'Quenched in the world's cold water !' cried
Alma, who had been pondering on De Vigne's
speech, and had never heard poor Curly's.   'It
never shall be, Sir Folko.   The fire of true enthusiasm is like the fires of Baku, which no water
can ever attempt to quench, and which burn

steadily on from night to day, and year to year, because their well-spring is eternal.'

'Or because the gases are poisonous, and nobody cares to approach them?' asked De Vigne mischievously.

I noticed that Alma was the first who had brought back in any degree the love of merriment and repartee natural to him in his youth; the first with whom, since his fatal marriage-day, he had ever cordially *laughed*. She called him Sir Folko, because she persisted in the resemblance between him and her favourite knight which she had discovered in her childhood, and because, as she told him, 'Major de Vigne' was so ceremonious. His manner with her, like that to a pretty spoilt child, had established a curiously familiar friendship between them, strangely different from the usual intercourse of men and young girls; for De Vigne received from her the compliments and frankly-expressed admiration that come ordinarily from the man to the woman. Somehow or other, it seemed perfectly natural between *them*, and, *après tout*, Eve's

> ' My author and disposer!—what thou wilst,
> Unargued I obey. God is thy law,
> Thou mine—'

is strangely touching, sweet, and natural.

Curly was enchanted with her; he went into
tenfold more raptures about her than the beauties
of the Drawing-room, with their perfect *tournures*
and sweeping trains, had ever extorted from him;
she was 'just his style;' a thing, however, that
Curly was perpetually avowing of every different
style of blonde and brunette, tall or small, statu-
esque or kittenish, as they chanced to chase one
another in and out of his capacious heart.

'She is a little darling!' he swore earnestly, as
we drove homewards, 'and certainly the very
prettiest woman I have ever seen.'

'Rather overdone that, Curly,' said De Vigne,
drily, 'considering all the regular beauties you
have worshipped, and that Alma is no regular
beauty at all.'

'No, she's much better,' said Curly, decidedly.
'Where's the regular beauty that's worth that
little dear's grace, and vivacity, and lovely
colouring?'

De Vigne put up his eyebrows, as if he would
not give much for the praise of such an universal
admirer as Curly was, of all degrees and orders.

CHAPTER III.

LE CHAT QUI DORMAIT.

'WHO is that Little Tressillian they were talking of at De Vigne's the other night?' Sabretasche asked me one morning, in the window at White's —his club, *par excellence*, where he was referee and criterion on all things of art, fashion, and society, and where his word could crush a belle, sell a picture, and condemn a coterie.

He shrugged his shoulders as I told him, and stroked his moustaches:

'Very little good will come of *that*; at least for her; for him there will be an amusement for a time, then a certain regret—remorse, perhaps, as he is very generous-hearted—and then a separation, and—oblivion.'

'Do you think so? I fancy De Vigne paid too heavy a price for passion to have any fancy to let its reins loose again.'

'Mon cher, mon cher!' cried Sabretasche, impatiently, 'if Phaeton had not been killed by that

thunderbolt, do you suppose that the *bouleversement*
and the conflagration would have deterred him
from driving his father's chariot as often as Sol
would let him have it?'

'Possibly not; but I mean that De Vigne is
thoroughly steeled against all female humanity.
The sex of the Trefusis cannot possibly, he thinks,
have any good in it; and I believe he only takes
what notice he does of Alma Tressillian from
friendship for her old grandfather and pity for her
desolate position.'

'Friendship—pity? For Heaven's sake, Arthur,
do not you, a man of the world, talk such nonsense. To what, pray, do friendship and pity
invariably bring men and women? De Vigne and
his *protégée* are walking upon mines.'

'Which will explode beneath them?'

'*Sans doute.* We are, unhappily, mortal, mon
ami! I will go down and see this little Tressillian some day when I have nothing to do. Let
me see; she is painting that picture for me, of
course, that I ordered of him from his unknown artist. He must take me down: I
shall soon see how the land lies between
them,'

Accordingly, Sabretasche one day, when De
Vigne and he were driving down to a dinner at

the Castle, took out his watch, and found De Vigne's clocks had been too fast.

'We shall be there half-an-hour too soon, my dear fellow. Turn aside, and take me to see this little friend of yours with the pretty name and the pretty pictures. If you refuse, I shall think Vane Castleton is right, and that you are like the famed dog in the manger. I have a right to see the artist that is executing my own order.'

De Vigne nodded, and turned the horses' heads towards St. Crucis, not with an over-good grace, for he knew Sabretasche's reputation, and the Colonel, with his fascination and his *bonnes fortunes*, was not exactly the man that, whether dog in the manger or not, De Vigne thought a very safe friend for his little·Tressillian. · But there was no possibility of resisting Sabretasche when he had set his mind upon anything. Very quietly, very gently, but very securely, he kept his hold upon it till he had it yielded up to him.

So De Vigne had to introduce the Colonel, who dropped into an easy chair beside Alma, with his eye-glass up, and began to talk to her. He was a great adept in the art of "bringing out." He had a way of hovering over a woman, and fixing his beautiful eyes on her, and talking softly and pleasantly, so that the subject under his skilful mesmerism developed talent that might otherwise never have gleamed out; and with Alma, who could talk with any and everybody on all subjects under the sun, from metaphysics and ethics to her kitten's collar, and who would discuss philosophies with you as readily as she would chatter nonsense to her parrot, Sabretasche had little difficulty.

De Vigne let the Colonel have all the talk to himself, irritated at the sight of his immovable and inquiring eye-glass, and the sound of his low, *trainante*, musical voice. Now and then, amidst his conversation, the Colonel shot a glance at him, and went on with his criticisms on Art, sacred, legendary, and historic; and on painting in the mediæval and the modern styles, with such a deep knowledge and refined appreciation of his subject as few presidents of the R. A. have ever shown in their lectures.

At last De Vigne rose, impatient past endurance, though he could hardly have told you why.

'It is half-past six, Sabretasche; the turbot and turtle will be cold.'

The Colonel smiled:

'Thank you, my dear fellow; there are a few things in life more attractive than turtle or turbot. The men will wait; they would be the last to hurry us if they knew our provocation for delay.'

De Vigne could have found it in his heart to have kicked the Colonel for that speech, and the soft sweet glance accompanying it. 'He will spoil that little thing,' he thought, angrily. 'No woman's head is strong enough to stand his and Curly's flattery.'

'I like your little lady, De Vigne,' said Sabre-tasche, as they drove away. 'She is really very charming, good style, and strikingly clever.'

'She is not *mine*,' said De Vigne, with a haughty stare of surprise.

'Well! she will be, I dare say.'

'Indeed no. I did not suppose your notions of my honour, or rather dishonour, were like Vane Castleton's.'

'Nor are they, *cher ami*,' said the Colonel, with that grave gentleness which occasionally replaced his worldly wit and gay ordinary tone. 'But like him I know the world; and I know, as you would, too, if you thought a moment, that a man of your age, cannot have that sort of friendly intercourse with a girl of hers, without its surely ripening into something infinitely warmer and more dangerous. You would be the first to sneer at an attempt at platonics in another; you are the last man in the

world to dream of such follies yourself. Tied as
you are, you cannot frequent her society without
danger for her; and for you, probably remorse—at
the least, satiety and regret. With nine men out
of ten the result would be a liaison lightly formed
and as lightly broken; but you have an uncommon
nature, and a young girl like little Tressillian
your warmth of heart would never let you desert.
I hate advising; I never do it to anybody. My
life has left me little title to counsel men against
sins and follies which I daily commit myself; nor
do I count as sins many things the world con-
demns as such. Only here 1 see so plainly what
will come of it, that I do not like you to rush into
it blindfold and repent afterwards. Because you
have had fifty such loves which cost you nothing,
that is no reason that the fifty-first may not cost
you some pain, some very great pain, in its forma-
tion or its severance—'

'You mean very kindly, Sabretasche, but there
is no question of "love" here,' interrupted De
Vigne, with his impatient hauteur. 'In the first
place, you, so well read in woman's character,
might know she is far too frank and familiar with
me for any fear of the kind. In another I have
paid too much for passion ever to risk it again,
and I hope I know too well what is due from

honour and generosity to win the love of a young
unprotected girl while I am by my own folly fettered and cursed by marriage ties. Sins enough
I have upon my soul, God knows, but there is no
danger of my. erring here. I have no temptation;
but if I had I should resist it; to take advantage
of her innocence and ignorance of my history
would be a blackguard's act, to which no madness,
even if I felt it, would ever make me condescend
to stoop!'

De Vigne spoke with all the sternness and impatience natural to him when roused, spoke in
overstrong terms, as men do of a fault they are
sure they shall never commit themselves. Sabretasche listened, an unusual angry shadow gathering in his large soft eyes, and a bitter sneer on his
features, as he leaned back and folded his arms to
silence and *dolce*.

'Most immaculate Pharisee! Remember. a
divine injunction, "Let him that standeth take
heed lest he fall."'

De Vigne cut his horses impatiently with the
whip.

'I am no Pharisee, but I am, with all my faults
and vices, a man of honour, I hope.'

Sabretasche answered nothing, but annoyance
was still in his eyes, and a sneer still on his lips.

De Vigne had one striking fault, namely, that if advised not to do a thing, that thing would he go and do straightway; moreover, being a man of strong will and resolve, and very reliant on his own strength, he was apt, as in his fatal marriage, to go headlong, perfectly safe in his own power to guide himself, to judge for himself, and to draw back when it was needful. Therefore, he paid no attention whatever to Sabretasche's counsels, but, as it chanced, went down to see Alma rather more often than he had done before; for she had said how much she wished she could exhibit at the Water-Colour Society, which De Vigne, knowing something of the president, and of the society in general, had been able to manage for her.

'What should I do without you?' said Alma, fervently, to him one day, when he went there to tell her her picture was accepted. 'You are so kind to me, Sir Folko!'

'I? Not at all, my dear child, I wish you would not exalt me to such a pinnacle. What will you say when I tumble down one day, and you see nothing of me but worthless shivers?'

'Reverence you still,' said Alma, softly. 'A fragment of the Parthenon is worth a whole spotless and unbroken modern building. If my ideal were to fall, I should treasure the dust.'

' But, seriously,' he interrupted her, ' I wish you would not get into the habit of rating me so high, Alma. I don't in the least come up to it. You do not guess—how should you?—you cannot even in fancy, picture the life that I, and men like me, lead ; you cannot imagine the wild follies with which we drown our past, the reckless pleasures with which we pass our present, our temptations, our weaknesses, our errors ; how should you, child as you are, living out of the world in a solitude peopled only with the bright fancies of your own pure imagination, that never incarnates the hideous fauns and beckoning bacchanals which haunt and fever ours? '

' But I can,' said Alma, earnestly, looking up to him. 'I do not go into the world, it is true, but still I know the world to a certain extent. Montaigne, Rochefoucauld, Rabelais, Goethe, Emerson, Bolingbroke, the translated classics, do you not think they teach me the world, or, at least, of what makes the world, Human Nature, better than the few hours at a dinner-table, or the gossip of morning calls, which you tell me is all girls in good society see of life? You know, Sir Folko, it always seems to me, that women, fenced in as they are, in educated circles, by boundaries which they cannot overstep, except to their own hindrance; screened from all temptations; deprived of all opportunity to wander, if they wished, out of the beaten track; should be gentle to your sex, whose whole life is one long temptation, and to whose lips is almost forced that Circean " cup of life" whose flowers round its brim hide the poisons at its dregs. Women have, if they acknowledged them, passions, ambitions, impatience at their own monotonous rôle, longings for the living life denied to them; but everything tends to crush these down in them, has thus tended through so many generations, that it has come to be an accepted thing that they must be calm, fair, pulseless statues; and when here and there a woman dares to acknowledge that her heart beats, and that nature is not wholly dead within her, the world stares at her, and rails at her, for there is no *bête noire* so terrible to the world as Truth! No, I can fancy your temptations, I can picture your errors and your follies, I can understand how you drink your poison one hour because you liked its flavour, and drink more the next hour to make you forget your weakness in having yielded to it at all. That my own solitude and imagination are only peopled with shapes bright and fair, I must thank Heaven and not myself. If I had been born in squalor and nursed in vice, what would circumstance and surroundings have made me? Oh, I think, instead of the Pharisee's presumptuous "I thank God that I am holier than he," our thanksgiving should be, "I thank God that I have so little opportunity to do evil!" and we should forgive, as we wish to be forgiven ourselves, those whose temptations, either from their own nature, or from the outer world, have been so much greater than our own.'

Her voice was wonderfully musical, with a strange pathos in it; and her gesticulation had all the grace and fervour of her Southern origin. Her words sent a thrill to De Vigne's heart; they were the first gentle and tolerant words he had heard since his mother had died. He had known but two classes of women: those who shared his errors and pandered to his pleasures, whose life disgusted, while their beauty lured him; and those whose illiberality and whose sermons only roused him to more wayward rebellion against the social laws which they expounded. It touched him singularly to hear words at once so true, so liberal, and so humble, from one on whose young life he knew that no stain had rested; to meet with so much comprehension from a heart, compared with his own, as pure and spotless from all error as the snow-white roses in her windows, on

which the morning dewdrops rested without soil.
And at her words something of De Vigne's old
nature began to wake into new existence, as, after
a long and weary sleep, the eyelids tremble before
the soul arouses to the heat and action of the
day.

A memory of the woman called his wife passed
over him—he could scarcely tell why or how—
with a cold chill, like the air of a pestilent
charnel-house.

'Alma, if women were like you, men might be
better than they are. Child, I wish you would
not talk as you do. You wake up thoughts and
memories that had far better sleep.'

She touched his hand gently :

'Sir Folko, what are those memories?'

He drew his hand away and laughed, not
joyously, but that laugh which has less joy in it
even than tears :

'Don't you know a proverb, Alma—" *N'éveillez
pas le chat qui dort?* " '

'But were the cat a tiger I would not fear it, if
it were yours.'

'But *I* fear it.'

There was more meaning in that than Alma
guessed. The impetuous passion that had blasted
his life, and linked his name with the Trefusis,

would be, while his life lasted, a giant whose throes and mighty will would always hold him captive in his chains!

He was silent; he sat looking out of the window by which he sat, and playing with a branch of the white rose. His lips were pressed together, his eyebrows slightly contracted, his eyes troubled, as if he were looking far away—which indeed he was—to a white headstone lying among fragrant violet tufts under the old elms at Vigne, with the spring sunshine, in its fitful lights and shadows, playing fondly round the name of the only woman who had loved him at once fondly and unselfishly.

Alma looked at him long and wistfully, some of his darker shadows flung on her own bright and sunny nature—as the yew-tree throws the dark shadows of its boughs over the golden cowslips that nestle at its roots.

At last she bent forward, lifting her soft frank eyes to his.

'Sir Folko, where are your thoughts? Tell me.'

Her voice won its way to his heart; he knew that interest, not curiosity, spoke in it, and he answered gently.

'With my mother.'

It was the first time he had spoken of her to
Alma—he never breathed her name to anyone.

'You loved her dearly?'

'Very dearly.'

Alma's eyes filled with tears, a passion very
rare with her.

'Tell me of her,' she said softly,

'No. I cannot talk of her.'

'Because you loved her so much?'

No. Because I killed her.'

This was the great remorse of his life; that his
folly had cost him his name and, as he considered,
his honour, was less bitter to him than that it
had cost his mother's life.

Alma, at his reply—uttered almost involuntarily
under his breath—gazed at him, horror-stricken,
with wild terror in her large eyes; yet De Vigne
might have noticed that she did not shrink from,
but rather drew the closer to, him. Her expres-
sion recalled his thoughts.

'Not that, not that,' he said hastily. 'My hand
never harmed her, but my passions did. My own
headlong and wilful folly sent her to her grave.
Child! you may well thank God if Temptation
never enter your life. No man has strength
against it.'

For the first time De Vigne felt an inclination

to disclose his marriage; to tell her what he would have told to no other living being: of all his own madness had cost him, of the fatal revenge the Trefusis had taken, of the headlong impetuosity which had led him to raise the daughter of a beggar-woman to one of the proudest names in England, of the fatal curse which he had drawn on his own head, and the iron fetters which his own hand had forged. The words were already on his lips, in another minute he would have bent his pride and laid bare his secret to her, if at that moment the door had not opened—to admit Alma's late governess.

Alma was very right—our life hinges upon Opportunity!

De Vigne never again felt a wish to tell her of his marriage.

CHAPTER IV.

PAOLO AND FRANCESCA.

MAY came; it was the height of the season; town
was full; Her Majesty had given her first levee;
Belgravia and Mayfair were occupied; the Ride
and the Ring were full, too, at six o'clock every
day, and the thousand toys with which Babylon
amuses her grown babies were ready, among others
the Exhibition of Fine Arts, where, on its first
day, De Vigne and I went to lounge away an
hour, chiefly for the great entertainment and fun
afforded to persons of sane mind by the eccen-
tricities of the pre-Raphaelite gentlemen.

In the entrance we met Lady Molyneux and
her daughter, Sabretasche and his young Grace of
Regalia with them. It was easy to see which the
Viscountess favoured the most.

'Are you come to be disenchanted with all
living womanhood by the contemplation of Messrs.
Millais and Hunt's ideals, Major de Vigne?' asked
Violet, giving him her hand, looking a very lovely

sample of 'living womanhood.' Ladies said she was very extravagant in dress. She might be; she was naturally lavish, and liked instinctively all that was graceful in form or colouring; but I only know she dressed perfectly, and, what was better, never *thought about it.*

'Perhaps we should suffer less disappointment if ladies *were* like Millais's ideals,' smiled De Vigne. 'From those rough red-haired, long-limbed women we should never look for much perfection; whereas the faces and forms of our living beauties are rather like Belladonna, beautiful to look at, but destruction to approach or trust!'

'You are incorrigible!' cried Violet, with a tiny shrug of her shoulders, 'and forget that if Belladonna is a poison to those who don't know how to use it, it is a medicine and a balm to those who do.'

'But for one cautious enough to cure himself, how many unwary are poisoned for life!' laughed De Vigne.

He said it as a jest, but a bitter memory prompted it.

'Send that fellah to Coventry, Miss Molyneux, do,' lisped Regalia; 'he's so dweadfully rude.'

'Not yet; sarcasms are infinitely more refresh-

ing than empty compliments,' said Violet, with a
scornful flash of her brilliant eyes.   The little
Duke was idiot enough to attempt to flatter Violet
Molyneux, to whom the *pas* in beauty and talent
was indisputably given!   'Colonel Sabretasche,
take my catalogue, I have not looked into it yet,
and mark all our favourites for me.   I am
going to enjoy the pictures now, and talk to
nobody.'

A charming ruse on the young lady's part to
keep Sabretasche at her side and make him talk
to her, for they passed over eleven pictures, and
lingered over a twelfth, while he discoursed on the
Italian and French, the German and the English
schools.

'Why have you never been to see me for four
days?' asked Violet, standing before one of the
glorious sea pieces of Stanfield.

Sabretasche hesitated a moment.

'I have had other engagements.'

Violet's eyes flashed.   'I beg your pardon,
Colonel Sabretasche; not being capricious myself,
it did not occur to me that you were so.   However, if it is a matter of so little moment to you,
it is of still less to me.'

'Did I not tell you,' whispered Sabretasche,
'that I like too well to be with you to dare to be

with you much. You cannot have forgotten our conversation at Richmond?'

'No,' she answered, hurriedly; 'but you promised me your friendship, and you have no right to take it away. I do not pretend to understand you, I do not seek to know more than you choose to tell me, but since you once promised to be my friend, you have no right—'

'Violet, for God's sake do not break my heart!' broke in Sabretasche, his voice scarcely above his breath, but full of such intense anguish that she was startled. 'Your friend I *cannot* be; anything dearer I *may not* be. Forget me, and all interest in my fate. Of your interest in me I am utterly unworthy; and I would rather that you should credit all the evil that the world attributes to me, and, crediting it, learn to hate me, than think that I, in my own utter selfishness, had thrown one shade on your young life, mingled one regret with your bright future.'

They were both leaning against the rail; no one saw Violet's face as she answered him.

'To speak of hate from me to you is folly, and it is too late to command forgetfulness. If you had no right to make me remember you, you have still less right to bid me forget you.'

'Violet, come and look at this picture of

Lance's, Regalia talks of buying it,' said her
mother's cold, slow, languid voice.

Violet turned, and though she smiled and spoke
about the picture in question with some of her
old vivacity and self-possession, her face had lost
its brilliant tinting, and her white teeth were set
together.

De Vigne joined them at that minute.

' Miss Molyneux, I want to show you a painting
in the Middle Room. It is just your style, I
fancy. Will you come and look at it?'

We all went into the Middle Room after him,
Sabretasche too, pausing occasionally to look at
some of the luckless exiles near the ceiling with
his lorgnon. By-the-way, what a farce it is to hang
pictures where one must have a lorgnon to look
at them; the exhibition of the Few is the sup-
pression of the Many!

'Voilà!' said De Vigne. 'Am I wrong?'
Don't you like it?'

' Like it!' echoed Violet. 'O, how beautiful!'

Quite forgetful that she was the centre of a
crowd who were looking at her much more than
at the paintings on the walls, she stood, the colour
back in her cheeks, her eyes lifted to the picture.
The painting deserved it. It was Love—old in
story, yet new to every human heart—the love of

Francesca and Paolo, often essayed by artists, yet never rendered, even by Ary Scheffer, as Dante would have had it, and as it was rendered here.

There were no vulgarities of a fabled Hell; there were the two, alone in that true torture—

‘ Ricordarsi del tempo felice nella miseria—’

yet happy because *together*. Her face and form were in full light, his in shadow. Heart beating against heart, their arms round each other, they looked down into each other’s eyes. On his face were the fierce passions, against which he had had no strength, mingled with deep and yearning regret for the fate he had drawn in with his own. On hers, lifted up to him, was all the love at sight of which he who beheld it ‘ swooned even as unto death ; ’ the love—

‘ ——piacer si forte
Che come vedi ancor non m’abbandona—’

the love which made hell, paradise ; and torture together, dearer than heaven alone. Her face spoke, her clinging arms circled him as though defying power in eternity strong enough to part them ; her eyes looked into his with unutterable tenderness, anguish for his sorrow, ecstasy in his presence !—and on her soft lips, still trembling with the memory of that first kiss which had been their ruin, was all the heroism and all the passion, all the fidelity, devotion, and joy in him alone, spoken in that one sentence—

'Questi che mai da me non fia diviso!'

The picture told its tale; crowds gathered round it; and those who could not wholly appreciate its wonderful colouring and skill were awed by its living humanity, its passionate tenderness, its exquisite beauty.

Violet stood, regardless of the men and women around her, looking up at the Francesca, a fervent response to it, a yearning sympathy with the warm human love and joys of which it breathed, written on her mobile features.

She turned away from it with a heavy sigh, and the flush deepened in her cheeks as she met Sabretasche's eyes, who now stood behind her.

'You are pleased with that picture,' he said, bending his head.

'Is it not beautiful?' cried Violet, passionately. 'It is not to be criticized; it is to be loved. It is art and poetry and human nature blended in one. Whoever painted it, interprets art as no other artist here can do. He has loved and felt his subject, and makes others in the force of his genius feel and love it too. Listen how every one is praising it! They all admire it, yet not nine out of ten of these people can understand it. Tell me who painted it, quick! Now you are looking in the last room, and it is 226, Middle Room. Oh! give me the catalogue!'

She took it out of his hands with that rapid vivacity which worried her mother so dreadfully as bad ton, and turned the leaves over till she reached '226. Paolo and Francesca—Vivian Sabretasche.

> "Amor che a nullo amato amar perdona,
> Mi prese del costui piacer si forte,
> Che come vedi ancor non m'abbandona
> Amor condusse noi ad una morte"'

She dropped the book; she could not speak but she held out her hand to him, and Sabretasche took it for an instant as they leaned over the rail together in the security and 'solitude of a crowd.'

'Do not speak of it here,' he whispered, as he bent down for the fallen catalogue.

''Pon my honour, Sabretasche,' whispered little Regalia ' we're all so astonished—turning artist, eh? Never knew you exhibited. Splendid picture—ah—really!'

'You do me much honour,' said Sabretasche, coldly—he hated the little puppy who was always

dawdling after Violet—' but I should prefer not to
be congratulated before a room full of people.'

'On my life, old fellow, I envy you,' said De
Vigne, too low for any one to hear him ; 'not for
being the talk of the room, for that is neither to
your taste nor mine, but for having such magnificent talent as you have given us here.'

'Cui bono?' said Sabretasche, with his slight
smile, that was too gentle for discontent, and too
sad for cynicism.

'I had not an idea *whose* Francesca I was bringing Miss Molyneux to see,' De Vigne continued.
'How came you to exhibit this year?'

'Oh, I have been a dabbler in art a long time,'
laughed the Colonel. 'Many of the Forty are my
intimate friends ; they would not have rejected
anything I sent.'

'They would have been mad to reject the Francesca ; they have nothing to compete with it on
the walls. I wish you were in Poland Street, Sabretasche, that one could order of you. You are
the first fine gentleman, since Sir George Beau-
mont, who has turned "artiste véritable," and you
grace it better than he.'

Sabretasche and his Grace of Regalia, De Vigne,
and I, went to luncheon that day with Lady Molyneux in Loundes Square, at which meal the Colonel

made himself so charming, lively, and winning, that
the Viscountess, strong as were her leanings to
her pet Duke, could not but admit that he shone to
very small advantage, and made a mental mem.
never to invite the two together again. The
Molyneux were devoting that morning to picture-
viewing. And from the Royal Academy, after
luncheon, they went to the French aquarelles, in
Pall Mall, and thence to the Water-Colour Exhibition, whither De Vigne and I followed them in
his tilbury.

'I wonder what they will say to Alma's picture,'
said De Vigne, as we alighted. 'I wish it may
make a hit, as it is her livelihood now, poor child!'

Strange enough, it was before Alma's picture
that we found most people in the room congre-
gated; and Violet turned to us:

'Come and look here, Major De Vigne; this
"Louis Dix-sept in the Tower of the Temple," by
Miss Trevelyan—Trevanion—no, Tressillian—whoever she be—is the gem of the collection to my
mind. There is an unlucky green ticket on it,
else I would purchase it. What enviable talent!
I wish I were Miss Tressillian!'

'How rash you are!' said De Vigne. 'How
can you tell but that Miss Tressillian may be some
masculine woman living in an *entresol*, painting

with a clay pipe between her teeth, and horses and cows. for veritable models in a litter adjoining, dressing like George Sand, and deriving inspiration from gin ? '

' What a shameful picture ! ' cried Violet, indignantly. ' I do not know her, nor anything about her, it is true, but I am perfectly certain that the woman who idealized and carried out this painting, with so much delicacy and grace, must have a delicate and graceful mind herself.'

' Or,' continued De Vigne, ruthlessly, ' she may now, for anything you can tell, be a *vieille fille* who has consecrated her life to art, and grown old and ugly in the consecration, and who—'

' Be quiet, Major De Vigne,' interrupted Violet. ' I am perfectly certain that the artist would correspond to the picture: Raphael was as beautiful as his paintings, Michael Angelo was of noble appearance, Mozart and Mendelssohn had faces full of music—'

' Fuseli, too, was,' said De Vigne, mischievously, ' remarkably like his grand archangels; Reynolds, in his brown coat and wig, is so poetic that one could have no other ideal of the " Golden Age ; " Turner's appearance was so artistic that one would have imagined him a farmer bent on crops ; fat and snuffy Handel is the embodiment of the beauty of the Cangio d'Aspetto—'

'How tiresome you are!' interrupted Violet
again, 'I am establishing a theory; I don't care
for facts—no theorists ever do in these days! I
maintain that a graceful and ennobling art must
leave its trace on the thought and mind and man-
ners of its expositors (I know you are going to remind me of Morland at the hedge-alehouse, of
Opie, and the "little Jew-broker," and of Nolli-
kens making the writing-paper label for the single
bottle of claret); never mind, I keep to my theory,
and I am sure that this Miss Tressillian, who has
had the happiness to paint the lovely face of that
little Dauphin, would, if we could see her, correspond to it; and I envy her without the slightest he-
sitation.'

'You have no need to envy any one,' whispered
Regalia.

Violet turned impatiently from him, and began
to talk to Sabretasche about one of those ever-
charming pictures of Mr. Edmund Warren. De
Vigne looked at me and smiled, thinking with how
much more grounds the little Tressillian had envied
Violet Molyneux.

'I wish I could tell you half I feel about your
Francesca,' said Violet, lifting her eyes to Sabretasche's face, as they stood apart from anybody
else in a part of the room little frequented, for

there were few people there that morning, and
those few were round Alma's pet picture. 'You
can never guess how I reverence your genius, how
it speaks to my heart, how it reveals to me all your
inner nature, which the world, much as it admires
you, never sees or dreams of seeing.'

Sabretasche bent his head ; her words went too
near home to him to let him answer them.

'All your pictures,' Violet went on, 'bear the
stamp of a master's talent, but this—how beautiful
it is! I might have known no other hand but
yours could have called it into life. Have you
long finished it ?'

'I finished the painting two years ago ; but
three *months* ago I saw for the first time the face
that answered my ideal, the face that expressed
all that I would have expressed in Francesca. I
effaced what I had painted, and in its stead I
placed—yours.'

Violet's eyes dropped ; the delicate colour in
her cheeks deepened. She had been dimly conscious of a resemblance in the painting, and De
Vigne's glance from Francesca to herself had told
her that he at the least saw it also ; and, indeed, the
face of the painting, with its delicate and impassioned features, and the form, with its voluptuous
grace, were singularly like her own.

Sabretasche looked closer at her.

'You could love like Francesca,' he said involuntarily.

It was not above his breath, but his face gave it all the eloquence it lacked, as hers all the response it needed.

She heard his short quick breathing as he stood beside her; she felt the passionate words which rose to his lips; she knew that if ever a man's love was hers his was then. But he was long silent, and when he spoke his voice was full of that utter anguish which had startled her twice before.

'*Keep* it, then, and give it to some man more worthy it than I!'

'Violet, my love, are you not tired of all this?' said Lady Molyneux, sweeping up. 'It is half-past four, and I want to go to Swan and Edgar's. Pictures make one's head ache so; I was never so ill in my life as I was after the Sistine chapel.'

Sabretasche took her to their carriage without another word between them.

The next day, to our surprise, the Colonel asked for leave, got it, and went away.

'What the deuce is that for, Colonel?' said I. 'Never been out of town in the season before, have you?'

'Just the reason why I should be now, my dear

fellow,' responded Sabretasche, lazily. 'Twenty
years of the same thing is enough to tire one of it,
if the thing were paradise itself; and when it
comes to be only dusty paves, whitebait dinners,
and club gossip, ennui is very pardonable. The
medical men tell me, if I don't give up Pleasure
for a little time, Pleasure will give up Me. You
know I am not over-strong; so I shall go to the
Continent, and look at it in spring, before there
are the pests of English touring about, with Mur-
ray's, carpet-bags, and sandwiches.'

He vouchsafed no more on the subject, but
went. His departure was talked of in clubs and
boudoirs; women missed him as they would have
missed no other man in London, for Sabretasche
was universal censor, referee, regulator of fashion,
his bow was the best thing in the Park, his fêtes
at Richmond the most charming and exclusive of
the season; but people absent on tours are soon
forgotten, like dead leaves sucked under a water-
wheel and whirled away; and after the first day,
perhaps, nobody save De Vigne and I remarked
how triste his house in Park Lane looked with the
green persiennes closed over its sunny bay-win-
dows.

Whatever his motive, the Colonel was gone to
that golden land where the foamy Rhône speeds

on her course, and Marseilles lies by the free blue
sea, and the Pic du Midi rears its stately head.
The Colonel was gone, and all the clubs, and
drawing-rooms, and journals were speaking of his
Francesca; speaking, for once, unanimously, in
admiration for its wonderful union of art and
truth. The Francesca was the theme of the
day in artistic circles: its masterly conception and
unexceptionable handling would for any pencil have
gained it fame; and in fashionable circles it only
needed the well-known name of Vivian Sabretasche to give it at once an interest and a brevet
of value. The Francesca was talked of by everybody, and strangely enough, the picture most
appreciated in another line by the papers and the
virtuosi, was the Little Tressillian's, which, with
its subject, its treatment, and the truthful ren-
dering of the boy's face, attracted more attention
than any woman's picture had done for a long
time; the art reviews were almost unanimous in
its praise; certain faults were pointed out—re-
viewers must always find *some* as a sort of voucher
of their own discernment—but for all that, Alma's
first picture was a very decided success.

Not long after the Exhibition, De Vigne, one
morning after early parade, ordered his horse
round, put some of the journals in his coat-pocket,

and rode towards Richmond, with the double purpose of having a cool morning gallop before the bother of the day commenced, and of seeing Alma, which he had not done since the success of her picture. He rode fast;—I believe it would have been as great a misery to him to be obliged to do a thing slowly as it would have been to Sabretasche to do it quickly!—and he enjoyed the fresh morning, with the free, pure air of spring. His nature was naturally a very happy one; his character was too strong, vigorous, and impatient to allow melancholy to become habitual to him; he was too young for his fate, however it preyed upon his pride, to be constantly before him; his wife was, indeed, a bitter memory to him, but she was *but* a memory to him now, and a man imperceptibly forgets what is never recalled to him. Except occasional deep fits of gloom and an unvarying cynical sarcasm, De Vigne had cured himself of the utter despondency into which his marriage had first thrown him; the pace at which he lived, if the pleasures were stale, was such as does not leave a man much time for thought, and now, as he rode along, some of his natural spirits came back to him, as they generally do in the saddle to a man fond of riding.

'At home of course?' he said to Mrs. Lee, as

she opened the door to him—said it with that careless hauteur which was the result of habit, not of
intention. De Vigne was very republican in his
theories, but the patrician came out in him malgré
lui!

'Yes, sir,' said the old nurse, giving him her
lowest curtsey. 'Yes, sir, she's at home, and
there's a young gentleman a calling on her. I'm
glad of it; she wants somebody to talk to bad
enough. 'Tain't right, you know, sir, for a merry
child like that to be cooped up alone; you might
as well put a bird in a cage and tie its beak up,
so that it couldn't sing! It's that young gentleman
as came with you, sir, the other day.'

De Vigne stroked his moustaches.

'Oh, ho! Master Curly's found his way, has
he. I dare say she'll be a confounded little flirt,
like all the rest of them, when she has the opportunity,' was his reflection, more natural than
complimentary, as he opened the door of Alma's
room, where the little lady was sitting, as usual
in the window, among the birds and flowers De
Vigne had sent her; Curly, lying back in a chaise
longue, talking to her quite as softly and far more
interestedly than he was wont to talk to the
beauties in his mother's drawing-room.

But Alma cut him short in the middle of a

sentence as she turned her head at the opening
of the door, and sprang up at the sight of De
Vigne.

'How glad I am! How good you are to come
so early.'

'Not good at all; the air is beautiful to-day,
one only wants to be fishing in a mountain burn
to enjoy it thoroughly. Hallo, Curly!' said De
Vigne, throwing himself into an arm-chair; 'how
are you? How did *you* manage to get up so early?
I thought you never were up till after one, except
on Derby Day?'

'Or other temptation greater still,' said Curly,
with an eloquent glance of his long violet eyes at
Alma.

'Do you mean that for a compliment to me?'
said the Little Tressillian, with that gay, rebel-
lious air which was so pretty in her. 'In the
first place, I do not believe it, for there is no
woman on the face of the earth who could attempt
to rival a horse; and in the second, I should not
thank you for it if I did, for compliments are only
fit for empty heads to feed on!'

'Meaning, you think yours the very reverse of
empty?' said De Vigne, quietly.

'Certainly. I am not a boarding-school girl,
monsieur,' said Alma, indignantly. 'I have filled

it with what food I can get for it, and I know at
least enough to feel that I know nothing—the
first step to wisdom the sages say.'

'But if you dislike compliments you might at
least accept homage,' said Curly, smiling,

'Homage? Oh! yes, as much as you like. I
should like to be worshipped by the world, and
petted by a few,'

'I dare say you would,' said De Vigne. 'I
can't say you rdesires are characterized by great
modesty!'

'Well, I speak the truth,' said Alma, naively.
'I *should* like to be admired by the thousands,
and loved just by one or two.'

'You have only to be seen to have your first
wish,' said Curly, softly, 'and only to be known to
have much more than your second.'

Alma turned away impatiently; she had a sad
knack of showing when she was annoyed.

'Really you are intolerable, Colonel Brandling.
You spoil conversation utterly. I say those things
because I mean them, not to make you flatter me.
I shall talk only to Sir Folko, for he understands
me, and answers me properly.'

With which lecture to Curly she twisted her low
chair nearer to De Vigne, and looked up in his
face, much as spaniels look up in their master's,

liking a kick from them better than a caress from
a stranger.

'Have you seen Miss Molyneux lately?'

'Yes; and not long ago I heard Miss Molyneux envying you!'

'Me! *I* envy *her*, if you like. How does she
know me! What has she heard about me? Who
has told her anything of me?'

'Gently, gently, *de grâce!* I don't know that
she has heard anything of you, or that anybody
has told her anything about you; but she has seen
something of yours, and admired it exceedingly.

'Ah! my picture!' cried Alma, joyously, her
envy and her wrongs passing away like summer
shadows off a sunny landscape. 'What has been
said about it? Who has seen it? Do the papers
mention it? Have the—'

'One question at a time, please, then perhaps I
may contrive to answer them:' said De Vigne,
smiling; 'though the best answer to them all will
be for you to read these. Here, see how you like
that!'

He took a critique by a well-known Art-critic
out of his pocket, and gave it to her, pointing out,
among many condemnatory notices of other works,
the brief words in praise of her own, worth more
than whole pages of warmer laudation but less dis-

criminating criticism, which Alma read with her eyes beaming, and her whole face in a rose flush of delight.

'Wait a minute; reserve your raptures,' said De Vigne, putting the 'Times' and other papers before her. 'If the first review sends you into such a state of exultation, we shall lose sight of you altogether over these.'.

'Ah, they make me so happy!' she cried, with none of the dignity and tranquil pride becoming to a successful artist, but with a wild, gleeful, triumph amusing to behold. 'I used to think my pictures would be liked if people saw them; but I never hoped they would be admired like this; and it is all owing to you; without you I should never have had it!'

'Indeed you would, though. You have nothing to thank me for, I can assure you.'

'I have! You knew how I could exhibit it; you did it all for me; but *for* you my picture would now be hanging here, unnoticed and un-praised; and you know well enough that your few words are of more value to me than all these!' With which Alma tossed over the table, with con-temptuous energy, the reviews which had charmed her a minute or two before.

'Very unwise,' said De Vigne, dryly. 'These

will make your fame and your money; my words can do you no good whatever.'

She twisted herself away from him with one of her rapid, un-English movements.

'How courteous he is! You are very forbearing, Miss Tressillian, to put up with him!' said Curly, who had been listening, half amusedly, half irritably, to this conversation, which excluded him.

Alma was angry with De Vigne herself, but she was not going to let anyone else be so too.

'Forbearing? What do you mean? I should be very ungrateful if I were not thankful for such a friend.'

'Now that is too bad,' said Curly, plaintively. 'I, who really admire your most marvellous talent, only get tabooed for being a flatterer, while he is thought perfection, and pleases by being most abominably rude.'

'You had better not measure yourself with him, Colonel Brandling,' said Alma, with that mischievous impudence which sat well upon her, though no other woman, I believe, could have had it with such impunity.

'Vous me piquez, mademoiselle,' said Curly, 'You will tempt me by your very prohibition to enter the lists with him. I should not care to

dispute the belt with him in most things, but for
such a prize—'

'What nonsense are you talking, Curly,' said
De Vigne, with that certain chill hauteur now so
customary to him, but which Alma had never yet
seen in him. 'A prize to be fought for must be
disputed. Don't bring hot-pressed compliments
here to spoil the atmosphere.'

'That's right, take my part,' interrupted Alma,
not understanding his speech as Curly understood
it. 'You see, Colonel Brandling, that sort of
high-flown flattery is no compliment; if the man
mean it, it says little for his intellect, for we are
none of us angels without wings, as you call us;
and if he do not mean it, it says little for ours, for
it is easy to tell when anyone is really liking or
only laughing at us.'

'Indeed!' said Curly. 'I wish we were as clear
when ladies were liking or laughing at us; it
would save us a good many disappointments, when
enchanting forms of life and light, who have softly
murmured tenderest words when they stole our
hearts away in tulle illusion at a hunt ball, bow to
us as chillily as to a first introduction when we
meet them afterwards en Amazone in the Ride,
with somebody as rich as he is gouty, on their off-
side.'

'Serve you right for being so credulous,' said De Vigne. ' Women are either actresses or fools; if they are amiable they are stupid, and if they are clever they are artful.'

' Like Thackeray's heroines,' suggested Curly.

' Exactly; shows how well the man knows life. The first thing the world teaches a clever woman is to banish her heart. Women may thrive on talent, they are certain to go to rack and ruin on feeling.'

' I don't agree with you,' said Alma, looking up, ready for a combat.

' Don't you, *petite?* ' laughed De Vigne, 'I think you will when you have a few more years over your head, and have seen the world a little.'

' No, I do not,' returned the Little Tressillian, decidedly, ' I believe that in proportion as you feel so do you suffer; but I deny that all clever women are actresses. Where will you go for all your noblest actions but to women of intellect and mind? Sappho's heart inspired the genius which has come down to us through such lengthened ages. Was it not love and genius in one, which immortalized Héloïse? Was it not intellect, joined to their love for their country, which have placed the deeds of Polycrita, Hortensia, Hersillia, Mademoiselle de la Rochefoucauld, among the records of patriot-

ism? One of the truest affections we have heard
of was that of Vittoria Colonna for Pescara, of the
woman who ranks only second to Petrarch, the
friend of Pope, and Bembo, and Catarini, the
adored of Michael Angelo, the admired of Ariosto!
Oh, you are very wrong; where you find the glowing imagination, there, too, will you find as ardent
affections; where there is expansive intellect there
and there only, will be charity, tolerance, clear
perception, just discrimination; with a large brain,
a large heart, the more cultured the intelligence,
the more sensitive the susceptibilities! Lucy
Edgermond would make your tea for you tolerably,
and head your table respectably, and blush where
she ought, and say Yes and No like a well-bred
woman : but in Corinne alone will you find passion
to beat with your own, intellect to match with
your own, sympathy, comprehension, elevation, all
that a woman *should* give to the man she loves!'

A Corinne in her own way I can fancy she looked,
too, her blue eyes scintillating like stars in her
earnestness, and her voice rising and falling in impassioned vehemence, accompanied with her viva-
cious and unconscious gesticulation, a trick, probably, of her foreign blood. Curly listened to her
with amazement, this was something quite new to
him; it was not so new to De Vigne, but it touched

him with something deeper, more like regret than
amusement. A glimpse of the golden land is pain
when we know the door is locked, and the key
irrevocably lost.

'Do you suppose, petite,' he said, with a bitter
smile, ' that if there *were* Corinnes in the land men
would be such fools as to go and take the Lucies
of modern society in their stead ? Heaven knows,
if there were women such as you describe, we might
be better men ; more earnest in our lives, more
faithful in our loves ! But you draw from the
ideal, I from the real, two altitudes very far wide
apart; as far apart, my child, as dawn and midnight.' •

His tone checked and saddened Alma's bright
and enthusiastic nature. She gave a heavy sigh.

' It is midnight with you, I am afraid, and I so
want it to be noon !

He answered with a laugh.

'If it be, it is like midnight at a *bal d'Opéra*,
with plenty of gaslights, transparencies, music, and
amusement enough to send the sun jealous, and
making believe the day has dawned !'

' But don't the gaslights, and transparencies, and
all the rest of your *bal d'Opéra* look tawdry and
garish when the day is really up and on them ?'

'We never let the daylight in,' laughed De

Vigne; 'and won't remember that we ever had any brighter light than our coloured lamps. Why should we? They do well enough for all intents and purposes.'

Alma shook her head:

'They won't content you always.'

'Oh yes, they will; I have no desires now but to live without worry, and die in some good hard fight in harness, like my father. What! are you going, Curly? I'll come with you.'

'Yes I must,' said Curly. 'I'm going to a confounded dejeuner in Palace Gardens, at that little flirt's, Jerry Maberly. I shall barely get back in time. How time slips in some places. If I promise to leave compliments, *i. e.* in your case, truth, behind me, may I not come again? Pray be merciful, and allow me.'

'How can I prevent you?' said Alma, in a laughing unconsciousness of Curly's meaning. 'Certainly, come if you like; it is kind of you, for I am very dull here all alone. I am no philosopher, and cannot make a virtue of necessity, and pretend to take my tub and cabbage-leaves in preference to a causeuse and delicate mayonnaise.'

'Capricious, like all your sex. You are asking for compliments now, Alma. " *On ne loue d'ordinaire que pour être loué*," ' said De Vigne, dryly.

'Am I? I did not mean it so,' answered the girl, innocently.

'Nor did I take it so,' said Curly, bending towards her as he took her hand; 'so I shall not say how I thank you for your permission, but only avail myself of it as often as I can.'

De Vigne stood looking disdainfully on, stroking his moustaches; and thinking, I dare say, what arrant flirts all women were at heart, and what fools men were to pander to their vanities.

He bid her good morning with that careless hauteur which he had often with everybody else, but very rarely with her. While he stood at the door waiting for his groom, he heard Alma's voice:

'Come back a minute.'

He went back, as in courtesy bound.

'Why did you speak so crossly to me?'

'I! I was not aware of it.'

'But I was, and it was not kind of you, Sir Folko.'

'Why will you persist in calling me like that knight *sans peur et sans reproche?*' said De Vigne, impatiently. 'I tell you I have nothing in common with him—with his pure life and his spotless shield. He did no evil; I do—Heaven knows how much! He surmounted his temptations; I have always succumbed to mine. He had a conscience at ease; mine might be as great a torture as the rack. His past was one of wise thoughts and noble deeds; mine can show neither the one nor the other.'

'Of your life you know best; but in your character I choose to see the resemblance,' replied Alma, always resolute to her own opinion. 'Was he not a man who feared nothing, who was fierce to his foes and generous to those who trusted him? As for his past, he had probably drawn experience from error, as men ever do; and learnt wisdom out of folly. And as for his stainless shield, is not your haughty De Vigne honour as unsullied as when it passed to you?'

'*No*,' said De Vigne, fiercely. 'My folly stained it, and the stain is the curse of my life. Child, why will you speak of such things? If you care for my friendship, you must never allude to my past.'

Deadly memories were stirring in him. Most women might have been afraid of him in his haughty anger. She was not. She looked up at him, bewildered, it is true, but with a strange mingling of girlish tenderness and woman's passion, both unconscious of themselves.

'Oh, I will not! Do forgive me!'

'Yes, yes, I forgive you,' said De Vigne, hastily. 'Don't exalt me into a god, Alma, that's all; for I am *very* mortal.'

He laid his hand on her shoulder, with the familiar kindness he had grown into with her.

In another second he was across his horse's back, and riding out of the court-yard with Curly, while she stood in the doorway looking after him, shading her eyes from the May sun, which touched up her golden hair and her bright-hued dress into a brilliant tableau, under the low, dark porch of her home.

Curly rode on quietly for some little way, busying his mind with rolling the leaves round a Manilla, and lighting it en route, while De Vigne puffed away at a giant Havannah, between regulating which and keeping his fidgetty Grey Derby quiet (he usually rode horses that would have thrown any other man but him or M. Rarey), he had little leisure for roadside conversation.

At last Curly broke silence, flicking his mare's ears thoughtfully.

'Well, De Vigne! I don't know what to make of it!'

'Don't know what to make of what?' demanded De Vigne, curtly.

He was a little impatient with his Frestonhills

pet. One may not care two straws for pheasant-
shooting—nay, one may even have sprained one's
arm, so that it is a physical impossibility to lift an
Enfield to one's shoulder—and yet, so dog-in-
mangerish is human nature, that one could kick a
fellow who ventures to come in and touch a head
of our *défendu* or uncared-for game!

'Of that little thing,' returned Curly musingly.
'I don't understand her.'

'Very possibly!'

'Why very possibly? I know a good deal of
women, good, bad, and indifferent, but I'll be
hanged if I can understand that Little Tressillian.
She is so frank and free one *might* take no end of
advantage of her; and yet, somehow, deuce take
it, one *can't*. The girl's truth and fearlessness are
more protection to her than other women's pru-
deries and chevaux-de-frise.'

De Vigne did not answer, but smoked silently.

'She is a little darling,' resumed Curly, medi-
tatively. 'One feels a better fellow with her
—eh?'

'Can't say,' replied De Vigne. 'I have generally looked on young ladies, for inflammable boys
like you, as dangerous stimulants rather than as
calming tonics.'

'Confound your matter-of-fact,' swore Curly.

'You may laugh at it if you like, but I mean it.
She makes me think of things that one pooh-
poohs and forgets in the bustle of the world. She's
a vast lot too good to be shut up in that brown
old house, with only a kitten to play with, and an
old nurse to take care of her.'

'She seems to have made an impression on
you !'

'Certainly she has !' said Curly, gaily. 'And,
'pon my life, what makes still more impression on
me, De Vigne, is, that you and I should be going
calling on and chatting with her as harmlessly as
if she were our sister, when we *ought* to be making
desperate love to her, if she hadn't such confounded trusting eyes of hers that they make one
ashamed of one's own thoughts! 'Pon my life, it's
very extraordinary !'

'If extraordinary, it is only honour,' said De
Vigne, with his coldest hauteur, ' towards a young,
guileless girl, utterly unprotected, save by her
own defencelessness. For my own part, as a
" married man " (how cold his sneer grew at those
words !), I have no right to " enter the lists " with
you, as you poetically phrased it to-day ; and for
yourself, you are too true a gentleman, Curly,
though it is " our way " to be unscrupulous in
such matters, to take unfair advantage of my in-

troduction. Indeed, if you did, I, to whom Mr. Tressillian appealed for what slight assistance I have it in my power to afford her, should hold myself responsible for having made you known to her, and should be bound to take the insult as to myself.'

Curly, at the beginning of De Vigne's very calm, but very grandiose speech, opened his lazy violet eyes, and stared at him; but as he went on, he turned to his old Frestonhills hero with his smile,—so *young* in its brightness:

'Quite right, De Vigne. You are a brick; and if I do any harm to that dear Little Tressillian, I give you free leave to shoot me dead like a dog, and I should richly deserve it too. But go and see her I must, for she is worth all the women we shall meet at Jerry's to-day, though they *do* count themselves the *crême de la crême.*'

'The *crême de la crême* can be, at the best, only skim!' said De Vigne, with his ready fling of sarcasm; 'but I am not going to the Maberlys', thank you. Early strawberries and late on dits are both flavourless to my taste; the fault of my own palate perhaps. I shall go and lunch at the U. S., and play a game or two at pool. How pleasant the wind is! Grey Derby wants a gallop.'

Palamon and Arcite were not truer or warmer friends than De Vigne and Curly; but, when a woman's face dazzled the eyes of both, the death-blow was struck to friendship, and the seeds of feud were sown.

CHAPTER V.

THE SKELETON WHICH SOCIETY HAD NEVER SEEN.

ON the 12th of May, Leila Countess of Puffdorff gave a ball, concert, and sort of moonlight fête, all three in one, at her charming dower-house at Twickenham. All our set went, and all of Ours, for *le feu* Puffdorff had been in the Dashers, and out of a tender memory of him, his young widow made pets ,of all the Corps; not, one is sure, because we were counted the handsomest set of men in all Arms, but out of pure love and respect for our late gouty Colonel, who, Georges Dandin in life, became a Mausolus when under the sod. Who upholds that the good is oft interred with our bones? 'Tisn't true though it *is* Shakspeare who says it; if you leave your family, or your pet hospital a good many thousands, you will get the cardinal virtues, and a trifle more, in letters of gold on your tomb; though if you have lived up to your income, or forgotten to insure, any penny-a-lining La Monnoye will do to

scribble your epitaph, and break off with ' *C'est
trop mentir pour cinq écus!* ' Le feu Puffdorff
became ' my poor dear lord,' as soon as the grave
closed over him; pour cause—' my poor dear
lord ' had left his Countess most admirably well
off, and with some of this ' last bequest' the little
widow gave us a charming fête on this 12th of May.

I went to the ball late; De Vigne chose
instead to go to a card party at Wyndham's,
where play was certain to be high. He preferred
men's society to women's at all times, and I must
say I think he showed his judgment! The first
person I saw was Violet, on Curly's arm, with
whom she had been waltzing. Brilliant and
lovely she looked, with all her high-bred grace
and finish about her; but she had lost her colour,
there was an absence of all that free spontaneous
gaiety, and there was a certain distraction in her
eyes, which made me guess the Colonel's abrupt
departure had not been without its effect upon our
most radiant beauty. She had promised me the
sixth dance the previous day in the Park, and as
I waltzed with her, pour m'amuser I mentioned
Sabretasche's name casually, when, despite all her
sang-froid, a slight flush in her cheeks showed
she did not hear it with indifference. When I
resigned her to Regalia, I strolled through the

rooms with the other beauté régnante of the night, Madame la Duchesse de La Vieillecour. Good Heavens! what relationship was there between that stately, haughty-eyed woman, with her Court atmosphere about her calm but finished coquetteries, and bright-faced, blithe-voiced Gwen Brandling, who had given me that ring under the trees in Kensington Gardens ten years before? Ah, well! Time changes us all. The ring was old-fashioned now; and Madame and I *made love* more amusingly and more wisely, if less truly than earnestly, than in those old silly days when we were *in love*, before I had learned experience and she had taken up prudence and ducal quarterings !

I was sitting under one of the luxuriant festoons of creepers in the winter garden with her Excellency; revenging, perhaps a little more naturally than rightly, on Madame de La Vieillecour the desertion of Gwen Brandling : and I suppose I was getting a trifle too sarcastic in the memories I was recalling to her, for she broke off our conversation suddenly, and not with that subtle tact which Tuileries air had taught her.

'Look! Is it possible? Is not that Colonel Sabretasche? I thought he was gone to Biarritz for his health.'

I looked; it *was* Sabretasche, to my supreme astonishment, for his leave had not nearly expired; and in a letter De Vigne had had from him a day or two previous, there had been no mention of his intending to return.

'How charming he is, your Colonel!' said Madame de La Vieillecour, languidly. 'I never met anybody handsomer or more witty in all Paris. Bring him here, I want to speak to him.'

'Surprised to see me, Arthur?' said Sabretasche, laughing, as I went up to him, obedient to her desires. 'I always told you never to be astonished at anything I do. Madame de La Vieillecour there? She does me much honour. Is she trying to make you singe your wings again?'

He came up to her with me, of course, and stood chatting some minutes.

'I am only this moment arrived,' he said, in answer to her. 'When I reached Park Lane this evening, I found Lady Puffdorff's card; so I dined, dressed, and came off, for I knew I should meet all my old friends here. Yes, I am much better, thank you; the sweet air of the Pyrenees must always do one good, and then they give all the credit to the Biarritz baths! Shockingly unjust, but what *is* just in this world?'

He stayed chatting some moments, though his eyes glanced impatiently through the rooms. The air of the Pyrenees had indeed done him good ; his listless melancholy, which had grown on him so much during the last month, had entirely worn off; there was a clear mind-at-ease look about him as if he were relieved of some weight that had worn him down, and there was a true ring about his voice and laugh which had not been there, gay as he was accounted, since I had known him, even when he was ten years younger than he was now. He soon left Madame de La Vieillecour, and lounged through the rooms, exchanging a smile, or a bow, or a few words with almost every one he met, for Sabretasche had a most illimitable acquaintance.

Violet Molyneux was sitting down after her waltz with Regalia, leaning back on a couch, fanning herself slowly, and attending very little to the crowd of men who had gathered, as they were certain to do, round the beauty of the season. She generally laughed, and talked, and jested with them all, so that her pet friends called her a shocking flirt, but to-night she was listless and silent, playing absently with her bouquet, though admiring glances enough were bent upon her, and delicate flattery enough breathed in her ears, to have roused the Sleeping Beauty herself from her trance.

It required more, however, to rouse her; that little more she had, in a voice well accustomed to give meaning to such words, which whispered:

'How can I hope I have been remembered when you have so many to teach you to forget?'

She looked up; her wild-rose colour came back into her cheeks; she gave him her hand without a word, and one of her vassals, a young Viscount, in the Rifles, relinquished his place beside her to Sabretasche. Then she talked to him, quietly enough, on indifferent subjects, as if neither remembered their last strange interview in the Water-colour Exhibition, as if the Francesca were not in both their minds, as if love were not lying at the heart and gleaming in the eyes of each of them!

Sabretasche asked her to waltz; she could not, since she had only the minute before refused Regalia; but she took his arm and strolled into the winter-garden, leaving the full rise and swell of the ball-room music with the subdued hum and murmur of Society, in the distance.

He spoke of trifles as they passed the different groups that were laughing, chatting, or flirting in the several rooms ; but his eyes were on hers, and spoke a more eloquent language. Violet never asked him of his sudden return or his abrupt departure. She was too happy to be with him again to care through what right or reason she was so. Gradually they grew silent, as they strolled on through the conservatories till they were alone. One side of the winter-garden was open to the still night, where the midnight stars shone on trees and statues, with lamps gleaming between, while the nightingales sang their chants of love, which give utterance in their unknown tongue to those diviner thoughts,. that yearning sadness, which lie far down unseen in Human nature.

The night was still, there was no sound save the distant music and the sweet gush of the nightingales' songs close by; the wind swept gently in till the air was full of the dreamy and voluptuous fragrance which lulls the senses and woos the heart to those softer moments which, could they but last, would make men never need to dream of heaven. Such hours are rare ; what wonder if to win them we risk all, if *in* them we cry, with the Lotus Eaters,

> " Let us alone. What is it that will last?
> All things are taken from us and become
> Portions and parcels of the dreadful Past.

Let us alone.   What pleasure can we have
To war with evil ?   Is there any peace
In ever climbing up the climbing wave?
All things have rest and ripen toward the grave
In silence ; ripen, fall, and cease.
Give us long rest, or death ; dark death or dreamful ease."

He, in the still beauty of the night, could listen
to every breath and hear each heart-throb of the
woman he loved, as he looked into her face with
its delicate and impassioned beauty—the beauty
of the Francesca.   All the passion that was in
him stirred and trembled at it ; the voluptuous
spell of the hour stole over his thoughts and senses ;
he stooped towards her :

'Violet !'

It was only one word he spoke : but in it all
was uttered to them both.

He drew her to his heart, pressing his lips on
hers in kisses long and passionate as those that
doomed Francesca.   And the stars shone softly,
and the nightingales sang under the early roses in
the fair spring night, while two human hearts met
and were at rest.

*   *   *   *   *   *   *

When they went back into the ball-room the
waltz had its charm, the music its melody, the
flowers their fragrance again, for Violet; for a
touch of the hand, a glance of the eyes were suffi-

cient eloquence between them, and his whispered Good night, as he led her to her carriage, was dearer to her than any flattery poet or prince had ever breathed. Nay, she was so happy that she even smiled brightly on Regalia, to her mother's joy—so happy, that when she reached the solitude of her own chamber, she threw herself on her knees in her glittering gossamer ball-dress, with as unchecked and impetuous tears of rapture as if she had been Little Alma in her cottage home, rather than the beauty of the Season, with Coronets at her feet.

Lord Molyneux was a poor Irish peer; Sabretasche was rich, of high family, a man whose word was law, whose pre-eminence in fashion and ton was acknowledged, whose admiration was honour, and at whose offer of marriage anyone would feel proud. His social position was so good, his settlements would be so unexceptionable, why! even our dear saint, the Bishop of Comet-Hock, though he shook his head over Sabretasche's sins, and expressed his opinion with considerable certainty concerning the warmth of his ultimate reception —you know where—would have handed him over with the greatest eagerness either of his pretty, extravagant daughters, had the Colonel deigned to ask for one of them. Therefore, when Sabretasche

called the morning after, and made formal propo-
sals for Violet, Jockey Jack, though considerably
astonished ; as society had settled that Sabretasche
would never marry, as decidedly as it had settled
that he was Mephistopheles in fascinating guise ;
was excessively pleased, assented readily, and had
but one drawback on his mind—*telling his wife*—
that lady having set her affections on things above,
namely, little Regalia's balls and strawberry-leaves.

When he came out of Molyneux's study that
morning, he naturally took his way to where his
young love sat alone. She sprang up as he entered,
with so fond a smile and so bright a blush, that
Sabretasche thought he had never seen anything
of half so much beauty, sated as he had been with
beauty all his days.

'How lovely you are !' he said, involuntarily,
some minutes after, as he sat beside her on the
couch, passing his hand over the soft perfumed
hair that rested against his arm.

'Oh ! do not tell me that. So many do !' cried
Violet. 'I like *you* to see in me what no one else
sees.'

'I see a great deal in you that no one else sees ;
whole tableaux of heart and mind, that no one
else can have [a glance at,' said Sabretasche,
smiling. 'But I am proud of your beauty, my

lovely Francesca, for all that; though it may be a fact patent to all eyes.'

'Then I am glad I have it! I would be a thousand times worthier of you if I could.'

'The difficulty "to be worthy" is not on *your* side,' said he, with a shade of his old sadness. 'I cannot bear to think that a life so pure as yours should be dedicated to a life so impure as mine. How spotless is your past, Violet—how dark is mine!'

'But how few have been my temptations—how many yours!' she interrupted him, softly. 'I shall not love you the less, through whatever fires you may have passed. A woman's office is to console, not to censure; and if a man have trust in her enough to reveal his past sins or sorrows, her pleasure should be to teach him to forsake them and forget them.'

'God bless you! If my care and tenderness can repay, your future shall reward you,' he whispered. 'What I have chiefly to tell you, is of wrongs done to me—wrongs that have sealed my lips to you till now—wrongs that have weighed on me for more than twenty long years, and made me the enigmatical and wayward man I probably have seemed. It is a long story, but one I would rather you should know before you fully give yourself to me.'

She looked up at him with a silent promise that
in heart she *was* already given to him; and leaning against him, Violet listened to the story—
which every different scandalmonger had guessed
at, and each separate coterie tried, and vainly
tried, to probe—the story of the Colonel's early
life.

'You know,' began Sabretasche, 'that I was
born and educated in Italy; indulged in all things
by my father, and accustomed to every luxury, I
grew up with much of the softness, voluptuousness,
and passion of the Italian character, while at fif-
teen I knew life as many a man of five-and-twenty,
brought up in seclusion and puritanism here, does
not.   But though I was in the Neapolitan service,
and first in pleasure and levity among the young
noblesse, I was still impressionable and romantic,
with too much of the poetry and imagination of
the country in me to be blasé, though I might be
inconstant.   I never recall the memory of my
youth, *up to three-and-twenty*, without regret, it
was so full of enjoyment.   In the summer of my
four-and-twentieth year I left Naples, during the
hot season, to stay with a friend of mine, whose
estates lay in Tuscany.   You were in Tuscany last
year.   How fair the country is under the shadow
of the Apennines, with its brown olive woods and

its glorious sunsets! It is strange how the curse
of its ingratitude to its noblest sons still clings to
it, so favoured by nature as it is! Della Torre's
place was some six or seven miles from Sienna.
I had gone up to Florence previously with my father,
whose oldest friend was consul there; and travelling across Tuscany where malaria was then rife, a
low fever attacked me. I was travelling vetturino
—there were no railways there in those days—
and my servant, finding that I was much too ill
to go on, stopped of his own accord at a village
not very far from Cachiano. The single act of
a servant, who would have died to serve either
me or my father, grew into the curse of my life!
The name of the village was Montepulto. I dare
say you passed through it; it is beautifully placed,
its few scattered houses, with their high peaked
roofs, standing among the great groves of chesnuts
and the gray thickets of olives, with vineyards and
woods of genista and myrtle lying in the glowing
sunlight. There Anzoletto stopped of his own
accord. I was too ill to dissent; and as the carriage pulled up before the single wretched little
inn the place afforded, the priest of the village,
who was passing, offered me the use of his own
house. I had hardly power to accept or refuse,
but Anzoletto seized on the offer eagerly; and I

was conveyed to the house, where, for many days,
I knew nothing of what passed, except that I
suffered and dreamt. When I awoke from sleep
one evening into consciousness, I saw the red sunset streaming through the purple vine around my
lattice, Anzoletto asleep by my bedside, and a
woman of great beauty watching me: of great
beauty, Violet, but not *your* beauty. It seemed
to me then the face of an angel: afterwards, God
forgive her! I knew it as the face of a fiend. She
was the niece, some said the daughter, of the priest
of Montepulto. She was then five-and-twenty—
when men love women their own age, or older, no
good can come of it—and very beautiful: a Tuscan
beauty, with blonde hair, and long, large, dark
eyes; a lovely woman, in fact, with a certain languid grace which charmed one like music. She
had, too, a certain aristocracy of air. The priest
himself was of noble though decayed family; a
sleek, silent, suave man, discontented with his
humble position in Montepulto, but meek and
lowly-minded, according to his own telling, as a
religieux could be. I awoke to see Silvia da'
Castrone by my bedside. I recovered to have her
constantly beside me, to gaze on her dangerous
charms in the equally dangerous lassitude of con-
valescence. There is a certain languid pleasure

in recovery from illness when one is young that makes all things seem *couleur de rose*; to me, with my impressionable senses and my Southern temperament, there was something in this seclusion, shared with one as beautiful as the scenes among which I found her, which appealed irresistibly at once to poetry and passion, then the two dominant elements in my character; and to my desires, with which no ambitions greater than those of pleasure, and no pains harsher than those of love, had at that time mingled. Sufficient to say, I began to love this woman; as I recovered my love grew, till sense, prudence, pride, all that might have restrained me, were submerged in it. I loved her tenderly, honourably, as ever man could love woman. I decked her in all the brilliant hues of a poet's fancy, I thought her the realization of all my sweetest ideals, I believed I loved for all eternity! I never stopped to learn her nature, her character, her thoughts; I never paused to learn if she in any way accorded to all my requirements and ideas; I loved her—I *married her!* Heavens, what that madness has cost me!'

The memory came over him with a deadly shudder; at its recollection the fell shade it had so long cast on him returned again, and he pressed Violet convulsively to his heart, as if with her

warm, young love to crush out the burden of that
cold and cruel dead one; the intelligence of his
marriage cast a death-like chill over her, but even
in its pain her first impulse was to console him.
She lifted her head and kissed his cheek, the first
caress she had ever offered him, as if to show
more tenderly than words could give them, her
sympathy and her affection. As silently he
thanked her: then with an effort he resumed his
story.

'We were married—by the priest Castrone, and
for a few weeks I believed my fairest dreams were
realized. Violet, do not let my story pain you.
All men have many early loves before they reach
that fuller and stronger one which is the crown
of their existence. I was happy, then, when I
was a boy, and when you were not born, my darling!—but you will give me greater happiness, as
passionate, and more perfect. We were married;
and for a week or two the surrender of my liberty
seemed trifling pay indeed for the rapture it had
brought me. The first shock back to actual life
was a letter from my father. I dared not tell him
of my hasty step; not from any anger that I
should have met, but from the grief it would have
caused him, for the only thing he had ever inter-
dicted to me was an early or an unequal marriage.

Fortunately, the letter was only to ask me to go to England on some business for him. I went, of course, taking Sylvia with me; and while in London, at her suggestion (it did not occur to me, or I should have made it), we had the ceremony again performed in a Protestant church. She said it pleased her to be united to me by the religion of my country as well as of her own. I loved her, and believed her, and was only too happy to make still faster, if I could, the fetters which bound me to a woman I idolized! We were a month or two in England; then we returned, and I bought her a little villa just outside Naples, where every spare moment that I had formerly given to dissipation or amusement, or idle dreaming by the sea-shore, I now gave to my wife. Oh, my love! my love! that any should have borne that title before you! Gradually now dawned on me the truth which she had carefully concealed during our earlier intercourse; that, graceful, gentle as she was in seeming, her temper was the temper of a fiend, her passions such as would have disgraced the vilest woman in a street-brawl! Fancy what it was to me, with my taste, over-refined, accustomed at home to the gentlest tones and softest voices, abhorring what was harsh, vulgar, or unharmonious; to hear the woman I wor-

i 2

shipped meet me, if I was a moment later than
she expected, or the presents I brought her a trifle
less costly than she had anticipated—meet me
with a torrent of reproaches and invectives, her
beautiful features distorted with fury, her soft eyes
lurid with flame, her coral lips quivering with
deadly venom, railing alike at her dogs, her servants, and her husband!—a fury—a she-devil!
Good Heavens! what fiercer torment can there
be for man than to be linked for life with a vixen,
a virago? None can tell how it wears all the
beauty of his life away; how surely, like the dropping of water on a stone, it eats away his peace;
how it lowers him, how it degrades him in his own
eyes, how it drags him down to her own level,
until it is a miracle if it do not rouse in him her
own coarse and humiliating passions! Looking
back on those daily scenes of disgrace and misery,
which grew, as week and month rolled by, each
time worse and worse, as my words ceased to have
the slightest weight, I wonder how I endured
them as I did; yet what is more incredible still,
I yet loved her despite the hideous deformity of her
fiendish nature, for a virago *is* a fiend, and of the
deadliest sort. Still, though my life grew a very
agony to me, and the weight of my secret from
my father unbearable—I dared not tell him, for

he was in such delicate health that the shock might have been fatal—I was never neglectful of her. Strange as it seems, little as the world would believe it, I *was* most constant to, and patient with her. I have done little good in my life, God knows, but in my duty as a husband to her, boy as I was, I may truly say I never failed. Some twelve months after our marriage she gave birth to a daughter. I was very sorry. I am not domestic—never shall be—and a child was the last inconvenience and annoyance I should have wished added to the ménage. I hoped, however, that it might soften her temper. It did not; and my life became literally a curse.

' At this time Sylvia's brother came to Naples, a showy, handsome, vulgar young man, with none of her exterior delicacy, who had been my detestation in Montepulto. Naturally he came to his sister's house, though he had no liking for me, for our antipathy was mutual; but he quartered himself on his sister, for he was poor, and had nothing to do. I generally, when I went to her after Castrone's arrival, found him and some of his friends—rollicking, do-nothing, *mauvais sujets*, like himself—smoking and drinking there; while Sylvia, decked with her old smiles, and adorned in the rich dress it had been my delight to bestow

on her, lay on her couch, flirting her fan or touching her guitar; her lovely voice had been one of
her greatest charms for me; but, once married,
she never let me hear it. The men were odious
to me, accustomed as I was to the best society of
the old Italian noblesse, but I was so sick and
heart-weary of the constant contentions which
awaited me in my wife's home, that I was glad of
the presence of other persons to prevent a scene
of passion and abuse. The chief visitor at Sylvia's
house was a friend of her brother's—an artist of
the name of Lani—a young fellow, exceedingly
handsome, in a coarse, full-coloured style, though
utterly detestable to me, with his loud voice, his
vulgar foppism, and his would-be wit. He pleased
Sylvia, however; a fact to which I never attached
any importance, for I was not at all of a suspicious
or sceptical nature then, and I am never one of
those who think that a woman must necessarily
be faithless to her husband because she likes the
society of another man; on the contrary, a husband's hold on her affection must be very slight,
if, to keep it, he must subject her to a seclusion
almost conventual. Fidelity is no fidelity unless
it has opportunity to swerve if it choose. So, to
be *jealous* of Lani never occurred to me. I could
never have stooped to it, had it even done so,

for I held my own honour infinitely too high
to dream that another could sully it. My trust
and my security were rudely destroyed! Six
months more went on. Sylvia clamoured cease-
lessly for the acknowledgment of our marriage;
in vain I pleaded to her that my father was on
his death-bed, that the physicians told me that
the slightest mental shock would end his existence, and that as soon as ever I had lost him,
which must be at farthest in a few months' time,
I would acknowledge her as my wife, and take
her to England, where large property had just
been left me. Such a plea would, you would
think, have been enough for any woman's heart.
It availed nothing with her; she made it the
occasion for such awful scenes of execration and
passion as I pray Heaven I may never see in
woman or man again. I refused to endanger my
father's life to please her caprices. The result
was one so degrading to her, so full of shame
and misery to me, that for several days I could
not bring myself to enter her presence again. My
love was gone, trampled down under her coarse
and cruel invectives. In the place of my lovely
and idolized wife I found a fiend; and I repented
too late the irrevocable folly of an Early Marriage,
the curse of so many men. When at last I went

to what *should* have been my home, and *was* my
hell ; the windows of some of the rooms stood
open ; I walked up the gardens and through those
windows into the rooms unannounced, as a man
in his own house thinks he is at liberty to do.
How one remembers trifles on such days of anguish
as that was to me ! I remember the very play of
the sunshine on the ilex-leaves, I remember how
I brushed the boughs of the magnolias out of my
path as I went up the verandah steps ! Unseen
myself, I saw Lani and my wife : his arms were
round her, her head upon his breast, and I caught
words which, though insufficient for law, told me
of her infidelity. God help me ! what I suffered!
Young, unsuspicious, acutely sensitive, painfully
alive to the slightest stain upon my honour, to be
displaced by this vulgar, low-bred rival! Great
Heavens ! how bitter was my shame.'

Violet's hands clenched on his in the horror of
his wrongs :

' Oh, my dearest, my dearest ! Would to Heaven
I could avenge you ! '

' Death has avenged me, my darling ! Those
few words which fell on my ear, in the first
paralysed moment of the treachery which had
availed itself of my unsuspecting hospitality to
rob me of my honour, were sufficient for me.

Even then I had memory enough to keep myself
from stooping to the degradation of a spy, and
from lowering myself before the man who had
betrayed me. I went farther into the room, and
they saw me. Lani had the grace to look guilty
and ashamed ;. for only the day before he had
asked me to lend him money, and I had complied.
I remember being perfectly calm and self-pos-
sessed ; one often is so in hours of the greatest
suffering or excitement. I motioned him to the
door; and he slunk like a hound afraid of a
double thonging. He went out, and I was left
alone—with my wife. Do you wonder that I
have loathed and abhorred that title, holding it
as a synonym with all that is base, and treacherous,
and shameful—a curse from which there is no
escape—a clog, rather than take which into his
life a man had better forego all love, all pleasure,
all passion—a mess of porridge with poison in the
cup, for which he must give up all the priceless
birthright of liberty and peace, never enjoyed
and never valued till they are lost for ever, past
recall?

'Do you think there was any shame, remorse,
repentance on her face, any regret for the abuse
of all my confidence, any consciousness of the
fidelity thus repaid, of the trust thus returned?

No ; in her face there was only a devilish laugh. She met me with a sneer and a scoff; she had the brazen falseness to deny her infidelity, for she knew that admission would divorce her and give me freedom ; and when I taxed her with it, she only answered with invectives, with violence, insult, and opprobrium. It seemed as if a demon entered into her when she became possessed with that fearful and fiend-like passion. I will not sully your ears with all the disgraceful details of the scene where a woman gave reins to her fell passions, and forgot sex, truth, all things, even common decency of language or of conduct : suffice it, it ended in worse violence still. As I rose, to leave her for ever, and end the last of these horrible interviews, which destroyed all my self-respect, and withered all my youth, she sprang upon me like a tigress, and struck at my breast with a stiletto, which lay on a table near, among other things of curious workmanship. Strong as I was at that time, I could scarcely master her —a furious woman is more savage in her wrath than any beast of prey; she clung to me, yelling hideous words, and striking blindly at me with her dagger. Fortunately for me, the stiletto was old and blunt, and could not penetrate through the cloth of my coat. By sheer force I wrenched

myself from her grasp, unclenched her fingers
from the handle of the dagger, and left her pros-
trate, from the violence of her own passions, her
beautiful hair unloosened in the struggle, her
hands cut and torn in her own wild fencing with
the stiletto, her eyes glaring with the ferocity of
a tigress, her lips covered with foam. From that
hour I never saw her face.—Last week I read the
tidings of her death.'

Sabretasche paused. He had not recalled the
dread memory of his marriage without bitter pain ;
never till now had his lips breathed one word of
his story to a living creature, and he could not
lift the veil from the secret buried for twenty
years without the murderous air from the tomb
poisoning the free, pure atmosphere which he now
breathed. All the colour fled from Violet's lips
and cheeks ; she burst into convulsive sobs, and
trembling painfully, shrank closer into his arms,
as if the dead wife could come and claim him
from her.

Gently and tenderly he caressed and calmed
her.

' My precious one, I would not have told you
my story if I had known how it would pain you.
I did not like you to be in ignorance of my previous marriage, and I could not tell you the fact,

without telling you also, the history of the
wretched woman who held from me the title you
have promised me to bear. But do not let it
weigh on you. Great as my wrongs were I can
forgive them now. She can harm me no longer;
and you will teach me in the sunshine of your
presence to forget the deadly shadow of her past.
I will tell you no more to-day, you look so pale.
What will your mother say to me for sending
away your brilliant bloom? She likes me little
enough already! Do you wish me to go on?
Then promise me to give me my old gay smiles;
I should be sad, indeed, for my early fate to cast
the slightest shade on your shadowless life! Well,
I left her, as I said. It is useless to dwell on the
anguish, the misery, the shame which had crowded
into my young heart. To have my name stained,
my wife stolen from me by that low-bred cur,
and to know that to this woman I was chained,
till one or other of us should be laid in the grave!
—it was enough to drive a man of four-and-
twenty to any recklessness or any crime. With
that shame and horror upon me, I had to watch
over the dying hours of my father. He died
shortly afterwards in my arms, peacefully, as he
had spent his life. I saw the grave close over
one from whom I had never had an angry word

or a harsh glance, and reckless and heart-broken,
I came to England. I took Counsel's advice about
my marriage; they told me it was perfectly legal
and valid, and that the evidence, however morally
or rationally clear, was not strong enough to
dissolve the unholy ties which bound me to one
whom in my heart I knew a virago, a liar, an
adulteress, who would, if she could, have added
murder to her list of crimes. Of her I never had
heard a word. I left her, at once and for ever,
to her lovers and her passions.'

'Did the child die?' asked Violet. 'I wish you
had had no child, Vivian. I am jealous of everything that has ever been yours! . . . Pray God
that I may live and make atonement to you!'

'My darling!' he murmured fondly. 'You
need be jealous of nothing in my past; none
have been to me what you are and will be. I
never remembered the child. She was nothing to
me; how could I even know that she was mine?
But some years afterwards, they told me she had
died in infancy. So best with such a mother!
What could she but be now? I came to England,
entered the army, and began the life I have led ever
since, plunging into dissipation, to still the fatal
memories that stirred within me; revenging myself on that sex whom I had before trusted and

worshipped; gaining for myself the reputation, to which your mother and the rest of the world still hold, of an unscrupulous profligate; none guessing how my heart ached while my lips laughed; how, sceptical by force, I yet longed to *believe;* and how the heart of my boyhood craved to love and be loved. Three years after my arrival here, the sight of Castrone recalled to me the past in all its hideous horror. What errand think you he, shameless as his sister, came upon me? None less than to extort money from me by the threat, in Sylvia's name, that she would come over to England and proclaim herself my wife. I was weak to yield his demand to him, and not to have the servants show him at once out of the house; but money was plentiful, his presence was loathsome; the idea of seeing that woman, of being forced to endure her presence, of having the mistress of young Lani known in England as my wife, was so horrible, that, without thinking, I snatched at the only means of security. I paid him what he asked —exorbitant, of course — and hung that other millstone round my neck for life! From that time, to within the last twelvemonths, her brother has come to me, whenever his or her exchequer failed; she was not above living on the husband she had wronged! For twenty years I kept my

secret; all I had to remind me of my fatal tie
was the annual visit of Castrone. Can any one
wonder that when I met you I forgot oftentimes
my own fetters, and, what was worse, your danger?
In my many loves I have only, I confess, sought
pleasure and revenged myself on Sylvia's sex—
how could I think well or mercifully of women?
But you roused in me something infinitely deeper,
and more tender. In you the soft idyls of my
lost dreams lived again; with you the grace and
glory of my lost youth returned. Before, as a
man of the world—bitterly as I felt the secret
disgrace of it—I experienced no inconvenience
from the tie. I wooed many lightly, won them
easily, forsook them recklessly. None of the
three could I do with you. *They* only charmed
my senses; *you* won into my heart; they had
amused me, you grew dear to me—a wide difference, Violet, in a woman's influence upon a
man. At first, I confess I flirted carelessly with
you. But when the full beauties of your heart
and mind unfolded themselves to me for the first
time, I remembered mercy, even while I learnt
that for the last time I loved! How great were
my sufferings I need not tell you. Unable to bear
the misery of constant intercourse with you, conscious in myself that if long under the temptation

I should give way under it, and say words for
which, when you knew all, you might learn to
hate me—'

'Oh, never, never!' whispered Violet, fondly.
'I should always love you, come what might.'

Sabretasche passed his hand fondly over her
brow :

'I knew well that you would. But it was the
very consciousness that *if* you loved, you would
love very differently to the frivolous and inconstant women of our set, which roused me into
mercy to you. I left for the south of France, to
give myself time for reflection, or—vain hope !—
to forget you, as I had forgotten many; to give
you time to find, if it so chanced, some one who,
more worthy of your attachment, would reward it
with the legitimate happiness which the world
smiles upon. In a week from leaving London I was
in the Pyrenees, intending to stay there for some
time for the sake of the sea-bathing; but the first
evening I was at Biarritz, I took up over my chocolate an Italian newspaper—how it chanced to
come there I know not—it was the 'Nazionale'
of Naples. Among the deaths I read that of
my wife ! Great heaven ! that a husband's first
thoughts should be a thanksgiving for the death
of the woman he once fondly loved, over whose

sleep he once watched, and in whom he once
reposed his name, his trust, his honour! I read it
over and over again, the letters danced and swam
before my eyes; I, whom the world says nothing
can disturb or ruffle, shook in every nerve, as I
leaned out into the evening air, dizzy and delirious with the rush of past memories, and future
hopes, that surged over my brain! With that one
fateful line I was *free!* No prisoner ever welcomed liberty with such rapturous ecstasy as I.
The blight was off my life, the curse was taken
from my soul, my heart beat free again as it had
never done during the twenty long years that
the bitter shame and misery of my marriage had
weighed upon me. Love and youth and joy were
mine again. A new existence, fresher and fairer,
had come back to me. My cruel enemy, who had
given my honour to a cur, and who had yet stooped
to live on the money she robbed from the boy-
husband she had wronged, was dead, and I at last
was free—free to offer to you the fondest love
man ever offered woman—free to receive at your
hands the golden gifts, robbed from me for so
long. Violet,—I know that I shall not ask for
them in vain?'

She lifted her face to his with broken words,
in her eyes gleaming unshed tears; and as his lips

lingered upon hers, the new youth and joy he coveted came back to Sabretasche, never, he fondly thought, to leave him again while both their lives should last.

CHAPTER VI.

ONE OF THE SUMMER DAYS BEFORE THE STORM.

THE Derby fell late that year. The day was a brilliant, sunshiny one, as it ought to be, for it is the sole day in our existence when we are excited and do not, as usual, think it necessary to be bored to death to save our characters. We confess to a wild anxiety at the magic word 'Start!' to which no other sight on earth could rouse us. We watch with thrilling eagerness the horses rounding the Corner as we should watch the beauty of no Galatea, however irresistible ; and we see the favourite do the distance with enthusiastic intoxication, to which all the other excitements on earth could never fire our blood! From my earliest recollection since I rode races with the stable boys at five years old, and was discovered indulging in that reprehensible pastime by my tutor (a mild and inoffensive Ch. Ch. man, to whom 'Bell's Life' was a dead letter, and the chariot-racing at Rome and

K 2

Elis the only painful reading in the classics), my
passion has been the Turf.   The Turf!—there
must needs be some strange attraction in our
English sport.   It has lovers more faithful than
women ever win; it has victims, voluntary holo-
causts upon its altars, more numerous than any
creed that ever brought men to martyrdom; its
iron chains are hugged where other silken fetters
have grown wearisome; its fascination lasts while
the taste of the wine may pall and the beauty of
feminine grace may satiate.   Men are constant to
its mystic charms where they tire of love's beguile-
ments; they give with a lavish hand to it what
they would deny to any living thing.   Olden
chivalry, modern ambition, boast no disciples so
faithful as the followers of the Turf; and, to the
Turf, men yield up what women whom they love
would ask in vain ; lands, fortunes, years, energies, powers; till their mistress has beggared them
of all—even too often robbed them of honour
itself!

To the Derby, of course, we went—Curly, I,
and some other men, in De Vigne's drag, lunched
off Rhenish, and Guinness, and Moët, and all the
delicacies Fortnum and Mason ever packed in a
hamper for Epsom; and drove back to mess along
the crowded road.   Dropping the others en route,

De Vigne drove me on to dine with him at his own house in Wilton Crescent.

'Come into my room first, old fellow,' he said, as we passed up the stairs. 'I bought my wedding presents for Sabretasche and his wife that will be, yesterday, and want to show them to you. Holloa! what the deuce is that fellow Raymond doing?— reading my letters as I live! I think I am fated to come across rascals! However, as they make up nine-tenths of the world, I suppose I can't be surprised at the constant rencontres!'

From the top of the staircase we saw, though at some distance, straight through into De Vigne's bedroom, the door of which stood open. At the writing-table in the centre sat his head valet, Raymond, so earnestly reading some of the correspondence upon it, that he never heard or saw us. De Vigne sometimes wrote his letters in his bedroom; he always read those by the first post over his matutinal coffee; and as he was immeasurably careless both with his papers and his money, his servants had always full opportunity to peruse the one and take the other. If he had seen the man taking ten pounds off his dressing-table, he would have had a fling at human nature, thought it was the way of that class of people, and kept the man on, because he was a useful servant, and no more of a thief, probably, than another would be. But—no matter in what rank—a dishonourable or a sneaky thing, a breach of trust in any way, always irritated him beyond conception ; he had been betrayed in greater or minor things so often, and treachery was so utterly foreign to his own frank and impetuous nature, that his impatience at it was very pardonable. I could see his eyebrows contract ominously; he went up, stretched his hand over the man's shoulder, and took the letter quietly out of his grasp.

'Go to Mills for your next month's wages, and leave this evening.'

Raymond, sleek, and smooth, and impenetrable as he was, started violently, and changed colour; but his answer was very ready.

'Why, Major? I was merely sorting your papers, sir. You have often ordered me to do that.'

'No lies—leave the room!' said his master, briefly, as he turned to me. 'Arthur, here are the things I mentioned. Come and look at them.'

His valet did not obey his order; he still lingered. He began again, in his soft, purring tone :

'You wouldn't dismiss me like this, Major, if you knew what I could tell you.'

'Leave the room, and send Robert to me,' said De Vigne, with that stern hauteur which always came up when people teazed him. He had had his own way from his infancy, and was totally unaccustomed to being crossed. It is bad training for the world for a man to have been obeyed from his cradle.

'You would give me a good deal, Major, to know what I know. I have a secret in my keeping, sir, that you would pay me handsomely to learn—'

'Silence—and leave the room!' reiterated De Vigne, with an impatient stamp of his foot.

Raymond bowed, with the grace becoming a groom of the chambers.

'Certainly, sir. I hope you will pardon me for having troubled you.'

Wherewith he backed out with all the sang-froid imaginable, and De Vigne turned to me:

'Cool fellow, isn't he?'

'Yes, but you might as well have heard what he had to say.'

'My dear fellow, why?' cried De Vigne, with his most grandiose and contemptuous smile. 'What could that man possibly know that

could concern me. It was only a ruse to get
money out of me, or twist his low-bred curiosity
in spying over my letters into a matter of moment. I was especially annoyed at it, because
the letter he was reading is a note from Alma;
nothing in it—merely to answer a question I
asked her about one of her pictures; but you
know the child has an enthusiastic way of ex-
pressing herself at all times—means nothing, but
sounds a great deal, and the "Dear Sir Folko,"
and "your ever grateful Little Alma," and all the
rest of it—the days are so long when I don't go
to see her, and she envies the women who are in
my set and always with me—and all that—reads
rather . . . . *I* know how she means it, but a common man like Raymond will put a very different
significance upon it.'

'Most probably. *I* know how she means it
too; still, you know the old saying, De Vigne,
relative to toying with edged tools?'

'No, I don't,' said De Vigne, curtly; 'or at
least I should say I know edged tools, when I
see them, as well as you do, and am old enough,
if I did come across them, not to cut myself with
them. I can't think what has possessed Sabretasche and you to try and sermonize to me!
Heaven knows you need to lecture yourselves,

both of you! I don't stand it very well from *him*; but I'll be shot if I do from you, you young dog, whom I patronized in jackets in Frestonhills! Get out with you, and let Robert take the Derby dust off you in the blue-room.'

And he threw Alma's note into a private drawer (to be kept, I wonder?), and pushed me out by the shoulders.

No Cup day ever was so ill-bred as to send dusky English rain-drops on the exquisite toilettes that grace the most aristocratic race in the universe, and we had 'Queen's weather' for Ascot. We had all betted on the Colonel's chesnut, who won the Ascot Cup, distancing all the rest of the first flight at an easy swinging gallop, without any apparent effort;* and when we had seen the race fairly run, we went up to the Molyneux carriage to congratulate the Colonel on his chesnut's triumph: Sabretasche being missed from his usual circle of titled betting-men and great turfites, and, for the first time in all his life, watching Ascot run, with his attention more given to the face beside him, than the course before.

His old-accustomed bay-window saw compara-

---

* I have taken a liberty with the Ascot of '54, which I trust will be pardoned me at the Corner!—*Ouida.*

tively little of him ; his mornings were given to
Violet in the tête-à-tête of her boudoir; in the
Ride and the Ring he was by her side or in her
carriage ; and the whist-tables of the United, the
guinea points of the Travellers', the coulisses,
the lansquenet parties, saw but very little of him.
The Colonel, for the time being, was lost to us
and to 'life,' which he had lived so recklessly and
graced so brilliantly for so many years ; and I
suppose his new occupation charmed him, for
when we did get an hour or two of him, he was
certainly more delightful than ever: there was
such a joyous ring in his ever-brilliant wit—such
gentleness, to all people and all things, out of the
abundance of his own happiness—such a depth of
rest and contentment, in lieu of that touching and
deep-seated melancholy, which had gone down so
far into his character under his gay and fashionable exterior, that it had seemed as if nothing
would uproot it. So happily does human life
forget its past sorrows in present joy, as the green
meadows grow dark or golden, according as the
summer sun fades on and off them ! His marriage was fixed to take place in a few weeks, and
all the prosaic details which attend on love in these
days of matter-of-fact and almighty dollars (how
often to tarnish and corrode it !) grew in his hands

into the generous gifts of love to love, the out-
ward symbols of the inward worship. So sur-
rounded, and with such a future lying before her,
in its brilliant colours and seductive witchery, can
you not fancy that our ever-radiant beauty looked
—how, words are not warm enough to tell; it
would need a brush of power diviner than Titian's
to picture to you Violet Molyneux's face as it was
then, the incarnation of young, shadowless, brilliant, impassioned life !

'I knew we should win !' she said, as we
approached her barouche. 'Did I not tell you
so, Major de Vigne?'

'You did, fair prophetess; and if you will
always honour me with your clairvoyant instruc-
tions, I will always make up my books accordingly.'

'The number of bets *I* have made to-day is
something frightful,' answered Violet. 'If that
darling horse had failed me I should have been
utterly ruined in gloves.'

'As it is, you will have bracelets and negligés
enough to fill Hunt and Roskell's ! You are most
dangerous to approach, Miss Molyneux, in more
ways than one,' said Vane Castleton, who was
leaning against the carriage door flirting with her
mother.

'Oh! pray don't, Lord Vane; you talk as if I were some grim and terrible Thalestris!' cried Violet, with contemptuous impatience, looking at Sabretasche with a laugh.

'Thalestris!' repeated Sabretasche, smiling. 'You have but very little of the Amazon about you; not enough, perhaps, if your lines had fallen in hard places.'

'Instead of rose-leaves! Yet I think I can fight my own battles?'

'Oh yes!' laughed Sabretasche. 'I never meant to hint but that you had, in very great perfection, that prerogative par excellence of woman, that Damascus blade, whose brilliant chasing makes us treat it as a toy, until the point has wounded us —the tongue!'

'If mine is a Damascus blade, yours is an Excalibur itself! *Le fourgon se moque de la pelle, monsieur!*'

'An English inelegance taking refuge in a foreign idiom! What true feminine diplomacy!' laughed Sabretasche, resting his eyes on her with that deep tenderness for her, for all she did, and said, and thought, which had grown into his life.

She laughed too—a sweet, gay laugh of perfect happiness.

'Ah! there is Her Majesty going off the stand —before Queen Violet goes too! Colonel Sabretasche tells me, Major de Vigne, that you know the artist of that lovely " Louis Dix-sept," and that she is a lady living at Richmond. May I go and see her?'

'Certainly, if you will be so kind.'

De Vigne felt a certain annoyance; why, I doubt if he could have told—a certain selfish desire to keep his little flower blooming unseen, save by his own eyes, acting unconsciously upon him.

'The kindness will be to me. Is she young?'

'Yes.'

'And very pretty?'

'Really I cannot say; ladies' tastes differ from ours on such points.'

'I hope she is,' said Violet, plaintively. 'I never did like plain people, never could! I dare say it is very wrong, but I think one likes a handsome face as naturally as one prefers a lily to a dandelion; and I am quite certain the artist of that sketch *must* be pretty—she could not help it.'

'She *is* pretty,' said Sabretasche; at least attractive—what you will call so.'

'Then will you take me to see her to-morrow,

Major de Vigne, and introduce us? Of course
you will; no one refuses me anything! You can
come with me, can you not, Vivian? We will all
ride down there early, shall we?'

'Yes, and lunch at the Dilcoosha, if Lady Molyneux permit?'

'Go where? Do what?' asked the Viscountess,
languidly, turning reluctantly from her, I presume,
interesting conversation with Vane Castleton.

Sabretasche repeated his question.

'To see an artist, and lunch with you? Oh
yes, I shall be very happy, I don't think we have
any engagements for to-morrow morning,' said
Lady Molyneux, turning again to Castleton.
'Are you going to the Lumleys to-night, Vane?'

The morning after, half-a-dozen of us rode down
out of Lowndes Square. First, the Colonel and
Violet; next, the Viscountess and her pet, Vane
Castleton; then De Vigne and I—De Vigne, I
must confess, in one of his most haughty, reserved,
and impatient moods, annoyed, more than he knew,
at having to take people to see Alma, whom he
had had to himself so long that he seemed to consider any other visit to her as an invasion on his
own 'vested interests.' Besides, he was irritated
to be tricked into taking Vane Castleton there, of
all men in the world! Lady Molyneux had asked

him; De Vigne knew nothing of his addition to the party until he had reached Lowndes Square, and to make any comment on, or opposition to it, would have been as useless as unwise.

'Does Miss Tressillian live alone with an old nurse, Major De Vigne?' Lady Molyneux was asking, in that voice which was langour and superciliousness embodied. 'How very queer— so young a girl! To be sure, she is only an artist! Artists *are* queer people generally. Still, it is very odd!'

'Artists, like other people, must live; and if they have happened to have lost their parents, they cannot live with them, I presume,' responded De Vigne, dryly. The Viscountess had always an irritating effect upon his nerves.

'No, of course not: still, there are plenty of places where a girl can take refuge that are most irreproachable—a school, for instance. She would be much better, I should fancy, as a teacher, or a—'

'She happens to be a gentlewoman,' interrupted De Vigne, quietly, 'and nurtured in as much luxury and refinement as your daughter.'

'Indeed!' said the Viscountess, with a nasty sneer and upraised eyebrows. 'Pray, is she quite a—quite a *proper* person for Violet to visit?'

De Vigne's slumbering wrath roused up; every vein glowed with righteous anger and scorn for the pharisaic Peeress, of whose own under-currents he knew a story or two not quite so spotless as might have been.

'Lady Molyneux, if the ladies your daughter meets in our set at Court and Drawing-room, balls and operas, the immaculate Cordelias and Lucretias of English Matronage, could lay claim to half as pure a life, and half as pure a heart, as the young girl you are so ready to suspect and to condemn, it might be better for them and—for their husbands!'

It was a more outspoken, and, in this case, more personal, speech than is customary to the bland reserve and reticence customary in ' good society,' where we may sin, but may not say we do, and where it is only permitted to ridicule or blackguard our friends behind their backs. The Viscountess reddened under her delicate rouge, and turned with a laugh to Castleton. The white gate and dark thatched gables of St. Crucis Farm were now close at hand, and De Vigne rode forward.

'What a picturesque place!' cried Violet, dropping her reins on her mare's neck. 'Oh, Vivian, do look at those little lovely yellow chickens, and that great China rose climbing all over the house, and the veritable lattice windows, and that splendid black cat in the sunshine! Wouldn't you like to live here?'

Sabretasche shook his head, and would have crossed himself had he been a Catholic.

'My dear Violet! Heaven forfend! I cannot say I should.'

'Nor she either,' laughed De Vigne. 'She will be much more in her element in its neighbour, your luxurious Dilcoosha.'

Sabretasche smiled, Violet's delicate colour deepened, to vie with the China roses she admired, while the Colonel lifted her from her saddle close to the objects of her attachment, the little lovely yellow chickens, surely the prettiest of all new-born things; humiliatingly pretty beside the rough ugliness of new-born man, who piques himself on being lord of all created creatures; God knows why, except that he is slowest in development, and quickest in evil!

Certainly the old farm-house looked its best that day, the grey stone, the black wooden porch, the dark thatch, with its sombre lichens, that had all appeared so dark and dreary in the dim February light in which we first saw them, were only antiquated in the full glow of the June sunlight.

The deep cool shadows of the two great chesnut trees beside it, with their large leaves and snowy pyramidal blossoms, the warm colours of the China roses and the honeysuckles against its walls, of the full-blossomed apple-trees, and the fragrant lilacs—those delicate perfumy boughs that Horace Walpole, the man of wit and gossip, courts and salons, patches and powders, still found time to love—gave it the picturesqueness and brightness which charmed Violet at first sight; for not more different is the view of human life in youth and age, than the view of the same place in summer and winter. If our life were but all youth! if our year were but all summer!

Out of the wide, low lattice window of her own room, half shadowed by the great branches of the chesnut-trees, with their mélange of green and white, yet with the full glow of the golden morning sunbeams, and the rose-hued reflex of the China roses upon her, Alma was leaning as we alighted. Like her home, she chanced to look her prettiest and most picturesque that day; a picture shrined in the dark chesnut-boughs and the glowing flowers—a picture which we could see, though she could not see us.

' Is that Miss Tressillian? How lovely she is!' cried Violet, enthusiastically.

Sabretasche, thinking of her alone, smiled at
her ecstasies. The Viscountess raised her glass
with supercilious and hypercritic curiosity. Castleton did the same, with the look in his eyes
that he had given the night before to the very
superior ankles of a new danseuse. De Vigne
caught the look—by George! how his eyes flashed
—and he led the way into the house, sorely wrathful within him. Alma's innate high breeding
never showed itself more than now when she
received her unexpected influx of visitors. The
girl had seen no society, had never been 'finished,'
nor taught to 'give a reception;' yet her inborn
self-possession and tact never deserted her, and
if she had been brought up all her days in the
salons of the Tuileries or St. James, it would have
been impossible to show more calm and winning
grace than she did at this sudden inroad on the
conventual solitude of her studio. Violet and
she fraternized immediately; it was no visit from
a fashionable beauty to a friendless artist, for
Violet was infinitely too much of a lady not
to recognize the intuitive aristocracy which in
the Little Tressillian was thoroughly stamped in
blood and feature, manner and mind, and would
have survived all adventitious circumstances or
surroundings. There was, besides, a certain re-

semblance, which we had often noticed, in their natures, their vivacity, and their perfect freedom from all affectations.

The Viscountess sat down on a low chair in a state of supercilious apathy. She cared nothing for pictures. The parrot's talk, which was certainly very voluble, made her head ache, and Vane Castleton was infinitely too full of admiration of Alma to please her ladyship. De Vigne, when he had done the introductory part of the action, played with Sylvio, only looking up when Alma addressed him, and then answering her more distantly and briefly than his wont. He could have shot Castleton with great pleasure for the free glance of his bold light eyes, and such a murderous frame of mind rather spoils a man for society, however great he may generally be as a conversationalist!

We, however, managed to keep up the ball of talk very gaily, even without him. It was chiefly, of course, upon art—turning on Alma's pictures, which drew warm praises from Violet and Castleton, and, what was much more, from that most fastidious critic and connoisseur, the Colonel. We were in no hurry to leave. Castleton evidently thought the *chevelure dorée* charming; women were all of one class to him—all to be bought; some with higher prices and some with lower, and he drew no distinction between them, except that some were blondes and some brunes. Violet liked leaning against the old oak window-seat scenting the roses, and listening to Sabretasche's classic and charming disquisitions upon painting, and Alma herself was in her element with highly-bred and highly-educated people. We were in no hurry to go; but Lady Molyneux was, and was much too bored to stay there long.

'You will come and see me?' said her daughter, holding out her hand to Alma. 'Oh yes, you must. Mamma, is not Thursday our next "At Home"? Miss Tressillian would like to meet some of our celebrities, I am sure; and they would like to see her, for every one has admired her "Louis Dix-sept." Have you any engagement?'

Of course Alma had none. She gave a glance at De Vigne, to see if he wished her to go, but as he was absorbed in teaching Sylvio to sit on his hind legs and hold a riding-whip on his nose, she found no responsive glance, and had to accept it without consulting him. Violet taking acceptance for granted, and her mamma, who did not care to contradict her before Sabretasche, joining languidly in the invitation, the Little Tressillian stood

booked for the Thursday soirée in Lowndes
Square.

Violet bade her good-day, with that suave
warmth which fashionable life could never ice out
of her, and the Viscountess swept out of the room,
and down the garden, in no very amiable frame of
mind. She rather affected patronizing artists of
all kinds, and had brought out several protégés,
though she unhappily had dropped them as soon as
their novelty had worn off; but to patronize a
girl's genius, whose face Vane Castleton admired,
was a very different matter, for my lady was just
now as much in love as she had ever been in love
with anything, except herself, and there is no passion more exigeant and tenacious than the fancy
of a woman, *passée* herself, for a young and handsome man! De Vigne was a little behind the
rest as he left the room, and Alma called him
back, her face full of the delight that Violet's
invitation had given her.

'Oh, Sir Folko! I am so happy. Was it not
kind of Miss Molyneux?'

'Very kind indeed.'

'Don't you like me to go?'

'I? What have I to do with it? On the
contrary, I think you will enjoy yourself very
much.'

'You will be there, of course?'

'I don't know. Perhaps.'

'Oh, you will,' cried Alma, plaintively. 'You
would not spoil all my pleasure, surely? But why
have you spoken so little to me this morning?'

'You have had plenty of others to talk to you,'
said De Vigne, coldly. 'At least, you have
seemed very much amused.'

'Sir Folko, that is very cruel,' cried Alma,
vehemently. 'You know as well as I can tell
you, that if you are not kind to me, all the world
can give me no pleasure.'

'Nonsense! Good-by, petite,' said De Vigne,
hastily, but kindly, for his momentary irritation
had passed, as he swung through the garden and
threw himself across his horse.

'What a little darling she is, Vivian?' said
Violet, as they cantered along the road. 'Don't
you think so?'

Sabretasche laughed:

'Really, I did not notice her much. There is
but one "darling" for me now.'

'Deuced nice little thing, that!' said Castleton
to me; 'uncommonly pretty feet she has; I
caught sight of one of them. I suppose she's
De Vigne's game, bagged already probably, else,
on my honour, I shouldn't mind dethroning La

Valdare, and promoting her, French women
have such deuced extravagant ideas.'

I believe if De Vigne had heard him he would
have knocked Castleton straight off his horse ! His
cool way of disposing of Alma irritated even *me* a
little, and I told him, a trifle sharply, that I thought
he had better call on his ' honour' to remember that
Miss Tressillian had birth and education, and that
she was hardly to be classed with the Anonyma
of our acquaintance. To which Castleton responded with a shrug of his shoulders and a twist
of his whiskers :

' Bless your soul, my dear fellow, women are all
alike!   Never knew either you or De Vigne scrupulous before ; ' and rode on with the Viscountess,
asking me, with a sneer, if I was ' the Major's
gamekeeper ? '

De Vigne was very quick to act, but he was unwilling to analyze. It always fidgeted him to reason on, to dissect, and to investigate his own feelings ; he was not cold enough to sit on a court-
martial on his own heart, to cut it up and put it in
a microscope, like Gosse over a trog or a dianthis,
or to imitate De Quincey's habit of speculating on
his own emotions. He was utterly incapable of
laying his own feelings before him, as an anatomist
lays a human skeleton, counting the bones, and

muscles, and points of ossification, it is true, but
missing the flesh, the colouring, the quick flow of
blood, the warm moving life which gave to that
bare skeleton all its glow and beauty. De Vigne
acted, and did not stop to ask himself why he did
so nine times out of ten; therefore he never in-
quired, or thought of inquiring, why he had experienced such unnecessary and unreasonable anger
at Castleton and Alma, but only felt remorsefully
that he had lacked kindness in not sympathizing
with the poor child in her very natural delight at
her invitation to Lowndes Square. Whenever he
thought he had been unkind, if it were to a dog,
he was not easy till he had made reparation; and
not stopping to remember that unkindness from
him might be the greater kindness in the end, he
sent her down on Thursday morning the best bouquet the pick of Covent Garden could give him,
clasped round with a *parure* of jewels, as delicate in
workmanship as rare in value, with a line, ' Wear
them to-night in memory of your grandfather's
friendship for " Sir Folko." '

De Vigne's virtues led him as often into
temptation as other men's vice. When he
sent those flowers and pearls to the Little
Tressillian, I am certain he had no deeper
motive, no other thought, than to make reparation

for his unkindness, and to give her as delicately as
he could ornaments he knew that she must need.
With him no error was foreplanned and premedi-
tated.   He might have slain you in a passion, perhaps, but he could never have stilettoed you in
cold blood.   There was not a taint of malice or
design, not a trace of the ' serpent nature ' in his
character.

CHAPTER VII.

HOW THE OLDEN DELIRIUM AWOKE LIKE A GIANT FROM HIS SLUMBERS.

THE Molyneux rooms in Lowndes Square were full; not crowded, the Viscountess knew too well the art of society to cram her apartments, as is the present habitude, till lords and ladies jostle and crush one another like so many Johns and Marys crowding before a fair—the rooms were full, and 'brilliantly attended,' as the morning papers had it next day, for though they were of the fourth order of nobility, the Molyneux had as exclusive a set as any in town, and knew 'everybody.' 'Everybody!' Comprehensive yet exclusive phrase! meaning, in *their* lips, just the crême de la crême, and nothing whatever below it; meaning, in a Warden's, all his Chapter; in a schoolgirl's, all her schoolfellows; in a leg's, all the ' ossy-men ;' in an author's, those who read him; in a painter's, those who praise him; in a rector's, those who tes-

timonialize and saint him! In addition to the
haute volée of fashion there was the *haute volée* of
intellect at the Viscountess's Reception, for Lady
Molyneux dearly loved to have a lion (though
whether a writer who honours the nations, or an
Eastern prince in native ugliness and jewellery,
was perhaps immaterial to her!) ; and many of our
best authors and artists were not only acquaint-
ances of hers, but intimate friends of Sabretasche's,
who at any time threw over the most aristocratic
crush for the simplest intellectual réunion, pre-
ferring, as he used to say, the God-given cordon
of Brain to the ribbons of Bath or Garter.

I went there early, leaving a dinner-party in
Eaton Square sooner than perhaps I should have
done, from a trifle of curiosity I felt to see how
the ' Little Tressillian ' comported herself in her
new sphere ; and I confess I did not expect to see
her quite so thoroughly at home, and quite so
much of a star in her own way as I found her to
be. I have told you she had nothing of Violet's
regular and perfect beauty—regular as a classic
statue, perfect as an exquisitely-tinted picture—
yet, someway or other, Alma *told* as well in her
way as the lovely Irish belle in hers ; told even better than the Lady Ela Ashburnington, our modern
Medici Venus—but who, alas! like the Venus,

never opens those perfectly-chiselled lips; or the
exquisite Mrs. Tite Delafield,—whose form would
rival Canova's Pauline, if it weren't made by her
couturière: or even Madame la Duchesse de la
Vieillecour, now that—ah me!—the sweet rose
bloom is due to Palais Royal shops, and the once
innocent lips only breathe coquetries studied be-
forehand, while her maid brushes out her long
hair, and Gwen'—pshaw! Madame la Duchesse
—glances alternately from Octave Feuillet's or
Feydeau's last novel, to her Dresden-framed
mirror.

Yes, Alma won upon all; whether it was her
freshness, whether it was her natural abandon,
whether it was her unusual talent, wit, and gay
self-possession (for if there is a being on earth
whom I hate, 'tis Byron's ' bread-and-butter miss '),
I must leave undetermined. Probably, it was
that nameless something which one would think
Mephistopheles himself had given some women,
so surely and so unreasoningly do men go down
before it, whether they will or no. The women
sneered at her, and smiled superciliously, but that
was of course! See two pretty women look at
each other—there is defiance in the mutual re-
gard, and each thinks in her own heart, ' *Je vais
me frotter contre Wellington!* ' One might have

imagined that those high-bred beauties, with their
style and their Paris dress, their acknowledged
beauty, and their assured conquests, could well
have spared Alma a few of the leaves out of their
weighty bay wreaths. Yet I believe in my soul
they grudged her even the stalks, and absolutely
condescended to honour her with a sneer (surest
sign of feminine envy) when they saw not only
a leaf or two, but a good many garlands of rose
and myrtle going to her in the Olympic game
of 'Shining.'

An R. A. complimented her on her talent, a
Cabinet minister smiled at her repartee, a great
littérateur exchanged mots with her, Curly fell
more deeply in love with her than ever, Castleton
was rapturous about her feet, very blasés men
about town went the length of exciting themselves to ask her to dance, and Attachés and
Guardsmen warmed into stronger admiration than
their customary *nil admirari*-ism usually permitted, about her. Yet she bent forward to
me as I approached her with a very eager
whisper:

'Oh, Captain Chevasney! isn't Major De Vigne
coming?'

I really couldn't tell her, as I had not seen
him all day, save for a few minutes in Pall Mall;

and the disappointment on her face was amusing. But a minute afterwards her eyes flashed, the colour deepened in her cheeks.

'There he is!' she said, with an under-breath of delight. And her attention to Curly, and Castleton, and the other men, began to wander considerably.

There he was, leaning against the doorway, looking bored, I was going to say, but that is rather too affected a thing, and not earnest nor ardent enough for any feeling of De Vigne's; it was rather the look of a man too impatient and too spirited for the quiet trivialities around him, who would prefer 'fierce love and faithless war' to drawing-room flirtations and polite character-damning; the look of a horse who wants to be scenting powder and leading a charge, and is ridden quietly along smooth downs where nothing is stirring, with a curb which he does not relish. Ostensibly, he was chatting with a member of the Lower House: absolutely, he was watching Alma with that look in his eyes, caused, I think, by a certain peculiarity of dropping the lashes over them when he was angry, which made me fancy he was not overpleased to see the men crowding round the little lady.

'He won't come and speak to me. Do go and

ask him to come,' whispered Alma, confidentially,
to me.

I laughed—he had not been more than three
minutes in the room!—and obeyed her behest.

'Your little friend wants you to go and talk to
her, De Vigne.'

He glanced towards her.

'She is quite as well without any attention from
me, considering the reports that have already
risen concerning us, and she seems admirably
amused as it is.'

'Halloa! are we jealous?'

'Jealous! Of what, pray?' asked my lord,
with supreme scorn.

And moving across the room at once in Alma's
direction (without thinking of it, I had suggested
the very thing to send him to her, in sheer defiance), he joined the group gathered round the
Little Tressillian, whose radiant smile at his approach made Castleton sneer and poor Curly swear
sotto voce under his moustaches.   De Vigne, however, did not say much to her; he shook hands
with her, said one or two things, and then talking
with Tom Severn (whom Alma had attracted to
her side) about the ties shot off at Hornsey Wood
that morning, left the little lady so much to the
other men, that though he was within a yard of

her, she thought she preferred him in her studio at St. Crucis than in the crowded salons of that 'set' of his in which she had wished to meet him.

De Vigne talked to those about him, but he meanwhile watched her dancing, lightly and gracefully as a Spanish girl or an Eastern bayadère; watched her, the fact dawning on him, with a certain warning thrill, that she was not, after all, a little thing to laugh at, and play with, and pet innocently, as he did his spaniel, but a woman, as dangerous to men as she was attractive to them, who could no more be trifled with without the trifling falling back again upon the trifler, than absinthe can be drunk like water, or opium eaten long without delirium.

Certain jealousies surged up in his heart, certain embers that had slumbered long began to quicken into flame; the blood that he had tried to chill into ice-water rushed through his veins with something of its natural rapidity and fire. He had pooh-poohed Sabretasche's earnest and my half-laughing counsels; he now heeded as little what ought to have roused him much more, the throbs of his own heart, and the passions stirring into life within him.

She was a child; his own honour was guard

sufficient against love growing up between them.
So he would have said if he had ever reasoned on
it. But he was not cold enough for such self-
examination, and even now, though jealousy was
waking up in him, he was wilfully blind to it, and
to the irritation, which the sight of the other
men crowding round, and claiming, her excited in
him.

' Don't you mean to dance with me ? ' whispered
Alma, piteously, as he passed her after the waltz
was over.

' I seldom dance,' he answered.

It was the truth : waltzing used to be a passion
with him, but since the Trefusis had waltzed his
reason away, the dance had brought disagreeable
associations with it.

' But you *must* waltz with me ! '

' Hush! All the room will hear you,' said De
Vigne, smiling in spite of himself. ' Let me look
at your list, then ! '

' Oh, I would not make any engagements. I
might have been engaged ten deep, Sir Folko, but
I kept them all free for you.'

' May I have the honour of the next waltz
with you, then, Miss Tressillian ? ' asked De
Vigne, in a louder tone, for the benefit of the
people round.

As he put his arm round her, and whirled her into the circle, he remembered, with a shudder at the memory, that the last woman he had waltzed with was the Trefusis. In India wilder sports and more exciting amusements had filled his time, and since he had been in England he had chiefly frequented men's society.

'You had my note, Sir Folko?' was Alma's first question. 'I could never thank you for your beautiful gifts, I could never tell you what happiness they gave me.'

'You have said far more than enough, petite,' said De Vigne, hastily.

'No;' persisted Alma, 'I could *never* say enough to thank you for all your lavish kindness to me.'

'Nonsense,' laughed De Vigne. 'I have given jewels to many other women, Alma, but none of them thought they had any need to feel any gratitude to me. The gratitude they thought was due to *them* for having allowed me to offer them the gift!'

He spoke with something of a sneer, from the memory of how—to him, at least—women, high and low, had ever been cheap, and worthless as most cheap things are; and the words cast a chill over his listener. For the first time the serpent

M 2

entered into Alma's Eden—entered, as in Milton's
apologue, with the first dawning knowledge of
Passion.   Unshed tears sprang into her eyes,
making them flash and gleam as brilliantly as the
gems he had given her.

'If you did not give them from kindness,' she
said, passionately, 'take them back, My happiness in them is gone.'

'Silly child!' said De Vigne, half smiling at
her vehement tones.   'Should I have given them
to you if I had not cared to do so?   On the contrary, I am always glad to give you any pleasures
if I can.   But do you suppose, Alma, that I have
gone all my life without giving presents to any
one till I gave them to you?'

Alma laughed, but she looked, half vexed, up
in his face even still :

'No, I do not, Sir Folko ; but you should not
give them to me *as* you gave them to other
women, any more than you should class me with
other women.   You have told me you did not?'

'My dear Alma, I cannot puzzle out all your
wonderful distinctions and definitions,' interrupted
De Vigne, hastily.   'Have you enjoyed the evening as much as you anticipated?'

'Oh, it is delightful!' cried the little lady,
with that rapid alternation from sorrow to mirth

due to her extreme susceptibility to external impressions.

De Vigne raised his eyebrows, and interrupted her again, somewhat unwarrantably:

'You are a finished coquette, Alma.'

Her blue eyes opened wide under their black lashes:

'Sir Folko! I?'

'Yes, you. I am not finding fault with you for it. All women are who can be. I only wonder where, in your seclusion, you have learned all those pretty wiles and ways that women, versed in society from their childhood, fail to acquire. Who has taught you all those dangerous tricks, from whom have you imitated your skill in captivating Curly and Castleton and Severn, and all those other men, however different their styles or tastes? You are an accomplished flirt, petite, and I congratulate you on your proficiency.'

He spoke with most unnecessary bitterness, much more than he was conscious of, and certainly much more than he ought to have used, for the Little Tressillian was just as much of a coquette—if you like to call it so—and no more of one, than De Vigne in reality liked; for he measured women by their power of fascination. But now the devil of jealousy had entered into him.

Her eyes flashed, her lips quivered a little;
Alma was not a woman to sit down tranquilly
under injustice; her nature was too passionate
not to be indignant under accusation, though it
was at the same time much too tender not to
forgive it as rapidly where she loved the of-
fender.

'For shame, Sir Folko! You are cruelly unjust: you know as well as I do that you do not
believe what you say, though Heaven knows *why*
you say it! I am not aware that I have any
"wiles and ways"—as you so kindly term them—
but I do know that no one has "taught" them to
me. What I think I say; what I feel I tell
people; if I am happy, I do not conceal it.
"Coquette!" I have heard you use that word to
women you despise. Coquette, I have heard you
say, means one to whom all men are equal. I
thank you greatly for your kind opinion of me!'

'Hush, hush! Heaven knows that was far from
my thoughts! Forgive me, I know you have no
artifice or affectation, and I should never attribute
them to you. Let nothing I say vex you. If
you knew all, you would not wonder that I am
sceptical and suspicious, and sometimes perhaps
unjust.'

He spoke kindly, gently, almost fondly. He

was angry with himself for having spoiled her
unclouded pleasure. She looked up in his face
with a saddened, reproachful tenderness, which
had never been in her eyes before, different to
their impetuous vexation, different still to their
frank, affectionate confidence:

'Yes; but trust *me* at least, if you doubt all
the world?'

'I do!'

He spoke in a low whisper, her heart throbbing
against his, her breath upon his cheek, his hand
closing tight upon hers in the caress of the waltz;
and with the voluptuous swell of the music, the
tender and passionate light of the eyes that were
lifted to his, for the first time there awoke, and
trembled in them both, the dawn of that passion
which the one had never before known, which
to the other had been so fierce and fatal a
curse.

At that moment the music ceased: De Vigne
gave her his arm in silence, and soon after seated
himself by her on one of the couches, while other
men came round her, taking ices and talking the
usual ball-room chit-chat. It was strange how much
that single evening did for Alma; she was admired,
courted, followed; she learnt her own power, she
received the myrtle crown due to her own attrac-

tions, to the grace and talent of Nature she
seemed to acquire the grace and talent of Society,
and to the charming and winning ways of her
girlhood, she added the witchery, wit, and fascination of a woman of the world. In that one
night she grew tenfold more attractive than
before; she was like a bird, who never sings so
well till he has tried his wings.

Not even Lady Ela, or Madame la Duchesse,
had more men anxious for the pleasure of taking
them to their carriages, than the young débutante.
Curly's soft words pleaded for the distinction;
Tom Severn would fain have had it; Castleton
tried hard to give her his arm; but De Vigne
kept them all off, and took her down with that
tranquil appropriativeness which he thought his
intimacy with her would warrant. He would not
have been best pleased if he had heard the laugh
and the remarks that followed them, from the
men that were on the staircase watching the
women leave! The gas-light shone on her eyes,
as she leaned forwards in the carriage, and put
out both her hands to him.

'Sir Folko! if I could but thank you as I
feel!'

'If I could but prove to you you have nothing
to thank me for!'

'At least, I have all the happiness that is in my life?'

'Happiness? Hush!' said De Vigne, passionately. 'How can you tell but that some day you may hate me, loathe me, and wish to God that we had never met?'

'I? O Heaven! no. If I were to die by your hand, I would pray with my latest breath that God might bless you.'

'You would? Poor child! Alma, good night!'

'Good night.'

Those two good nights were very soft and low —spoken with a more tender intonation than any words that had ever passed between them. His hands closed tightly upon hers; the love of woman, his favourite toy in early youth, the stake on which he risked so much in early manhood, was beguiling him again. His head was bent so that his lips almost touched her brow; perhaps they might have touched, and lingered there— but, 'Way for the Duchesse de la Vieillecour's carriage!' was shouted; the coachman started off his horses, and De Vigne stood beneath the awning, with the bright gas glare around and the dark street beyond him, while his heart stirred and his pulses quickened as, since his marriage-

day, he had vowed they never should again for
any woman's sake.

He walked home alone, without waiting for his
night-cab, or, indeed, remembering it, smoking as
he paced the streets, forsaken in the early morning save by some wretched women reeling out of a
gin-palace, or some groups quitting a casino with
riotous mirthless laughter. He walked home,
restless, impatient, ill at ease, with two faces
before him haunting him as relentlessly as in the
phantasmagoria of fever--the faces of the Trefusis
and of Alma—the one with her sensual, the other
with her spiritual loveliness ; the one who had
destroyed his youth, the other who had given it
back to him, side by side in their startling and
forcible contrast, as in the Eastern fable the good
angel sits on the right shoulder and the bad angel
on the left, neither leaving us, each pursuing us
throughout the day and night.

CHAPTER VIII.

THE COST OF HONOUR.

THE ball at Lady Molyneux's was on the 25th of June. On the day after, just a fortnight before the 10th, which was fixed as his marriage-day, Sabretasche gave a fête at his Dilcoosha. That exquisite place, which had always reminded me of Vathek and of Fonthill, it had been a whim of his to embellish in every possible way before his engagement; and now he seemed to take a delight in making Violet's home as luxurious as his wealth and his art could combine to render it. I went over it with him one day, and I told him that if ever I wanted to do up old Longholme as lavishly, I hoped he would come and act as superintendent of the works. Certainly, if Violet had married the highest peer in the realm, she could not have had a more lovely shrine than the Dilcoosha. Regalia's grim and grand old castle in Merioneth-shire would have looked very dull and dark after Sabretasche's villa. The grounds were artificially

made as wild and luxuriant as any woodland in the
heart of the provinces, while yet all the resources
of horticulture were lavished on them. The
conservatories excelled Chatsworth's; with here
and there, among their glories of blossom and
colouring, a marble group or a single statuette,
such as the rifling of Parisian, and Florentine, and
Roman studios could give him. The suite of
drawing-rooms opened out of them, a soft, demi-
lumière streaming through rose-hued glass on a
thousand gems of art that were gathered in
them. Violet's morning room (I hate the word
'boudoir;' stockbrokers' Hackney or Peckham
villas boast their ' boudoirs,' and tradesmen's
wives sit puffing under finery in ' boudoirs,' while
their lords take invoices in white aprons, or ad-
vertise their ' Nonpareil trousers,' their genuine
Glenlivat, or *ne plus ultra* coats!) was hung in
pale green and gold, with a choice library collected
in quaint mediæval book-stands, the deep bay-
window opening on to the river view the
grounds afforded, the walls painted in illustration
of Lallah Rookh, and the greatest gems the house
contained in sculpture or in art shrined here in
her honour. Her bedroom and her dressing-room
were unrivalled; the bed was of carved ivory, the
curtains of rose silk and white lace, caught up by

a chain of flowers, moulded and chased in silver;
all the hangings of the rooms were rose and silver,
while silver lamps swung from the ceiling, giving
out perfume as they burned. It was a home fit
for an imperial bride, and though a still fairer
shrine, and for a purer deity, made me think of
Luciennes, where the 'very locks of the doors
were works of art and *chefs-d'œuvre* of taste.'

On the 26th Sabretasche gave a fête at the
Dilcoosha, a day to be spent, according to Violet's
programme, so that, as she said, 'she might catch
a glimpse of the Summer, and forget the Season
for an hour or two;' and as the Colonel's Dilcoosha
was known to afford, if anything could, the requi-
sites for enjoying a long day, no one, even the
most *ennuyé*, was bored at the prospect, especially
as his invitations were invariably very exclusive,
and I know people who would rush into that
quarter where is written—

"Lasciate ogne speranza, o voi ch'entrate,"

if the admissions were exclusive; and would de-
cline Paradise if its golden gates were opened to
the multitude!

The luncheon was gay and brilliant; repartee
flowed with the still Aï, and mots sparkled with
the Johannisberg. Sabretasche showed nowhere

to better advantage than as a host; his Chester-
field courtesy, his graceful urbanity, his careful
attention to everybody, and every trifle, above all,
his art in starting conversation and drawing people
out, always made parties at his house more charming than at any other.

During the luncheon, De Vigne sat next to
Leila Puffdoff, who, as I have before hinted, was
willing to make more love to him than Granville
cared to make to her. De Vigne was much set upon
by fine ladies, and she flirted with him desperately
during the luncheon, and made him row her on
the river afterwards, part of the grounds of the
Dilcoosha sloping downwards to the Thames, and
drooping their willow and larch boughs into the
water. De Vigne took the sculls, as in duty
bound, and rowed her a good way down, under
the arching branches; but though Lady Puffdoff
put out all her charms, she could not lure him
into anything as warm or tender as she would
have liked; she was piqued—possibly what he
wished to make her—bid him scull her back to
the Dilcoosha, and, as soon as she was landed,
went off to listen to Gardoni, with Crowndiamonds,
Castleton's eldest brother. De Vigne was pro-
foundly thankful to be released; he had a fancy
to leave all these people and scenes, which were

so stale, and go where his heart inclined him, go
and see Alma Tressillian.

He knew the way by the river to St. Crucis;
took the oars of the little boat which the Countess
had just vacated, and pulled himself up Thames
to a point where he knew a path led to the
farm-house, as he had once or twice walked down
to the bank with Alma by it, and rowed her
a mile or so on the water, amused with *her*
amusement in seeing those steamers, barges, and
cockle-shell boats in which Cockneys love
to disport themselves on that unodoriferous
stream.

He moored the boat to the bank, thinking of
the careless days when he had pulled up the river
with the Eton Eight, enjoying the glories of success at the Brocas and Little Surley; and walked
onwards to St. Crucis, with that swinging cavalry
step which had beaten many good pedestrians and
stalwart mountain guides in both hemispheres.
He strode along, too, to uneasy thoughts; he was
conscious of a keener desire to see the Little
Tressillian than he would confess to himself, and,
at the same time, he had a remorseful conviction
that it might be better to stay away, a suggestion
to which he was equally reluctant to listen. A
quarter of an hour brought him in sight of St.

Crucis; but with that sight he saw, too—Curly,
who had apparently forsaken the Dilcoosha for the
same purpose as himself. Curly had just pushed
open the gate and entered, as if he liked his des-
tination; and De Vigne paused a moment behind
him, under the road-side trees, wavering in his
mind whether he should follow him or not.
Where he stood he could see the garden, in all
its untrained profuse summer beauty; the great
chesnuts, with their snowy blossoms, that the wind
was scattering over the turf beneath; and under
the trees he saw Alma, and beside her, bending
eagerly forward, Vane Castleton! He, too, then,
had left Sabretasche's fête to find his way after
Alma! 'Curse the fellow! swore De Vigne, in
his teeth, ' how dare he come after her?' If he
had followed his instinct, he would have taken
Castleton up by his coat-collar and kicked him out
of the garden like a dog; though probably, for
that matter, Castleton had as much right there as
himself?

Curly had pushed open the gate and entered,
and Alma, catching sight of him as he went across
the garden, sprang up, left Castleton rather unce-
remoniously, and came to meet him with a glad
greeting, and something of that gay, bright smile
which De Vigne liked to consider his own and his

unshared property. Curly answered it with an
air more tender than mere compliment, and sat
down beside her, giving Castleton such a glance
as a man only gives to a rival who has forestalled
him.

De Vigne took in the whole scene at a glance,
and construed it, as his scepticism and his knowledge of women suggested to him. The darker
passions of his character rose up; the venom of
jealousy entered into him again.

'She is a thorough-paced coquette, like all the
rest,' he thought. 'I will not add another to the
fools who pander to her vanity.'

He swung round and retraced his steps, leaving
Alma sitting under her chesnut with Castleton
and Curly. It cut him to the soul that those
men should be near her, teaching her the power,
and, with the power, the artifices of her sex,
gaining—who could say they would not, one or
other of them?—their way into her heart! He
was mad with himself for the jealousy he felt; and
fiercely and futilely he tried to persuade himself,
tried till at last he succeeded, that it was but his
regret at the inevitable fate which would await
Boughton Tressillian's adopted child if she listened to the love of Castleton, or even of Curly;
for Curly, though frankhearted and honourable as

a man could be, was young, wild, and held women lightly.

All the fire which lay asleep under the armour of ice which he had put on to guard himself from a sex that had wronged him, was stirred and kindled into flame. He might as yet seek to give them, and to conceal them to himself under, other names, but at work within were his old foes —jealousy and passion. The gay glitter of society, as he joined a group under the fragrant lines of the Dilcoosha, where Violet, Madame de la Vieillecour, and others, were competing in skill as Toxopholites for the prizes Sabretasche had rifled from Howell and James's stores, seemed strangely at variance with the tempest working up in his heart ; and while he laughed and jested with the women there, he could not forget for one instant the Little Tressillian, as he left her smiling on those men ! It was a far greater relief to him than he would own to himself, when not long afterwards he saw Castleton discussing the merits and demerits of her bow with Ela Ashburnington ; and in half an hour's time, or a trifle more, heard Curly chatting frothy badinage with Mrs. Tite Delafield : though, following the dictate of his nature, there was no bodily injury he could not have found it in his heart to wreak upon them both, even on his own Frestonhills pet, for having won those gay bright smiles under the chesnuts at St. Crucis.

He would scarcely have been less wrathful if he had heard Crowndiamonds saying to his brother,

'Where the deuce have you been to, Vane? Helena sent me to look for you, but I couldn't find you anywhere.'

'I was after something far prettier than the old woman,' was Castleton's graceful reply.

'Helena' was nobody less than my Lady Moly-neux, with whom this noble scion of the House of Tiara had been *lié* in a closer friendship than Jockey Jack would have relished had he not been taught to take such friendships as matters of course.

'I've been to see that little girl Tressillian—called to look at her pictures, of course; studios are deuced nice excuse, by Jove!'

And Lord Vane curled his whiskers and laughed at some joke not wholly explained.

'What, that little thing who was at Helena's last night,' asked Crowndiamonds, 'that you and the other fellows made such a fuss about? Heaven knows why! she's too petite for me. Besides, somebody said she was De Vigne's property!'

'What if she were? If he dont't take care

of his game, other men may poach it, mayn't
they ?'

Meanwhile that summer day passed away in
colours to Violet as glorious as those that tinged
its evening sky when the sun went down behind
the limes. Bright as the western light were her
present and her future; secure she dreamed from
the grey twilight or the starless night, which over-
shadow the brightest human life, not less surely
than they overtake the fairest summer day. Of
twilight taint, much less of midnight shadow,
Violet knew no fear. I have never seen on earth
—not even imagined in song nor idealized in art
—any face so expressive of brilliant youth as hers.
When it was in repose there was the light of a
smile on her lips; and the joyousness of the spirit
within seemed to linger far down in the sunny
depths of her eyes, as on the violet waves of the
Mediterranean we have seen the gleam and the
glow of the rays from a sunrise hidden from our
view. There was something in her face that
touched the most cynical amongst us, and subdued the most supercilious or systematic of all
those women of the world into a vague regret for
the spring-time of their days, when they, too, were
in their golden hours, and they, too, believed in
Love and Life.

Never had Violet given freer rein to the joyous spirits of her nature than on that day; never had he more completely surrendered himself to the new happiness he had won! He loved her with a strangely tender love. He loved her, as we love very rarely, for

> ' As those who dote on odours pluck the flowers,
> And place them on their breast, but place to die ;
> Thus the frail beings we should fondly cherish
> Are laid within our bosoms but to perish ! '

He loved her *better* than himself.

' Ah! Violet, time has leaden wings ! ' he whispered to her as, when they escaped unnoticed from the crowd, he led her through her own apartments, locked to the ingress of others. 'A fortnight is not long, yet to me, while it keeps you from me, it seems eternity ! Would to God you were mine now !'

The soft hue that wavered in her cheeks, the low sigh, love's tenderest interpreter, that parted her lips, re-echoed his wish, though words were silent.

' You will love me thus always Vivian,' she whispered, ' never less tenderly, never less warmly, never calmly, chillily, as men learn, they say, to love women whom they have won ?'

' Never, my own love! Calm, chill affections were

death to me as to you. My love has ever been as warm as my native Southern suns; for you it will be as eternal.'

'Then what can part us?' murmured Violet, lifting her face to his, with a smile upon her lips, and in her eyes the joy secure from all terror and all tarnish. 'No power on earth! And so well do we love, that if death took one, he would strike the other!'

'Hush!' whispered Sabretasche, fondly. 'Why speak of death or sorrow, my dearest? Our fate is life and joy; and life and joy together! We love; and in that word all happiness earth can know is given to us both.'

He paused, and the silence that is sweeter than any words supplied his broken words—cold interpreters at best of the heart's most eloquent utterances.

When all his other guests had left the Dilcoosha, Lady Molyneux gave him the third seat in her carriage back to town. The summer dawn was very bright and still, with not a trace of human life abroad, save in some gardeners' carts wending their way slowly to Covent Garden with their fresh pile of newly-gathered vegetables or fragrant load of nodding hothouse flowers—flowers destined to wither in the soft, cruel hand

of some jewelled beauty, or droop and die, pining
for their native sunlight, under the smoke-shroud
of the Great City, as sweet natures and warm
hearts shrink or harden, under the blight of a chill
world, or the pressure of an uncongenial existence.
There was no sign of human life, but the birds
were lifting up sweet gushes of natural song, the
dew was among the daisied grass, and the southerly
wind was tossing the wayside boughs up in its
play, and filling the air with a fragrance, brought
miles and miles on its rapid wings from the free,
fresh woodlands far away.

There was a soft beauty in the summer dawn
that chimed sweet cadence with their thoughts as
Violet and Sabretasche drove homewards; while
Lady Molyneux—worked throughout the season
for fashion's sake as hard as Hood's poor shirt-
maker for very life—slept, though she would have
denied it, tranquilly and well. They enjoyed the
sweet daybreak as people do whose hearts are full
of gladness; she, with that love of all fair things
and that susceptibility to externals natural to
youth and to a heart which has never yet known
care; he, with that poetic keenness to all things
in life and nature which had in boyhood made the
mere murmur of the Mediterranean waves, or the
setting of the sun, or the sighing of winds among

the olive-groves, pleasure to his senses. When the future is fair to us, how fair looks the green and laughing earth !

And she looked up in her lover's eyes :

' Oh, Vivian, how beautiful is life ! '

' With love ! '

Life and love were both beautiful to him as he whispered a farewell but for a few hours in Violet's ear, bent his head for one soft hurried kiss from the lips whose caresses were consecrated to him, and descended from the carriage at the door of his house in Park-lane.

It was past six o'clock when he reached his home, and threw himself down on one of the couches of that favourite room of his on the ground-floor, which adjoined and opened into his studio, where the morning light fell full on his easel, on a portrait of Violet in pastel. He lay smoking his narghilé with that voluptuous indolence habitual to him — looking at the picture where his own art had re-created the beauty of his young love—feeling in memory the loving, lingering touch of her lips— and dreaming over that fresh happiness whose solitary reveries were dearer to him now than society or sleep.

His life had never seemed so sweet, the peace he had won so perfect; and when his servant

rapped gently at the door, though infinitely too
sweet-tempered, and, truth to tell, too lazy, to
irritate himself about trifles, he was annoyed to be
disturbed.

'I told you not to interrupt me till I rang for
my chocolate.'

'I beg your pardon, Colonel,' answered his man,
submissively. 'I should not, but there is a person asking to see you upon business, and, as he
said it was of great importance, I did not know,
sir, what would be best to do.'

'What is always best to do is to obey me to the
letter—you can never be wrong then. The person could have waited. What is his name?'

'He would not give it, sir; he wished to see
you.'

'I see no one before two o'clock in the day.
Go tell him so.'

The man obeyed; but in a minute or two he
returned.

'The gentleman will take no denial, Colonel.
He begs you to see him.'

'What an impertinent fellow!' said Sabretasche, with surprise. 'Tell him I will *not* see
him, that is sufficient. I see no one who does not
send in his card.'

'But, sir—but—'

'Well, what? Speak out,' said Sabretasche, irritated at the disturbance. It seemed to let in the disagreeables of outer life.

'But, sir, he says his business concerns you, and —and Miss Molyneux, sir.'

The man hesitated—even servants living with Sabretasche caught something of his delicacy and refinement, and he knew intuitively how the mention of her name would annoy his master. A flush of astonishment and anger rose over Sabretasche's forehead. He was but too sensitive over Violet, perhaps, from what he considered as the deep disgrace of his first marriage, and he almost disliked to hear servants' lips breathe his idol's name. 'Show him in,' he said briefly, signing the man away. His past had been too fateful for him to join in Violet's cloudless and fearless trust in the future. One of the bitterest curses of sorrow is the *fear* that it leaves behind it; making us, with the sweetest cup to our lips, dread the unseen hand that will dash it down, hanging the funeral pall of the past over the most glittering bridal clothes of the present, and poisoning the sunshine that lies before us with the memory of those clouds which, having so often come before, must, it seems to us, come yet again. When sorrow has once been upon us, we have no longer

faith in life—we have but Hope, and Hope, God-
given as she is, is but fearful, and fluttering, and
evanescent at her best.

He lay still; the sunlight falling upon him and
upon the brilliant face on the easel at his side.
Vulgar and cruel eyes looked in on the scene—
at the luxurious and beautiful studio, where every
trifle was a gem of art, and at the man with all
his grace and beauty, all his delicate and artistic
surroundings: and a vulgar and cruel mind gloated
with delight on the desolation and torture it had
power to introduce into that peaceful life. Sabretasche lifted his eyes indolently—as he did so the
slight flush upon his face died away; he grew
pallid as death.   For he saw the man who was
linked with his hours of greatest shame, of most
bitter misery—the brother and the emissary of his
faithless wife!   Involuntarily he rose, fascinated
by the sight of the man connected with the deepest
wrong and greatest shame of his life: and the
Italian looked at him with a smile that showed
his glittering white teeth, as a hound, who has
seized the noblest of Highland royals at bay,
shows his in the cruel struggle.

'Signór Castrone, this is a very unexpected intrusion,' said Sabretasche, in Italian, with all the
loathing that he felt for this scoundrel who had

stooped to live upon gold wrung from the husband
whom his own sister had wronged. 'Your negotiations with me are at an end. Allow me to request
you to withdraw.'

'Wait one moment, Signór Sabretasche,' answered the Neapolitan, with a cunning leer in his
bright sharp eyes. '*Are* our negotiations at an
end?'

'So entirely, that if you do not leave my presence I shall be compelled to bid my servants ·
make you.'

The Italian laughed. The cold, contemptuous
tone stung him, and gave him but the greater
gusto for his task.

'Not so fast, buon' amico, not so fast; we are
brothers-in-law, remember! It would not do for
us to quarrel.'

The blood crimsoned Sabretasche's face up to
his very temples.

'The tie you dare to mention, and appeal to,
ought to be your bitterest disgrace. Since you
are dead to shame, I need feel none for you; and
if you do not leave the room, my servants will
compel you.'

'Per fede!' said the Italian, with a scoffing
laugh. 'You will scarcely call your household in
to witness your connection with me. They can

hear the secret if you choose; it matters nothing
to me; only I fancied that now, of all times, you
would rather have kept it underhand. You are
going to be married, caro, I hear, to a lovely
English aristocrat—is it so?'

Sabretasche answered nothing, but stretched
out his hand to the bell-handle in the wall nearest
him. He felt it was beneath him to bandy words
with such a man as Giuseppe da' Castrone, who, a
sort of gentlemanlike lazzarone, half swindler,
half idler, a Southern *Bohémien*, had lived on his
wits till he had lost all the traces of better feeling
with which he perhaps might have begun life.
He touched Sabretasche's wrist as the Colonel's
white, slender hand was approaching the bell.
Sabretasche flung off the grasp as if it had been
pollution; but before he could ring the Neapolitan interposed with a smile, half cunning, half
malicious:

'Would it not have been wiser, Eccelenza, before you had taken one wife to have made *sure*
you had lost the other?'

Despite his nerve and habitual impassiveness,
Sabretasche started: a deadly anguish of dread
fastened upon him.

'Yours is a very stale device,' he said, calmly.
'Too melodramatic to extort money from me. ·If

you want a few scudi to buy you maccaroni, or
game away at dominoes, ask for them in plain
words, and I may give you them out of charity.'

He stood leaning his arm upon the top of his
easel; his tall and graceful figure erect; pride,
scorn, loathing written on his features, and in the
depths of his eyes; speaking gently and slowly,
—but very bitterly!—in his low and silvery voice.
The tone, the glance, woke all the malice that
slept in the Italian's heart for his sister's high-born
and high-souled husband.   His eyes glittered like
an angry animal's; he dropped the smoother tone
which he had used before, for one of coarse and
malicious vindictiveness.

'Santa Maria! don't take that proud tone with
me, carissimo, or I may make you glad to change
it, and turn your threats into prayers! You are
not quite so near happiness as you fancy, my fine
gentleman.   That is your young love's picture, no
doubt?   Ah! it is a fair face; it will go hard
to lose it, I dare say?   It would go harder
still if the proud, fastidious Vivian Sabretasche
were tried for bigamy!   It would not look
pretty in the London papers, where his name
has been so often as a leader of fashion
and—'

Before he could end his sentence Sabretasche

had sprung at him, rapidly and lightly as a panther, and seized him by the throat:

'Wretch, you lie! How dare you to insult me! By Heaven! if it were not too great honour for you, I would kill you where you stand!'

So fierce was the grasp of his white slender fingers in the passion into which his gentle nature was at length roused, that the Italian, almost throttled, struggled with difficulty from his hold.

'You lie!' said Sabretasche, flinging him off with a force that sent him reeling from him. 'The woman whom you dare to recall as my wife is dead!'

'Per Dio, is she? You will find to the contrary, bel signór. Basta! but your hands have no baby's grasp; you had better have joined them in prayer, best brother-in-law. If you marry the English beauty, you will have two wives on your shoulders, and *one* has been more than you have managed!'

Sabretasche's eyes were fixed upon him, fascinated by horror as an antelope by a rattlesnake. 'Two wives—two wives!' he muttered incoherently, like a man in delirium. 'She is dead, I tell you—she is dead!'

Then the sense, and transparent falsity, of what

the Neapolitan had said came clearer to his mind, and, with an effort, he regained his calm and haughty tone, speaking slowly between his teeth. Signór Castrone, once more I will request you, for your own sake, to leave this house quietly, without compelling me to the force I am loth to use. With her, the grave buries all past errors; but with you, I still shall treat as with any other swindler. I am not a likely person to be terrified by secret inuendoes or open insults. This time I will let you go—you are beneath my anger—but if you intrude yourself into this house, or venture to approach me again, I shall call in the law to rid me of a pest.'

Something in his voice, which, soft as it was in his native Italian, bore a subtle magic of command, had awed the coarser nature into silence while he spoke; but when he paused, Castrone broke out into a long, discordant, malicious laugh, jarring like jangled bells upon every nerve and chord in his listener's heart.

'Diavolo! buon' amico, it will be I more likely who will have the law upon *you !* Sylvia is alive —alive! and your lawful wife, from whom nothing but death can ever divorce you. I do not think she loves you well enough, milor, to let another woman reign in her stead, without making you

pay the heaviest penalty she can, for your double
marriage! Wait! you saw the death of a Sylvia
da' Castrone in an Italian paper, I dare say? You
had the certificate of such a death from Naples?
Very possibly, but her aunt Sylvia da' Castrone
died last May in Naples, and it was her obituary
that you saw. If Sylvia died (as Santa Maria
forbid!), it would be recorded as what she is, and
what she will be while life lasts—the wife of
Vivian Sabretasche. She lives—nay, she is in
London, ready to proclaim her right to your
name to your new love—or, if your union take
place before she can do so, she will then prose-
cute you according to your English law. She was
married in England, you remember; she has not
lost the certificate, and the register is correct—I
saw it but this morning. It is no idle tale, I tell
you, buon' amico. I know you too well to try
and palm one off upon you unless I could sub-
stantiate it. Your wife is alive, cognato mio! I
fear me there will be some few difficulties in the
way of your marrying your young beauty?'

As the Italian spoke, his coarse malicious laugh,
like the hissing of a serpent, falling like seeth-
ing fire on his listener's heart, Sabretasche stood
gazing upon him. In his parted lips, in his eyes
wide open with the horror of amazement, on every

feature, already blanched and wan, was marked
the deadly anguish of despair,—then, as the full
meaning of the words he heard, cut gradually into
his brain, his strength gave way, and he sank
down upon his couch, covering his face with his
hands, while cold drops of agony stood upon
his brow, and a bitter cry broke from the great
passion that had grown and strengthened and en-
twined itself around his heart, till it were easier
to drain that heart of its life-blood than its love.

And the Neapolitan stood by, gloating at the
ruin he had wrought. He had longed for years
to revenge the silent scorn, the cutting contempt,
the high-bred hauteur with which the man upon
whose gold he had lived had treated him—he
had thirsted for the time to come when Sabretasche should be humbled before him—when
it should be his turn to hold the power which
could at will remove or let fall the sword that
hung above his victim's head—when it should be
his to see, writhing in anguish before him, the
haughty gentleman at whose glance and whose
word he had so often flinched and slunk away.
He stood by and watched him, and Sabretasche
had forgot all sense of his presence, all memory
of the coarse, cruel eyes which looked on the
grief of one who so long had persuaded the world

that he valued life too little to give it aught but
smiles; and Castrone laughed, the laugh of a demon, at his own fell work.

'Milor does not seem charmed to hear of his
wife; it does not seem to bring him the con-
nubial rapture one would expect?'

The jeer, the taunt, the mockery of his woe,
stung to madness the heart of the man who shrank
even from the sympathy of friends, and who had
oftentimes won the imputation of callousness of
feeling, because he felt too deeply to bear to unveil his sorrows to the glare of daylight and
the sneers of men.

Sabretasche started, as at the sharp touch of
the knife searching a fresh wound, and shivered as
if with the cold of death. He lifted his face, aged
in those brief moments as by long years of woe,
and *there* the brother of his wife read desolation
enough to satiate a fiend.

'If this were your errand,' he said, with effort—
and his voice was hollow almost to inarticulateness,
'you have no further excuse for intrusion. I shall
take means for verifying your story; and now
begone, while I can keep my hands off you.'

'Here is your proof, Eccellenza!'

Sabretasche mechanically read the paper held
out to him; it contained but two lines.

'If you will, you can see me once more to-day;
—but only to remind you that while I live no
other can call herself, your Wife.'

Though he had not seen it for more than twenty
long years, he knew the writing to be his wife's.
All hope died in him then; he *knew* that she
lived—the woman who had wedded him to
misery and disgrace; the woman who now
came forward, after the absence and the silence of
a score of years, to ban him from the better life
to which a gentler and a purer hand was about
to lead him.

'*I see* her!' he cried, his passionate anguish, his
loathing hatred, breaking out in a rapid rush of
words, '*I* see the woman who disgraced my name,
who betrayed my love; who for twenty years has
lived upon my gold, yet never addressed to me
one word of repentance or remorse; never one
word to confess her crimes; never one prayer to
ask forgiveness of her sin! *I* see her! How dares
she ask it? How dares she sign herself by the
name she has polluted? Go! tell her that I
will bribe her no more, that she is free to do her
worst that devils can prompt her, that she may
proclaim her marriage with me far and wide; *I*
care not! She may write her lying story in all the
papers if she will; she may persuade all England

and all Italy that she is a fond, deserted wife, and
I a cruel faithless husband : she may bring my
name into Law Courts if she choose to sue me for
her maintenance ; but tell her, once for all, I give
her no more bribes. *I* disown her, though the
world will not divorce me. Now go ; go, I
tell you, or by God I will not let you leave in
peace !'

The fierce but coward nature of the Neapolitan
quailed before the passion of the usually gentle
and impassive Englishman. He spoke softly, more
timidly, smoothing down the coarseness of his
tone.

'But, signore, listen. If you feel thus towards
my poor sister, and will not believe that your
hatred to her is without cause, would you not
rather that the world knew nothing of your marriage?'

'Since it cannot be broken, all the world may
know it. I will bribe you no longer. Begone !'

'Nay, one word—but one word, signore. If I
could show you how you might still wed your
young English love—'

The fierce gesture of his listener warned him to
hasten, if he would be heard ; and Castrone's instinct told him how sharper than a dagger's thrust,
and more bitter than poison to the man of reserve

and refinement, was this rending of the veil of
the one sacred temple by a coarse and sacrilegious
hand !

'Listen,' he said, in his sweet swift language,
with a glitter in his keen bright eyes. 'No one
living knows of your union with my sister save
ourselves; men do not dream that you are married,
much less will they think of turning over registers
for a date of more than twenty years ago. Your
young love, her father, her friends, all your circle,
need never know your wife is living unless you or
Sylvia, or I tell them. If any question ever arose
about your first marriage, your word would be
amply sufficient. They would never insult a
gentleman like Vivian Sabretasche by doubting
him and prying into details of his past ! Sylvia
and I are poor; per Baccho, she has luxurious
habits, and I—an Italian who is noble—cannot
soil his hands with work ! Signor mio, we are as
poor as the rats in the Vicaria; and if, as you say,
you will not support your wife as you have done
hitherto, she must apply to your law for maintenance. She *will* do so, and, basta! it is no more
than her rights; had she followed my counsels,
she would not have let them lie unasserted so
long. But she bids me make you this offer. If
you will pay us down ten thousand—it is but

a drop in the ocean out of all your wealth—we are very moderate; we will bind ourselves by every oath most sacred in your eyes and in ours (and we Catholics keep *our* oaths; we are not blasphemers like your churchmen, who kiss the book in courts and perjure themselves five seconds after!) never to reveal your marriage. You may wed your young English aristocrat, she will never know that another lives who might dispute her title. Men say you love her strangely well—and you are more than half Southern, signor; yours will be no calm and frigid happiness, such as content the cold tame English? You need have no scruple, for, since you say you disown her, whatever the law decree, you must feel as divorced as though men's words had unlocked your fetters, and—per Dio! if twenty long years' separation is not divorce in Heaven's sight, what *is?* Accept our offer—your marriage is virtually dissolved as though no tie of law existed; and long years of love and happiness await you with the woman you idolize? Refuse it, your marriage will be known all over England; and you will see your English love the wedded wife of some other and some happier-fated man? Choose, signor—the choice is very easy—you who have never hesitated to pay any price for Pleasure, will hardly refuse so small a price for Happiness!

Choose, signor, you hold the game in your own
hands.'

With subtle ingenuity, devilish skill, was the
temptation put! The Neapolitan watched the
speeding of his poisoned arrows, and saw that they
had hit their quarry. Sabretasche leaned against
the wall, his lips pressed in to keep down the
agony within him to which he would not give vent;
a shiver passing over his frame which was burning with feverish passions; he breathed in quick,
short gasps, as if panting for very life; while his
eyes were fixed on that brilliant face, whose loving
gaze turned on him from the canvas, tempted him,
how fiercely! how pitilessly! as woman's beauty
has ever tempted man's honour to its fall.

There on the lifeless easel beamed the fair, fond
face, pleading for her joy and his own. Before
him stretched two lives : one radiant and blessed,
full of the rest for which his heart was weary, the
beloved companionship, that makes existence of
beauty and of value ; the other desolate, with no
release from the chains that fettered him as the
bonds which bound the living man to the dead
corpse, no relief from the haunting passions, which
would burn within, till stilled in the slumber of
the grave! All wooed him to the one ; all manhood rebelled against the other !

All urged him to listen to his tempter—all—
save the honour, which shrank from the stain of
a Lie. He had paid down all prices save this
for pleasure; he would not pay this now, even
though the barter were hell for heaven. His eyes
were still fastened upon her picture, and there her
own answered his—clear, fond, true, even while
tempting him his better angel still. He could not
win *her* by wrong, woo *her* with deception; he
loved her too well to wed her by a fraud, and
the knightly soul that slept beneath the worldly
exterior of the man of fashion and of pleasure,
revolted from the shame of betraying a heart
which trusted him, by concealment and by falsehood. He would not give her his name, knowing
it was not hers; call her his wife, knowing the
title was denied her; live with her day by day,
knowing at every moment he had wronged her
and deceived her; receive her innocent caresses,
with the barrier of that deadly shadow between
them, which, if she saw it not, could never leave
his sight, nor rid him of its haunting presence.
Deadly was the temptation—deadly its struggle.
Great drops stood upon his brow, his lips turned
white as in the agonies of death, his hands clenched
as in the combat with some actual foe, and the
anguish of his heart broke out in a bitter moan:

'My God! I have no strength for this!'

'Why endure it, then?' whispered the low, subtle voice of the Italian. 'Freedom is in your own hands.'

But the tempter had lost his power!—the man whom the world said denied himself no pleasure and no wish, and called a heartless and selfish libertine, put aside the joys which could only be bought with Dishonour. Again with the spring of a panther he leapt forward; the blood staining his face, and about his lips a black and ghastly hue, as he caught the Italian in his grip:

'Hound! you tempt me to wrong *her!*—take your price!'

He lifted him from the ground with his left hand, opened the door, and threw him down the steps that parted the studio from the corridor. The Italian lay there, stunned with the fall; Sabretasche closed the door upon him, and went in again alone—alone, in what a solitude!

Long hours afterwards he re-issued from his chamber and entered his carriage, drawing down both blinds. A strange silence fell upon his house; many of his servants loved him, through a service of kindness on the one hand, and fidelity

on the other, and they knew that some great
sorrow had fallen on their master. The footmen
in Lowndes Square, accustomed to his entrance,
were about to show him, unasked, to the room
where Violet was; but Sabretasche signed them
back, and he went up the stairs to her chamber
alone. At the door he paused—what wonder?
Could his heart but fail him when he was about
to quench all radiance from the eyes that took
their brightness only from him? to carry the
chill of death into a life which had hitherto not
known even a passing shade? to say to the
woman pledged to be his wife, ' I am the husband
of another!' It is no exaggeration that he would
have gone with thanksgiving to his own grave;
life could have no greater bitterness for him
than this.

Many moments passed; the time told off by
the thick, slow throbs of his heart:—then he
opened the door and entered.

She looked up as the handle turned, dropped her
book, and sprang forwards, her hands outstretched,
her smile full of gladness; not even a trace of
long passed shadows on the fair young brow that
had never known care, or sorrow, or remorse.
In her joy, not noticing the change upon his face,
she welcomed him with fond words and fonder

caresses, her arms stealing softly round his neck;
and each touch of her lips, to him, like scorching
fire.

'Oh, Vivian!' she cried, 'you said you would
be here four hours ago, you should never be away
from me? You know I don't believe in military
duties! *I* should be your only thought.'

She looked up in his face as she spoke, and as
she did so, her gay smile faded, and the sweet
laughter from her eyes was quenched in the
shadow that already fell upon her from the curse
he bore.

'Vivian! you are not well? Oh, Heaven! what
is it?'

He pressed her in his arms. 'Hush, hush, or
you will kill me.'

Then the colour fled from her face; her eyes
grew full of pitiful fear and half-conscious anguish,
like a startled deer catching the first distant ring
of the hunters' feet. She hid her face upon his
breast, and clung to him in dread of the unknown
horror, while her voice rose in a plaintive
cry, 'Vivian, dearest! what is it—no evil—to
you?'

He held her in his arms as if no earthly power
should rend her from him; and his lips quivered
with anguish. 'I *cannot* tell you—the worst that

could happen to us both! Would to God that I had died ere I linked your fate to mine!'

Clinging to him more closely, she looked up into his eyes ; there she read, or guessed, the truth, and, with a bitter wail, her arms unloosed their clasp, and she sank down from his embrace, lying on the ground in all her delicate beauty, stricken by her great grief, crushed and unconscious, like a broken flower in a tempest.

CHAPTER IX.

HOW A WOMAN WOKE FEUD BETWIXT PALAMON AND ARCITE.

CAN you not fancy how eagerly all town, ever on the *qui vive* after scandal and gossip, darted like the vultures on a dying lion on the story of Vivian Sabretasche's marriage? They were so outraged at its having been so long and carefully concealed, that those who collected scandals of their neighbours, as industriously and persistently as Paris chiffoniers their rags, grubbing for them often in quite as filthy places, revenged themselves for the wrong he had done them, by telling it, garbled and distorted in every way. Heaven knows through whom it first chiefly spread, whether from the lips of my Lady Molyneux, who hated him and loved the telling, or through his wife and her brother, who probably supplied the *Court Talebearer*, the *St. James's Tittletatler*, and such like journals, with the vague, yet damning, versions that appeared in them, of the ' Early

history of a Colonel in the Queen's Cavalry, well
known in fashionable circles as a dilettante, a *lion*,
and a leader of ton, who has recently sought the
hand of the beautiful daughter of an Irish Peer,
and would have led her to the altar in a few days'
time, but for the unhappy, yet, considering the circumstances, fortunate discovery of the existence
of a first marriage, concealed by Colonel S. for the
space of twenty years; during which period, it is
said, the unfortunate wife has lived upon extra-
neous charity, denied even the ordinary necessities
of existence by her unnatural husband, who, having wooed her in a passing caprice, abandoned her
when one would have supposed his extreme youth
might have preserved him from the barbarity, and
we, the moral censors of the age, must say, however reluctantly, villainy of such a course!!'

How it spread I cannot say. I only know it
flew like wildfire. There were many who hated
him, and all his 'dearest friends' glutted over
the story so long hidden from their inquiring eyes.
Old dowagers mumbled it over their whist-tables,
married beauties whispered it behind their fans,
loungers gossiped of it in club-rooms; and in all
was the version different. Men in general took his
part; but women, the soft-voiced murderers of so
much fair fame—sided, without exception, against

him ; called him villain ! betrayer ! all the names
in their sentimental vocabulary ; pitied his 'poor
dear wife ; ' doubted not she was a sweet creature
sacrificed and thrown away ; lamented poor darling Violet's fate, sighed over her infatuation for
one against whom they had all warned her, and
agreed that such a wretch should be excluded
from society !

'I knew it ! ' said Lady Molyneux, with calm
satiric bitterness, and that air of superiority which
people assume when they give you what Madame
de Staël wisely terms that singular consolation,
' *Je l'avais bien dit !* ' 'I knew it—I always told
you what would come of that engagement—I was
always certain what that man really was. To
think of my sweet child running such a risk ! If
the marriage had taken place before this *éclaircis-
sement*, I positively could not have visited my own
daughter ! Too terrible—too terrible ! '

'If it had, Helena,' answered her husband, ' I
think you might have " visited " poor Vy without
disgrace. She would have been, at least, faithful
to *one*, which certain stories would say, my lady,
you are not always so careful to be ! '

The Viscountess deigned no reply to the coarse
insinuation, but covered her face in her handker-
chief, only repeating :

'I knew it! I knew it all along! If *I* had
had my way, Violet would now be the honoured
wife of one of the first Peers of the—'

'If you *did* know it, madame,' interrupted
Jockey Jack, sharply—'if you did know poor
Sabretasche's wife was alive, it's a pity you did not
tell us so. I won't have him blamed; I tell you
he's a splendid fellow—a splendid fellow—and the
victim of a rascally woman. He can't marry Vy,
of course—more fools those who make the laws!
—but I won't turn my back on him. He's not
the only husband who has very good motives for
divorce, though the facts may not be quite clear
to satisfy the courts.'

With which fling at his wife, Jockey Jack,
moved with more or less sympathy from personal
motives for his daughter's lover, took his hat and
gloves, and banged out of the house, meeting on
the door-step the Hon. Lascelles Fainéant, who
had received that morning in his Albany chambers
a delicate missive from his virtuous Viscountess,
commencing, '*Ami choisi de mon cœur.*'

So the journals teemed, and the coteries gos-
sipped, of depths they could neither guess at nor
understand. Sabretasche's fastidious delicacy could
no longer shield him from coarse remark. The
marriage which he considered disgrace, the love

which he held as the most sacred part of his life,
were the themes of London gossip, to be treated
with a jeer, or, at best, with what was far more
distasteful to him, pity.   Scandal was however
innocuous to him now ; he was blind and deaf to
all things, save his own anguish, and that of the
woman who loved him.

It was piteous, they tell me, to see the change
in Violet under the first grief of her life—and
such grief!   Such a shock from a bright and
laughing future to the utter desolation of a beggared present, has before now unseated intellects
not perhaps the weaker for their susceptibility.
From wild disconnected utterances of passionate
sorrow she would sink into a silent, voiceless suffering, worse to witness than any tears or laments.
She would lie in Sabretasche's arms, with her
bright-haired head stricken to the dust, uttering
low plaintive moans that entered his very soul
with stabs far keener than the keenest steel;
then she would cling to him, lifting her blanched
face to his, praying to him never to leave her, or
shrink still closer to him, wishing she had died
before she had brought sorrow on his head.   It
must have been a piteous sight—one to ring up
from earth to Heaven to claim vengeance against
the curse of laws that join hands set dead in

wrath against each other, and part hearts formed for each other's joy and linked by holiest love!

It did not induce brain fever, or harm her *so*, belles lectrices. If we went down under every stroke in that way as novelists assume, we should all be loved of Heaven if that love be shown by early graves, as the old Greeks say.

Violet's young life flowed in her veins still purely and strongly under the dead weight that the mind bore. But for a day or so her reason indeed seemed in danger, both were alike perilous to it, her delirious agony or her mute tearless sorrow; and when her mother approached her, pouring in her common-place sympathies, Violet gazed at her with an unconscious look in those eyes, once so radiant with vivid intelligence, which made even Lady Molyneux shudder with a vague terror, and a consciousness of the presence of a grief far beyond her powers to cure or calm. Sabretasche alone had influence over her. With miraculous self-command and self-sacrifice, while his own heart was breaking, he calmed himself to calm her: he alone had any power to soothe her, and he would surrender the right to none.

'You had better not see her again,' her father said to him one day—'much better not, for both of you. No good can come of it, much harm

may. You will not misunderstand me when I
say I must put an end to your visits. It gives
me intense regret. I have not known you these
past months without learning to admire and to
esteem you ; still, Sabretasche, you can well understand, that for poor Vy's sake—'

'Not see her again?' repeated Sabretasche,
with something of his old sneering smile upon
his worn, wearied, haggard features. 'Are you
human, Molyneux, that you say that coldly and
calmly to a man who, to win your daughter,
would brave death and shame, heaven and hell,
yet who loved her better than himself, and would
not do her wrong, even to purchase the sole paradise he craves, the sole chance of joy earth will
ever again offer him ?'

'I know, I know,' answered Jockey Jack,
hastily. 'You are a splendid fellow, Sabretasche.
I honour you from my soul. I have told my wife
so, I would tell any one so. At the same time,
it is just *because*, God help you! you have such a
passion for poor Vy, that I tell you—and I mean
it, too, and I think you must see it yourself—that
you had far better not meet each other any more,
and, indeed, I cannot, as her father allow it—'

' No?' said Sabretasche, with a sternness
and fierceness which Lord Molyneux had never

imagined in his nature. 'No? You side then, my Lord Molyneux, with those who think, because misfortune has overtaken a man, he must have no mercy shown him. Listen to me! You are taking dangerous measures. I tell you that, so well does Violet love me, that I have but to say to her, "Take pity on me, and give yourself to me," and I could make her leave you and her mother, her country and her friends, and follow me wherever I chose to lead her. If I exert my power over her, I believe that no authority of yours can or will keep her from me. It is not your word, nor society's dictum, that holds me back; it is solely and entirely because, young, pure-hearted, devoted as she is, I will not wrong her fond trust in me, by turning it to my own desires. I will not let my passions blind me to what is right to her. I will not woo her in her youth to a path which, in maturer years, she might live to regret, and long to retrace. I will *not* do it. If I have not spared any other woman in my life, I will spare her. But, at the same time, I will not be parted from her utterly; I will not be compelled to forsake her in the hour of suffering I have brought upon her. As long as she loves me, I will not entirely surrender her to you or to any other man. You judge rightly; I *dare* not

be with her long. God help me! I should have
no strength. A field is open now to every soldier;
if my Corps had not been ordered out, I should
have exchanged, and gone on active service. My
death would be the happiest thing for her; dead,
I might be forgotten and—replaced; but for our
farewell, eternal as it may be, I will choose my own
hour. No man shall dictate or interfere between
myself and Violet, who now *ought* to be—so near
to one another!'

Sternly and passionately as he had spoken, his
lips quivered, his voice sank to a hoarse whisper,
and he turned his head away from the gaze of his
fellow-man. The honest heart of blunt, simple,
obtuse Jockey Jack, stirred for once into sympathy
with the susceptible, sensitive, passionate nature
beside him. He was silent for a moment, re-
volving in his mind the strange problem of this
deep and tender love his daughter had awakened,
musing over a character so unlike his own, so far
above any with which he had come in contact.
Then he stretched out his hand with a sudden
impulse:

'Have your own way, you are right enough. I
put more faith in your honour than in bars and
bolts. If you love Violet thus, *I* can't say you
shall not see her; her heart's nigh broken as it is.

God help you both! I'll trust you with her as I would myself!'

I think Sabretasche had pledged himself to more than he could have fulfilled. It would have been beyond the strength of man to have seen her brilliant and laughing eyes heavy with tears wrung from her heart's depths, her head, with its wealth of chesnut hair, bowed and bent with the weight of an anguish too great to bear;—to have heard the low moan with which she would lie for hours on the cushions of her boudoir, like a summer rose snapped off in the fury of a tempest—to have been tortured with the touch of her hands clinging to him, with her wild entreaties to him not to leave her, with her words in calmer moments promising eternal fidelity to him, and vowing to keep true to him, true as though she were his wife—it had been more than the strength of man to have endured all this, and kept his word so constantly in sight as never to whisper to her of possible joy, never to woo her to a forbidden future.

He *did* keep it, with iron nerve and giant self-subjection, wonderful indeed in one, born in the voluptuous South, and accustomed to an existence, if of most refined, still of most complete, self-indulgence. He did keep it, though his heart would have broken—if hearts did break—in the agony

crowded into those few brief days. Had his torture lasted longer, I doubt if he would have borne
up against it; for, strong as his honour was, his
love was stronger still. But the English and
French troops were gathering in the East; months
before, the Guards had tramped through London
streets in the grey of the morning, with their band
playing their old cheery tunes, and their Queen
wishing them God speed. For several months in
Woolwich Dockyards transports had been filling
and ships weighing anchor, and decks crowding
with line on line of troops. Already through England, after a forty years' peace, the military
spirit of the nation had awoke; the trumpet-call
rang through the country, sounding far away
through the length and breadth of the land, arousing the slumbering embers of war that had slept
since Waterloo ; already bitter partings were taking place in stately English homes, and by lowly
farmstead hearths; and young gallant blood warmed
for the strife, longing for the struggle to come,
and knowing nothing of the deadly work of privation and disease, waiting, and chafing, and dying
off under inaction, that was to be their doom.
Ours were ordered to the Crimea with but a fortnight's time for preparation; where sharp work
was to be done the Dashers were pretty sure to

be in request. We were glad enough to catch a glimpse of active service and real life, after long years of dawdling in London drawing-rooms, and boring ourselves with the routine of pleasures of which we had long tired. We had plenty to do in the few days' notice; fresh harness, fresh horses, new rifles, and old liaisons; cases of Bass and cognac; partings with fair women; buying in camp furniture; burning the souvenirs of half a dozen seasons; the young ones thinking of Moore and Byron, the Bosphorus and veiled Haidées—we of Turkish tobacco, Syrian stallions, Miniés, and Long Enfields. We had all plenty to do, and the Crimea came to us as a good bit of fun, to take the place that year of the Western Highlands, the English open, or yachting up to Norway, or through the Levant.

'Colonel Brandling wishes to speak to you, Major,' said his man to De Vigne, one morning when Granville was dressing, after exercising his troop up at Wormwood Scrubs.

'Colonel Brandling? Ask him if he'd mind coming up to me here, if he's in a hurry,' answered De Vigne, going on brushing his whiskers. He did not bear Curly the greatest good will since seeing him under the chesnut-

trees at St. Crucis—where, by the way, he himself had not been since.

'May I come in, old fellow?' asked Curly's
voice at the door.

'Certainly. Entrez! You are an early visitor,
Curly,' said De Vigne, rather curtly. 'I thought
you'd prefer coming up here instead of waiting
ten minutes while I washed my hands and put
myself en bourgeois.'

'Yes, I have come early,' began Curly, so
abstractedly that De Vigne swung round, and
noticed with astonishment that his light-hearted
Frestonhill's pet seemed strangely down in the
mouth. Curly was distrait and absent; he looked
worried, and there were dark circles beneath his
eyes as of a man who has passed the night tossing
on his bed to painful thoughts.

'What's the matter, Curly?' asked De Vigne.
'Has Heliotrope gone lame, Lord Ormolu turned
crusty, Eudoxie Lemaire deserted you, or what
is it?'

Curly smiled, but very sadly.

'Nothing new; I have made a fool of myself,
that's all.'

'And are come to me for auricular confession?
What is the matter, Curly?'

'Imprimis, I have asked a woman to be my

wife,' answered Curly, with a nervous laugh, playing with the bouquet bottles on the table.

De Vigne started perceptibly; he looked up with a rapid glance of interrogation, but he did not speak, except a rather haughty and impatient 'Indeed!'

Curly did not notice his manner, he was too ill at ease, too thoroughly absorbed in his own thoughts, too entirely at a loss, for the first time in his life, how to express what he wanted to say. Curly had often come to De Vigne with the embarrassments and difficulties of his life; when he had dropped more over the Oaks than he knew exactly how to pay, or entangled himself where a tigress grip held him tighter than he relished; but there are other things that a man cannot so readily say to another.

'Well?' said De Vigne, impatient at his silence, and more anxious, perhaps, than he would have allowed to hear the end of these confessions. 'Certainly the step shows no great wisdom. Who has bewitched you into it?'

'You can guess, I should say.'

'Not I; I am no Œdipus; and of all riddles, men's folly with women is the hardest to read.'

'Yet you might. Who can be with her and resist her—'

'Her?—who? Speak intelligibly, Curly,' said
De Vigne, irritably.   'Remember your lover's
raptures are Arabic to me.'

'In a word then,' said Curly, hurriedly, 'I love
Alma Tressillian, and I have told her so.'

De Vigne's eyebrows contracted, his lips turned
pale, and he set them into a hard straight line,
as I have seen him when suffering severe physical
pain.

'She has accepted you, of course?'

Had Curly been less preoccupied, he must
have thought how huskily and coldly the question
was spoken.

Curly shook his head.

'No?' exclaimed De Vigne, his eyes lighting
up from their haughty impassibility into passionate eagerness.

'No! Plenty of women have loved me, too;
yet when I am more in earnest than I ever was,
I can awaken no response.   I love her very
dearly, Heaven knows.   I would give her my
name, my rank, my riches, were they a thousand
times greater than they are.   Good Heavens!
it seems very bitter that love like mine should
count for nothing, when other men, only seeking
to gratify their passions or gain their own selfish
ends, win all before them.'

His voice trembled as he spoke! his gay and careless spirits were beaten down; for the first time in his bright butterfly life Sorrow had come upon him. Its touch is death, and its breath the chill air of the charnel-house, even when we have had it by us waking and sleeping, in our bed and at our board, peopling our solitude and poisoning our Falernian, rising with the morning sun and with the evening stars;—how much heavier then must be the iron hand, how much more chill its breath, ice cold as the air of a grave, to one who has never known its presence!

> ‘ Wer nie sein Brod mit Tränen ass,
> Wer nicht die kummervollen Nächte.
> Auf seinem Bette weinend sass
> Der kent euch nicht ihr himlischen Mächte.’

Curly's voice trembled; he leaned his arm on the dressing-table, and his head upon his hand; his rejection had cut him more keenly to the heart than he cared another man should see. De Vigne stood still, an eager gladness in his eyes, a faint flush of colour on his face, his heart beating freely and his pulses throbbing quickly; that vehement and exultant joy of which his nature was capable, stirred in him at the thought of Curly's rejection. We never know how we value a thing till its loss is threatened!

He did not answer for some moments; then he laid his hand on Curly's shoulder with that old gentleness he had always used to his old Freston-hills favourite.

'Dear old fellow, it *is* hard.   I am very—'

He stopped abruptly, he would have added, 'sorry for you,' but De Vigne knew that he was *not* sorry in his heart, and the innate truth that was in the man checked the lie that conventionality would have pardoned.

Curly threw off his hand and started to his feet. Something in De Vigne's tone struck on his lover's keen senses with a suspicion that before had never crossed him, absorbed as he had been in his own love for the Little Tressillian, and his own hopes and fears for his favour in her eyes.

'Spare yourself the falsehood,' he said, coldly, as *he* had never spoken before to his idolized 'senior pupil.'   'Commiseration from a rival is simply insult.'

'A rival?' repeated De Vigne, that fiery blood of his always ready—too ready, at times— to rise up in anger.

'Yes, and a successful one, perhaps,' said Curly, as hotly, for at the sting of jealousy the sweetest temper can turn into hate.   'You could not say

on your honour, De Vigne, that my rejection by
her gives you pain. If you did your face would
belie you! You love her as well as I; you are
jealous over her; perhaps you have already taken
advantage of her youth and her ignorance of the
world and her trust in you, to sacrifice her to
your own inconstant passions—'

'Silence!' said De Vigne, fiercely. 'Your
very supposition is an insult to my honour.'

'Do you care nothing for her, then?'

The dark blood of his race rose over De Vigne's
forehead; his eyes lighted; he looked like a lion
longing to spring upon his foe. *He* to have his
heart probed rudely like this—to endure to have
his dearest secrets dragged to daylight—*he* to be
questioned, counselled, arraigned in accusation by
another man! Curly had forgotten his character,
or he would have hardly thought to gain his
secret by provocation and condemnation. De
Vigne restrained his anger only by a mighty effort
of will, and he threw back his hand with that
gesture, habitually expressive with him of contemptuous irritation.

'If you came here to cross-question me, you
were singularly unwise. I am not very likely to
be patient under such treatment. Whatever my
feelings might be on any subject of the kind,

do you suppose it is probable I should confide
them to you ? '

So haughtily careless was his tone, that Curly,
catching at straws as men in love will do, began
to hope that De Vigne, cold and cynical as he had
been to women ever since his fatal marriage,
might, after all, be indifferent to his protégée.

'If it be an insult to your honour, then,' he
said, eagerly, ' to hint that you love her, or think
of her otherwise than as a sister, you can have no
objection to do for me what I came to ask of
you.'

' What is that?' asked De Vigne, coldly. He
could not forgive Curly any of his words; if he
resented the accusation of loving Alma, because it
startled him into consciousness of what he had
been unwilling to admit to himself, he resented
still more the supposition that he cared for Alma
as a sister, since it involved the deduction that she
might love him—as a brother! And that fra-
ternal calmness of affection ill chimed in with an
impetuous nature that knew few shades between
hate and love, between profound indifference or
entire possession ?

' Alma rejected me!' answered poor Curly; all
the unconscious dignity of sorrow was lent to his
still girlish and Greek-like beauty, and a sadness

strangely calm and deep for his gay insouciant character had settled in his blue eyes. ' I offered her what few men would have thought it necessary to offer her, unprotected as she is. Yet she rejected me, though gently and tenderly, for she has nothing harsh in her. But sometimes we know a woman's refusal is not positive. I thought that perhaps (you have great influence over her) you could put this before her; persuade her at the least not to deny me all hope; plead my cause with her; ask her to let me wait? If it were even as long as Jacob for Rachel, I would bear it. I would try to be more worthy of her, to make her fonder of me. I would shake off the idleness and uselessness of my present life. I would gain a name that would do her honour. I would do anything, everything, if *only* she would give me hope !'

He spoke fervently and earnestly ; pale as death with the love that brought no joy! his delicate girlish face stamped pitifully with the anguish of uncontrollable anxiety, yet with a new nobility upon it from the chivalric honour and high devotedness which Alma had awakened in him.

He was silent—and De Vigne as well. De Vigne leaned against one of the windows of his bedroom, his face turned away from Curly, and

his eyes fixed on the gay street below. Curly's
words stirred him strangely; they revealed his own
heart to him; they contrasted with such love as
he had always known; they stung him with the
thought, how much better sheltered from the
storms of passion and the chill blasts of the world
in Curly's bosom, than in his own, would be this
fragile and soft-winged little dove, now coveted
by both.

Curly repeated his question in low tones.

'De Vigne, will you do it? Will you plead
my cause with her? If she be so little to you it
will cost you nothing!'

Again he did not answer, the question struck
too closely home. It woke up in all its force the
passion which had before slumbered in some unconsciousness. When asked to give her to another,
he learned how dear she was to him himself.
Hot and jealous by nature as a Southern, how
could *he* plead with her to give the joys to his
rival of which a cruel fate had robbed him? how
could *he* give the woman he would win for himself, away to the arms of another?

'Answer me, De Vigne. Yes or no?'

'No!'

And haughtily calm as the response was, in his
heart went up a bitter cry, 'God help me. I *cannot!*'

'Then you love her, and have lied!'

De Vigne sprang forward like a tiger at the
hiss of the murderous and cowardly bullet that has
roused him from his lair; the fire of just anger
now burned in his dark eyes, and his teeth were
set like a man who holds his vengeance with
difficulty in check. Involuntarily he lifted his
right arm; another man he would have struck
down at his feet for that dastard word. But with
an effort—how great only those who knew his
nature could appreciate—he held his anger. in, as
he would have held a chafing and fiery horse with
iron hand upon its reins.

'Your love has maddened you, or you would
scarcely have dared to use that word to me. If I
did not pity you, and if I had not liked you since
you were a little fair-faced boy, I should make
you answer for that insult in other ways than
speech. If I *were* to love any woman, what right
have you to dictate to me my actions or dispute
my will? You might know of old that I suffer no
man's interference with me and mine.'

'I have no power to dispute your will,' interrupted Curly, 'nor to arrest your actions. Would
to heaven I had! But as a man who loves her
truly and honourably himself, I will tell you,
whether I have a right or no, that no prevarica-

Q 2

tion on your part hides from me that you at least share my madness. I will tell you, too, though you slew me to-morrow for it, that she is too pure to be made the plaything of your fickle passions, and cast off when you are weary of her face and seek a newer mistress. I will tell you that the man who wrongs her trust in him, and betrays her guileless frankness, will carry a sin in his bosom greater than Cain's fratricide. I will tell you that, if you go on as you have done from day to day concealing your marriage, yet knitting her heart to yours—if you do not at once reveal your history to her, and leave her free to act for herself, to love you or to leave you, to save herself from you or to sacrifice herself for you, as she please, that for all your unstained name and unsuspected honour, *I* shall call you a coward!'

'My God!' muttered De Vigne, 'that I should live to hear another man speak such words to me. I wonder I do not kill you where you stand!'

I wonder, too, he kept down his wrath even to the point he did, for De Vigne's nature had no trace of the lamb in it, and to attack his honour was a worse crime than to attack his life. Deadly passion was between those two men then, sweeping away all ancient memories of boyish days, all gentler touches of brighter hours and kinder com-

munion. Their eyes met—fierce, steady, full of
fire, and love, and hate; De Vigne's hand clenched
harder on his breast, and with the other he signed
him to the door. The wildest passions were at war
within him; his instinct thirsted to revenge the
first insult he had ever known, yet his kingly soul
at the daring that defied him, yielded something
like that knightly admiration with which the
Thirty looked upon the Thirty when the sun went
down on Carnac. '

'Go—go! I honour you for your defence of
her, but such words as have passed between us, no
blood can wash out, nor after words efface!'

Curly bent his head and left him; he had done
all he could. When they met again—! Ah!
God knows if our meetings were foreseen, many
voices would be softer, many farewells warmer,
many lips that smile would quiver, many eyes that
laugh would linger long with salt tears in them,
many hands would never quit their clasp that
touch another with light careless grasp, at partings
where no prescience warns, no second-sight can
guide!

Curly left him, and De Vigne threw himself into
an arm-chair, all the fiery thoughts roused in him
beating like the strong pinions of chained eagles.
The passions which had already cost him so much,

and which from his fatal marriage-day he had
vowed should never regain their Circean hold
upon him, were now let loose, and rioted in his
heart. He knew that he loved, as he had sworn
to himself never to love woman ; that the honour
and the pride on which he had piqued himself had
been futile to save him from the danger which he
had so scornfully derided and recklessly provoked ;
that his own iron-will, on which he had so fear-
lessly relied, had been powerless to hold him back
from the old intoxication, whose fiery draught had
poisoned him even in its sweetness, and to whose
delirium he had vowed never again to succumb.

He loved her, and De Vigne was not a man
cold enough, or, as the world would phrase it, virtuous enough, to say to the woman he idolized,
' Flee from me—society will not smile upon our
love.' Yet Curly's words had struck into his brain
with marks of fire. ' Going on as you have done
day by day, deceiving her by concealment of your
marriage, yet knitting her heart to yours !' These
stung him cruelly, for, of all sins, De Vigne
abhorred concealment or cowardice ; of all men,
he was most punctilious in his ideas of truth and
honour, and his conscience told him that had he
acted straightforwardly, or, for her, wisely, he would
have let Alma know in the earliest days of their

intimacy of the cruel ties of Church and Law
which fettered him with so uncongenial and so unmerited a chain.   True, he had never concealed it
from bad motives; it was solely his disgust at
every thought of the Trefusis, and the semi-ob-
livion into which—never seeing his wife to remind
him of it—the bare fact of his so-called marriage
had sunk, which had prevented his revealing it.
He had never thought the matter would be of
consequence to her; he had looked on her as a
mere acquaintance, and it had no more occurred to
him to tell her his history, than it had done to talk
it over in the clubs.   The imputation of want of
candour, of lacking to a young girl the honour he
had been ever so scrupulous in yielding to men,
stung him however to the quick.   Other words, too,
lingered on his mind, bringing with them keen,
sharp pain.   The doubt whether his love was returned
was to him like the bitterness of death.   It *should*
not have been, we know, had he been unselfish as
he ought; he *should* have prayed for punishment
to fall upon his head, and for her to be spared the
fruits of his own imprudence ; but what man
amongst us can put his hand upon his heart, and
say before God that he could have summoned up
such unselfishness under such a temptation ?   Not
I—not you—not Granville de Vigne, for, as

Sabretasche would have said, we are unhappily mortal, mon ami!

One resolution he made amidst the whirl of thoughts and feelings which the stormy scene with Curly had so unexpectedly called into life— that was to tell her of his marriage at once. Perhaps there mingled with it some thought that by Alma's reception of it he would see how little or how much she cared for him. I know not; if there were I dare throw no stone at him. How many of my motives—how many of yours—of any man's, are unmixed and undefiled? He resolved to tell her, to be cold and guarded with her, to let her see no sign or shadow of the passion she had awakened. All his past warnings had failed to teach him wisdom; he still trusted in his own strength, still believed his will powerful enough to hold his love down without word or token of it, while it gnawed at his heart-strings in the very presence of the woman who had awakened it! Once more De Vigne had gone down before his old foe and syren, Passion; like Sisera before the treacherous wife of Heber the Kenite, at her feet he bowed and fell.

CHAPTER X.

THE ORDEAL BY FIRE.

THERE was the beauty of the 'summer-time' in the fragrant air, and on the moistened roads, and on the rich green woodlands, but it never reached his eyes or heart as De Vigne rode to Richmond, spurring his horse into a mad gallop, with that one world within him which blinds a man to all the rest of earth. He galloped on and on, never slackening his pace; for the first time in all his soldier's life he felt *dread*—dread of telling the woman he loved, that he was tied to the woman he hated! His pulse throbbed and his heart beat loudly as he came in sight of the farmhouse of St. Crucis, and saw coming out of the little gate, and taking his horse's bridle off the post—Vane Castleton.

'Good Heavens!' thought De Vigne, with a deadly anguish tightening at his heart, 'is she, then, like the rest? Has she duped us all? Is her guileless frankness as great a lie as other women's artifice?'

Castleton did not see him; he threw himself across his bay, and rode down the opposite road. De Vigne wavered a moment; sceptical as he was, he was almost ready to turn his horse's head and leave her, never to see her again. If she chose Castleton, let him have her! But love conquered; the girl's face had grown too dear to him for him of his own act never to look upon it again. He flung his bridle over the gate, pushed the little wicket open, and entered the garden. In the window, with her eyes lifted upwards to a lark singing far above in the blue ether, the chesnut-boughs hanging over her in their dark green framework, the honeysuckles and china roses bending down till they touched her shining golden hair ; her cheeks a little flushed, was Alma. At the sight of her he trembled like a woman with the passion that had grown silently up and ripened into such sudden force. How *could* he give her up to any living man? Right or wrong, how could he so tame down his inborn nature as to wish to win from such a woman only the calm, chill affection of a sister?

That mad jealousy which had awoke in all its fire at the sight of Castleton, and the suspicion that it was for Castleton's sake and not for his own that she had rejected Curly's suit, drove all memory of the Trefusis, all recollection of what he came to avow to Alma, from his mind!

He stood and looked at her—the rush of that delirium, half rapture and half suffering, which, for long years, none of her sex had had the power to rouse in him, told him that he should not dare to trust himself in her presence, for no will, however strong, could have strength enough to tame its fever down and chill his veins into ice-water. Still he lingered, not master of himself. The man's nature, alive and vigorous, rebelled against the stoicism he had thought to graft upon it, and flung off the cold and alien bonds of the chill philosophy circumstances had taught him to adopt. His heart was made for passionate joys; and against reason it demanded its rights and clamoured for his freedom. He lingered there loth— who can marvel?—to close upon himself the golden gates of a fuller, sweeter, more glorious existence; and turn away to bear an unmerited curse alone—a wanderer from that Eden which was his right and heritage as a man. He lingered —then she looked up and saw him, her lips parted with a low, glad cry, the rose flush deepened in her cheeks, the first blush she had ever given for him. She sprang down from the window, which was scarcely a foot above the ground, ran across the lawn as lightly as a fawn, and stood by his side.

'Oh, Sir Folko! how long you have been away!'

How could he leave her then?

She came and stood by him; her golden hair nearly touching his arm, her fingers still on his hand, her glad beaming face turned up to his with the full glow of the afternoon sunshine upon it. She stood by him, only thinking of her happiness at seeing him, never dreaming of the torture her presence was to him—a torment yet an ecstasy, like the exultation and the awakening of an opium-smoker combined in one. Seeing her thus, with her hand in his, her eyes looking upwards to him, so near to her that he could count every breath that parted her soft warm lips, it was hard for him to keep stern and cold to her, repress the words that hung upon his lips, chain down the impulse that rose in him with irresistible longing to take her to his heart, and carry her far away where no man could touch her, and no false laws deny him the love that was his common birthright among men.

'What a long time you have been away, Sir Folko!' began Alma again. 'Ten whole days! You have never been to see me since that beautiful ball. I thought you were sure to come the next day, or the day after, at the latest. Have you been out of town?'

'Oh no!' said De Vigne, moving towards the house without looking at her.

'Then why have you been so long?'

'I have been engaged, and you have had plenty of other visitors,' he answered, his jealousy of Vane Castleton working up into a bitterness he could not wholly conceal.

She coloured. Looking aside at her, he saw the flush in her cheeks. She had never looked confused before at any words of his, and he put it down, not to his own abruptness, but to the memory of his rival.

'No visitors whom I care for,' said Alma, with that pretty petulance which became her so well. 'I have told you till I am tired of telling you that nobody makes up, or ever could make up, to me for your absence!'

'Still, when I am absent,' he said, with that satire which with him was often a veil to very deep feeling, 'you can console yourself very agreeably with other men!'

They had now passed into her room. He leant against the side of the window, playing impatiently with sprays of the honeysuckle and

climatis that hung round it, snapping the sprays
and throwing the fragrant flowers recklessly on the
grass outside the sill, careless of the ruin of
beauty he was causing. She stood opposite to
him, stroking the parrot's scarlet crest unconsciously—she and her bird making a brilliant
picture.

'If I thought so,' she answered quickly, 'I
should not honour the woman I suspected by any
visits at all, were I you.'

'Is that a hint to me to leave your new friend
Castleton the monopoly?' asked De Vigne, between his teeth.

'Sir Folko !'

That was all she deigned to answer—her eyes
flashing fire in their dark-blue depths, her cheeks
hot as the crimson roses above her head, her expressive lips full of tremulous indignation, her
attitude, all fire and grace and outraged pride,
said the rest. There was fascination about her
then sufficient to madden any man who loved
her !

'Would you try to make me believe, then, that
you do not know that Castleton loves you?'
asked De Vigne, fiercely.

Alma's cheeks glowed to a warmer crimson still,
and resentment at his tone flashed from under her

black lashes, like azure lightning. He had put
her passions up now.

'You must be mad to speak to me in that tone!
I bear no imputation of a falsehood even from you.
I do not suppose Lord Vane loves me, as you
phrase it! That he flatters me, and would talk
more foolish nonsense still, I know.'

'You will be very unwise if you give ear or
weight to his "foolish nonsense;" many a girl, as
young and as fair as you, have been ruined by
listening to it,' interrupted De Vigne.   He was so
mad that Vane Castleton should even have dreamt
that he would win her; he was so rife with passions wild and reckless, that rather than stand
calmly by the girl, he must upbraid her; and the
storm that was in his heart found vent in cruel and
sarcastic words, being denied the softer and natural
outlet of love vows and fond caresses.   The love
that murdered Desdemona, and condemned He-
loise to a living death, is not dead in the world yet.
'Castleton *can* love, not as you idealize it, perhaps,
but as he holds it.   There is no man so brutal, so
heartless, or so egotistical, but can love—as he
translates the word, at least—for his own private
ends or selfish gratification.   "Love" is men's
amusement, like horse-racing, or gaming, or drinking, and you would not find that "bad men"

abstain from it—rather the contrary, I am afraid!
Castleton will love you, I dare say, if you let him,
very dearly—for a month or two!'

Alma gazed at him, her large eyes wide open,
like a startled gazelle's, her cheeks crimson with
the blush his manner and his subject awoke.

'Sir Folko, what has come to you? *Are* you
mad?'

'Perhaps,' said De Vigne, between his teeth.
'All I say is, that you are unwise to receive Castleton's visits and listen to his flattering compliments. Many women have rued them.'

'Sir Folko! What right have you to speak to
me like this?' interrupted Alma, with a passionate
gesture. 'What right have you to suppose that I
should stoop to Vane Castleton, or any other
man? If you had listened to me you would have
heard that his fulsome compliments are detestable
to me, that I hate them and loathe them, that I
told him so this very afternoon, and that I shall
have strangely mistaken him if ever he repeats
his visits here again. Would you wish to give me
over to your friend? Would you think so meanly
of me as to—Oh, Sir Folko, Heaven forgive
you!'

She stood beside him passionate as a little
Pythoness, with all the fervour of her moiety of

Italian nature awoke and aroused; her cheeks
crimson with her indignation, her grief, and her
vehemence, her lips just parted with their rush of
words, her head thrown back in defiance, her
hands clenched together, and in her large brilliant
eyes inexpressible tenderness, reproach, and wistful agony. Her gaze was fixed upon him even
while her heart heaved with the new emotions his
words had aroused; and tears rose in her throat
and gathered in her eyes—those tears of blood,
the tears of woman's love. All his passions surged
up in De Vigne's heart with resistless force ; that
love which had crept into his heart with such
insidious stealth, and burst into such sudden flame
but a few hours before, mastered and conquered
him. In her strange and brilliant fascination, in
her fond and childlike frankness, in her newly-
dawned and impassioned tenderness she stood before him. Will, power, reason, self-control were
shivered to the winds, he was no statue of clay, no
sculptured god of stone to resist such fierce temptation—to pass over and reject all for which
nature, and manhood, and tenderness pleaded—to
put away with unshaken hand the love for which
every fibre of his being yearned !

She stood before him in all her witchery of
womanhood, and before her De Vigne's strength

bowed down and fell; the love within him wrest-
led with and overthrew him; every nerve of his
frame thrilled and throbbed, every vein seemed
turned to fire; he seized her in his arms where
she stood, he crushed her slight form against his
heart in an embrace long and close enough for a
farewell, while he covered her flushed cheeks and
soft warm lips with 'lava kisses melting while
they burned.' He needed no words to tell him
he was loved; between them now there was an
eloquence compared to which all speech is dumb.

Those moments of deep rapture passed un-
counted by De Vigne, conscious only of that
ecstasy of which he had been robbed so long,
which was to his heart as the flowing of water-
springs through a dry land; all the outer world
was forgotten by him, all his unnatural and cruel
ties faded from his memory; all he remembered
was—that he loved and was loved! Holding her
still in his arms he leaned against the side of the
window, the soft summer wind fanning their
brows, flushed with their mutual joy; his passion
spending itself in broken sighs and deep delight,
and hurried words and fond caresses.

'You love me, Alma?' he whispered eagerly.

'For ever!' she murmured, looking up into
his face, while warm blushes tinged her cheeks

and brow. ' How could I choose but love you ?'

She paused abruptly with a deep-drawn sigh, awed at the depth and vehemence of her own love. How could he think of anything save the heaven shrined for him in those fond words and loving eyes? He clasped her closer still against his breast, pressing his lips on hers with all the fire of his vehement nature.

' My God! Would to heaven I could reward you for it!'

Alma, who knew not his meaning, looked up with a smile, half shy, half mournful, yet inexpressibly beautiful, with its frank gladness and deep tenderness.

' Ah, what reward is there like your love ?'

De Vigne kissed her lips to silence; he dare not listen to the eloquence that lured him in its unconscious innocence with such fierce temptation. For, now that the first moments of wild rapture had passed, came the memory of his marriage, of his resolves, of his duty, shown him by a much younger, and in such matters equally latitudinarian a man, and acknowledged to himself by reason and honour, justice and generosity ; of his right to tell her fully and freely of the fetters that held him, and the woman whom Law decreed to be,

though heart and nature refused ever to acknowledge as, his wife.   All these rushed on him, and
stood between him and his new-won heaven, as
we have seen the dark and spectral Shadow
of the Hartz Mountains rise up cold, and grim,
between us and the sweet rose-hued dawn which
is breaking over the hills and valleys, and chasing
away with its golden glories, the poisonous shades
and shapes of night.

He had no power to end with his own hand this
fresh and glorious existence which had opened before him.   If he had ended with absinthe or with
laudanum his own life, men would have prosed
sermons over him, and printed his condemnation
in glaring letters ; yet, alas ! for charity or judgment, they would have condemned him equally
because he shrank from this far worse and more
cruel self-murder—the assassination of joy, the
suicide of the soul.   By Heaven, men need be
gods to conform to all the laws of men !   We
must love life so well, that when it is at its
darkest, its loneliest, brimful with misery, bitter
and poisonous as hemlock, we must never, in our
hardest hours of solitude, feel for an instant
tempted to flee from its fret and anguish to the
silent sleep of the tomb.   Yet—we must love it
so little, that when it smiles the sweetest, when it

is fair as the dawn and generous as the sunshine, when it has led us from the dark and pestilent gloom of a charnel-house back to a laughing and joyous earth, when it has turned our tears into smiles, our sorrow into joy, our solitude into a heaven of delight, *then* with an unhesitating hand we are to put aside the glorious cup of life, and turn away, without one backward glance, from our loved Eden into the land of darkness, of silence, and of tears. Alas! if God be as harsh to us as man is to his fellow-man!

'How well do you love me, Alma?' he said, abruptly, as they sat beside the open bay-window, his arms round her, her head leaning against his breast, and on her face the flush of joy too deep to last.

'How well do I love you?' she repeated, with her old, arch, amused smile playing round her lips. 'Tell me, first, how many petals there are in those roses, how many leaves on the chesnut-boughs, how many feathers in that butterfly's wings—then perhaps I may tell you how well I love you, Sir Folko!'

De Vigne could not but smile at the poetry and enthusiasm of the reply—so like Alma herself; but as he smiled he sighed impatiently.

'I am "Sir Folko" no longer, Alma; the name

was never appropriate. I have always told you
I am no stainless knight. Call me Granville. I
have no one to give me the old familiar name
now.'

'Granville!' murmured Alma, repeating the
name to herself, with a deeper flush on her
cheeks. 'Granville! Yes it is a beautiful name,
and I love it because it is yours; yet I love Sir
Folko best, because others have called you Granville before me, but "Sir Folko" is all my own!'

Her innocent speech stung him to the heart;
he remembered how truth, and honour, and justice demanded of him to tell her *who* had 'called
him Granville before her.'

He interrupted her hastily:

'But you have not answered my question.
How much do you love me? Come, tell me!'

'How *can* I tell you?' she answered, looking
up in his face with that smile so tender that it
was almost mournful. 'It seems to me that no
one could ever have loved as I do you. How
much do I love you? Oh! I will tell you when
you number the rose-leaves or count the river
waves, then, but not till then, could I ever gauge
my love for you!'

He pressed her closer to him, yet he asked a
cruel question:

'But if I left you now—if I were ordered on foreign service, for instance, and died in battle, could you not find fresh happiness without me?'

She clung to him, all her radiant joy banished, her face white and her eyes wild with a prescient dread :

'Oh! why do you torture me so? such jests are cruel! I do not tell you I would die for you, that is a hackneyed phrase not fit for deep and earnest love like ours, though, Heaven knows, existence would be no sacrifice if given up to serve you; but I would live for you—I *will* live for you as no woman ever lived for man. I will increase all talents God has given me that you may be prouder of me; I will try and root out all my faults, that you may love me better. If ever you lose your wealth, as rich men have done, I will work for you, and glory in my task. To share the pomp of others would be misery, to share your poverty, joy. I will pray to Heaven that I may always be beautiful in your eyes; but if you ever love another, do not tell me, but kill me, as Alarcos slew his wife: to lose my life would be sweeter than to lose your love. If war calls you, I will follow—death and danger would have no terror by your side—and if you died in

battle, I would be truer to you, till we met
beyond the grave, than woman ever was to any
living love.   But—my God! you *know* how well
I love you; why do you torture me thus!'

She had spoken with all that impassioned
fervour natural to her, but passion so intense
treads close on anguish ; all the soft bloom of
youth and joy forsook her lips, and her head
drooped upon her bosom, which heaved with
uncontrollable sobs.   Poor child! they were the
first of those waters of Marah which flow side by
side with the hot springs of Passion.   De Vigne
pressed her to his heart, lifted her face to his,
and called back life to her cheeks with breathless
caresses, as if he would repay with that mute
eloquence the love which touched him too deeply
to answer it in words.   It struck far down into his
heart, this generous, and high-souled tenderness.
All its devotion and heroism ; all its unselfishness,
and warmth, and trust; all the diviner essence
which breathed in it, marking it out from man's
and woman's ordinary loves, brutal on the one
side, exigeant and egotistical on the other; struck
home to his better nature and there came upon
him a mortal anguish of regret and shame that
here he should give nothing, but gain all.   In
those few hours she had grown unutterably dear

to him, though, save a few murmured and feverish words, his passions were too strong to form themselves to speech. But one other question he put to her:

'Darling, if you love me like this, would you be content with me for your sole companion, away from the pleasures of society, alone in a solitude of the heart? For me, with me, could you bear the world's sneer? With the warmth of love around you, would you care what the world said of you? Should I be sufficient for you, if others look coldly and neglected you?'

Even now his literal meaning did not occur to her; she neither knew nor dreamt of any ties that bound him; and she still thought he was trying to see how little or how much she loved him.

'Why do you ask me?' she said, almost impatiently, her eyes growing dark and humid with her great love for him. 'You know well enough that "for you," and "with you," are talismans all-powerful with me. Your smile is my sole joy, your coldness my sole sorrow. You are all the world to me; Sir Folko—Granville, why *will* you doubt me?'

'I do *not* doubt you! It would be better for you if your love were less true, or mine more worthy it. Oh, Alma! Alma! Would to God we had met earlier!'

But she did not hear his muttered words, nor see the hot tears that stood in his eyes; tears wrung from his very heart's depths; tears of gratitude, regret, remorse, and wholly of tenderness, as he bent over her, pressing his burning lips to her flushed brow and soft cheeks, warm with a feverish glow, the glow of joy, predestined not to last.

And now the sun was near his setting, and all the earth was brilliant with the imperial glories that attend the gorgeous burial of a summer-day. Mingling rays of crimson and of gold stretched across the sky, steeping in light the snow-white fleecy clouds that rose up on the horizon, like the silvery mountain range of some far-off and Arcadian land. The roses glowed a deeper hue, the chesnut-boughs drooped nearer to the earth; the flowers hung their heads, drunk with the evening dew; the birds were rocked by the warm west wind; delicious odour from the lime-leaves filled the air, while already on the warm and radiant day descended the tender and voluptuous night.

The Sunset hour, when the busy day still lingers on the earth, bowed down with the weight of sins

and sorrows with which in one brief twelve hours the
sons of men have laden her ; and the night sweeps
down with noiseless wing from heaven, to lay her
soft hand on weary human eyes, and lead them
into dream-land, to rest awhile from toil and care ;
is ever full of Nature's deepest poetry. The working man at sunset, leaves his plough and his hard
toil for daily bread, and catches one glimpse of
God's great mystery of beauty, as he sees the
evening dew glisten in the dying buds of the
flowers his plough has slain. The Ave Maria at
sunset, wings its solemn chant over the woods and
mountains, golden in God's own light, and min-
gles its human worship with the pure voiceless
prayer of the fair earth. The soul of man at sunset, shakes off the dust of the working world, and
with its rest has time to listen to the sweeter
under-notes and more spiritual harmonies which
lie under the rushing current of our outer life;
and at sunset our hearts grow tenderer to those
we hate, and more awake to all the silent beauty
of existence which our strife, and fret, and follies
mar and ruin ; and—when we love—as the warm
sunset fades, and the dreamy night draws on, all
the poetry and passion that lie in us wake from
their slumber, and our heart throbs with its subtle
and voluptuous beauty.

The golden rays of the sun, while it still lingered over the earth, as a lover loth to part, fell upon Alma's hair, and lit up her features with a strange radiance, touching the lips and cheeks into a richer glow, and darkening her eyes into a still deeper brilliance. They were silent; they needed no words between them, a whisper now and then was all; their thoughts were better uttered by the caresses he lavished upon her, in the vehemence of his new-born love. The dangerous spell of the hour stole upon them; her soft arms were round his neck; his lips rested on her flushed brow; while one hand played with a thick silky lock of her golden hair which had escaped from the rest and hung down to her waist, twisting it round his fingers and drawing it out, half in admiration of its beauty, half in absence of thought. And as the sun sank out of sight below the horizon, and the little crescent of the moon rose clearer in the evening mists, and the air grew sweeter with the perfume of the early night, Alma might have known that the heart on which her young head rested, was throbbing loudly with fiercer and more restless passion than the loving and tender joy which made *her* heart its own unclouded heaven.

And still he had not told her of his marriage;

and still he said to himself, ' I ought to leave her, but, God forgive me! *I cannot.*'

On their delicious solitude the sound of a horse's hoofs broke suddenly, with the harsh clang and clamour of the outer world. All was so still around Alma's sequestered home, especially in the summer evenings, when the animal life about the farm was at rest, that the unusual sound brought, by its sudden inroad, the serpent of social life into the solitude of the heart, from which for a while all memory of the prying and fretting world had been excluded.

The horse's gallop ceased at the little gate, and the wicket was opened with a clash of its iron latch. De Vigne started, with a vague dread that some one had come to try and rob him of his new-won treasure. The strongest nerves grow highly strung at times; and when the poetry of life wakes in the hearts of men of action, and passion rises up out of their ordinarily calm existence, their whole souls stir with it, as the great seas, that do not move for light showers or low winds, arise at the sound of the tempest, till all nature is awed at their vehemence, and their own lowest depths tremble with the convulsion.

' What is the matter?' whispered Alma, as she

saw his eyes straining eagerly to see who the new comer was.

'Nothing, nothing,' he answered hastily. He could not tell her that the vague dread upon him (upon him! he who had laughed at every danger, and held his own against every foe) was the terror and the horror of that woman whom the Law called his Wife. He gave a deep sigh of relief as he saw that it was only his own groom, Warren, coming up the path with a note in his hand; but the blood mounted to his forehead in anger at the interruption. With the contradictory wayward-ness of human nature, while he knew that he should never leave Alma, unless some imperative call aided him to drag himself from her side, he could have found it in his heart to slay the man who would force him, however innocently, from his paradise!

The note was merely from Dunbar, major of Ours, to ask to see him at once, on business of urgent military importance; but as the envelope was marked outside 'Immediate,' his confidential servant had sent a groom off with it as soon as he had seen it.

De Vigne read the note in silence, only point-ing to Alma the words on it, 'Let me see you, if

possible, early this evening,' and sat still, tearing
the paper into little pieces, with his teeth set, his
face deadly pale, and a bitter struggle in his heart
—a struggle more hard and cruel, even than to
most men, to one who had followed all his impulses, whose will had been unbridled from his
cradle, with whom to wish and to have had always
been synonymous, and whose passions were as
strong as renunciation was unaccustomed. With a
fierce oath muttered in his teeth he sprang to his
feet; half awed by the sternness on his face, the
grey pallor of his cheek, and the flashing fire of
his eyes, she took his hands in her own with the
caressing fondness of her usual manner.

'Must you go? Can't you give me one half
hour more? The hours were always so long when
you were away; what will they be now? Give
me ten minutes more—just ten minutes!'

Her loving, innocent words, the clinging touch
of her hands, the witchery of her face, lifted up to
his in the twilight shadows—what torture they
were to him!

'Hush, hush!' he said, fiercely, crushing her in
a passionate farewell embrace. 'Do not ask me;
for God's sake, let me go while I can! Kiss me
and forgive me, my worshipped darling, for all the

sins in my past, and my acts and my thoughts, of which your guileless heart never dreams!'

She did not understand him; she had no clue to the wild desires rioting in his heart; but love taught her the sympathy, experience alone could not have given; her kisses, warm and soft as the touch of rose-leaves, answered his prayer, and her words were fond as human words could be.

'Since I love you, how could I help but forgive you whatever there might be? No sin that you could tell me of would *I* visit upon you. I do not know what your words mean, but I do know how well I love you; too well to listen what others might ever say of you; too well to care what your past may have been. There is nothing but tenderness and faith between us; there never can be, there never shall be. Good night. God bless you!'

'God bless you!' murmured De Vigne, incoherently. 'Let me go, let me go, Alma, while I have strength!' . . . .

In another moment the ring of his horse's hoofs rung loud on the stony road, growing fainter and fainter on the evening air, till it died away to silence; while Alma leaned out under the chesnut-boughs, looking up to the stars that were shining in the deep blue sky, now that the golden sunset had faded, with tears of joy on her long black lashes and sighs of delight on her warm lips, dreaming her sweet love idyll, and thinking of the morrow that would bring him to her again.

CHAPTER XI.

A BITTERNESS GREATER THAN DEATH.

As soon as De Vigne reached town he drove to
Dunbar's, who in a very few words told him what
he wanted of him, which was to exchange with
him back into the Dashers, and go out to the
Crimea in his stead; but in lieu of the eager
assent he had anticipated from so inveterate a
campaigner and thorough-bred a soldier, he was
astonished to see De Vigne pause, hesitate, and
wait irresolute.

'I thought you would like it, old fellow,' said
Dunbar.   'The exchange would be easily effected.
I should be no good in the Crimea; the winter
season would send me to glory in no time with
my confounded bronchia, while you seemed to
enjoy yourself so thoroughly out in India, polish-
ing off those black devils, that I thought you'd be
delighted to get a chance of active service again.'

'I enjoy campaigning; no man more so,' said

De Vigne, shortly; 'and to give up a chance of active service is almost as great a sacrifice to me as anything. At the same time, circumstances have arisen which make me doubt whether I can go in your stead or not. Will you give me twenty-fours to decide?'

'Very well—if you like. I know you will tell me this time to-morrow that you have already ordered your cases of Bass, and looked over your new rifles. You will never be able to resist the combined seductions of Turkish liaisons and Russian spearing,' laughed Dunbar.

De Vigne laughed too; though, Heaven knows, laughter was far enough from his heart:

'Very possibly. I'll send you a line to-morrow evening, yes or no.'

'Oh! it's sure to be yes,' said Dunbar. 'You were always the very deuce for war and women, but I think campaigning carried the day.'

De Vigne laughed again, par complaisance; but he thought of one woman he had learnt to love more dearly than anything else in earth or heaven. He left Dunbar, went back to his house, and shut himself in his own room. He lit his cigar, opened the window, and leaned out into the night. His honour and his love were at war, and the calm and holy midnight irritated and inflamed,

where at another time it might have soothed him.
Never in all his life, with its errors, its hot in-
stincts, its generous impulses, its haughty honour,
never stained by a mean thought, but often
hazarded by reckless passions, had his nature
been so fairly roused as now. He knew that he
had fallen far from his standard of truth and candour, in the concealment of his marriage, which
had gone on from day to day till he had won the
deepest love he had ever had, ostensibly a free
man ; and that knowledge cut him to the soul,
and gave him the keenest remorse which he had
ever known ; for though he had done much
sin in haste, his conscience was ever tender,
and nothing could ever blunt him to any derelic-
tion from frankness and honesty. But he knew,
too now, that the evil was done, and that to leave
her would be to quench all the youth and glory from
her young days, and refuse her the sole consolation
in his power to give her, which was his love, no light
treasure to a woman of her mind and nature.

'God help her!' he muttered to himself, as he
looked down into the dark and silent street ; ' I
will be truer to her than any husband ever was to
wife. She *is* my wife by love, by reason, by right,
and when others sneer at her or pass her coldly by
because she has sacrificed herself for me, I will

atone to her for all—I will give up the world, and
live for her alone. Since I have crushed my little
flower in my headlong path, I will make up to
her by guarding her from all blight or storm.
Would to Heaven I were worthy of her!'

That night his resolve was made. To-morrow
he would tell her of his marriage—tell her all. If
she still loved him, and still wished to live for him,
entirely as his heart was bound to the Service, he
would throw up his commission and take her to
Italy or the Ionian Isles, where he would lavish on
her all the luxuries and pleasures wealth could
bring, and give her what would be all-sufficient to
her affectionate and unselfish nature—love. He
would live for her alone ; if, in time, he missed
the glare and excitement of his past life with men'
this sacrifice, in return, he at the least owed her ;
he would not bring her to the din of cities where
coarse glances might pain the heart that had as yet
known no shame, and where coarse judges would
class her with the base Floras and Leilas of her
sex.

Military duties kept him until late the next day.
A soldier's life is not all play, though the foes to a
standing army are given to making it out such.
Several things called his attention that morning,
and he had afterwards to attend the first sitting of

a court-martial on one of those low practical jokes with which raw boys, bringing their public school vulgarities with them, stigmatize a Service that enrols the best gentlemen, the highest courage, and the most finished chivalry of Europe, whose enemies delightedly pounce on the exception to uphold it as the rule.

The court-martial was not over till between two and three; De Vigne then hastily got unharnessed, and threw himself across his horse. When he had once determined on a thing he never looked back; sometimes it had been better for him if he had. Yet, in the long run, I have known more mischief done by indecision of character than anything else in the world, and he is safe to be the strongest and stoutest-hearted who never looks back, whether he has determined on quitting Sodom or on staying in it. The evil lies in hasty judgment, not in prompt action.

Right or wrong, however, he never *had* looked back in any course. His mind was made up—if Alma still loved him on hearing all, to take her to some southern solitude, and give up his life to her; if she reproached and condemned him, to fight in the Crimea till he fell—and nothing would have stirred either of his resolves. He rode at a gallop from London to Richmond—rode to the

fevered thoughts that chased each other through
his mind, many of them of bitter pain and sharp
stinging regret, for to the man of honour it was
no light trial to say to the woman who had trusted
him, 'I have deceived you!'—some of them of
involuntary self-reproach at the memory of how
little he had merited and fulfilled the trust
Boughton Tressillian had placed in him, 'as a
man who will not misjudge my motives nor wrong
my confidence.' Yet all fears were crossed, and
all remorse silenced, and outweighed by that wild
joy of which his nature was capable.

All more gloomy memories vanished, as shadows
slink away before the noon, as he came within
sight of Alma's home. He pulled up his horse
with such abruptness that the beast reared and fell
back on his haunches; he threw himself off the
saddle with a headlong impetuosity that might
have lost him life or limb, flung the bridle over
the post, and entered. The morning was grey and
wet—strange contrast to the radiant summer
night before—the birds were silent, the flowers
were snapped off their stems, their scattered petals
lying stained and trodden on the moist gravel ;
his hurried steps stamped the discoloured rose-
leaves into the earth, and the dripping chesnut-
boughs shook raindrops on him as he passed.

He brushed past the dank bushes in haste, careless, indeed unconscious, of·the rain that fell upon him. With all the impatience of his nature he glanced up at the house as he approached. He expected to find her looking out for him, to see her eyes fixed wistfully upon the gate, and to watch the radiance of joy dawn upon her face as she beheld him. He wanted to see that her thoughts and moments were consecrated to him, in his absence as well as his presence, and to have in her joyous welcome and her rapid bound to meet him, sure evidence still of her love.

With a strange, disproportionate anxiety he brushed past the dripping boughs, ran up the steps of her bay-window, pushed open the glass door, and entered. There were her easel, her flowers, her little terrier, Pauline upon her stand pluming her feathers, and congratulating herself on her own beauty, one of his own books, 'Notre Dame,' open on her low chair, with some moss-roses flung down in a hurry on its leaves; her colours, and brushes, and half-finished sketches scattered over the room—but the mistress and queen of it was absent. There was no sweet welcome for him, no loving radiant face uplifted to his, no rapid musical voice to whisper in his ear earnest impassioned words, no soft caresses to linger on his lips, no warm young heart to beat against his own.

He glanced hastily round on the still deserted chamber, then opened the door, and called her by her name. The house was low and not large, and he knew she would come at the sound of his voice as a spaniel at its master's call. There was no reply; the building was silent as death, and his heart beat thickly with a vague and startled dread. He went on to the staircase and repeated her name; still there was no reply. Had she been anywhere in the house, small as it was, he knew she would have heard and answered him. A horrible unexplained fear fastened upon him, and he turned into a dark old-fashioned bedchamber, the door of which stood open, for in its farther window he caught sight of the old woman, her nurse, alone, in her wicker-chair, her head covered with her apron, rocking herself to and fro in the silent and querulous grief of age.

It is no metaphor that the beating of his heart stood still as he beheld her grief, which, mute as it was, spoke to him in a hundred hideous suggestions. She started up as his step rang on the bare floor, and wrung her hands, the tears falling down her wrinkled cheeks :

'Oh, sir! oh, sir! my poor young lady—my pretty darling—'

His hand clenched on her arm like an iron vice.

' My God ! what has happened ?'

' That ever I should live to see the day,' moaned the old woman. ' That ever I couldn't have died afore it. My pretty dear—my sweet little lady that I nursed on my knee when she was a little laughing—'

His grasp crushed on to her wrist, while his words broke from him inarticulate in his dire agony :

'Answer me—what is it ? Where is she ? Speak—do you hear ?'

The woman heard him, and waved to and fro in the garrulous grief of her years.

' Yes, sir—yes ; but I am half crazed. She's gone—my poor dear darling !'

' Gone—*dead ?* '

The hue of death itself spread over his face. He let go his hold upon her arm and staggered backwards, all life seeming to cease in the mortal terror of suspense and dread.

'No, sir—no, thank Heaven !' murmured the woman, blind to the agony before her in her own half-fretful sorrow. ' Not dead, the pretty dear, though some, I dare say, would sooner see her in her coffin, and sure she might be happier in her grave than she'll be now, poor child!'

The blood rushed back to his brain and heart; his strong nerves trembled, and he shook in every limb in the anguished agitation of that brief moment which seemed to him a ceaseless eternity of torture. If not dead she could not be lost to him; no human hand had power to take her from his arms!

He seized the garrulous woman in a grasp whose fervency terrified her :

' Where is she then? Speak—in a word—without that senseless babble.'

' Yes, sir, yes,' sobbed the old nurse, half lost in her quavering sorrow, but terrified at his manner and his tone. ' She's gone away, sir, with that soft, lying, purring villain—oh, Lord ! what is his name ?—that false, silky, girl-faced lord—a duke's son they said he was—who was always hankering after her, and coming to buy pictures, and cared no more for pictures than that cat. She's gone off with him, sir, and he'll no more marry her than he'll marry me ; and he'll leave her to starve in some foreign land, and I shall never see her face again. Oh, Lord ! oh, Lord ! sir, you men have much to answer for—'

'She is gone!—with *him* !'

If she had not been so wrapped in her own rambling regrets she must have noticed the unutterable anguish in his hoarse and broken words as he grasped her arm with almost the wild, unconscious ferocity of madness:

'Woman, it is a vile plot—a lie! She has been trapped, deceived. She has not gone of her own will!'

'Yes, sir, she is—she's gone of her own mind, her own choice,' moaned the old nurse.

'I tell you she did *not*—it is a lie,' swore De Vigne. 'He has stolen her, tricked her, fooled her away. It is a lie, I tell you, and you have been bribed to forge it. He has decoyed her away, and employed you for his accomplice, to pass this tale on me. My God! if you do not acknowledge the truth I will find a way to make you!'

Terrified at his violence the old woman shook with fear, tears falling down her pale and withered cheeks:

'I tell you truth, sir—before Heaven I do. Do you think *I* should injure her, my pretty little lady, that I've loved like my own child ever since my poor master brought her from foreign lands, a little, lisping, gold-haired thing? Do you think

I should join in a plot against her, when I've loved her all her life? Don't you think, sir, I'd be the first to screen her and the last to blame her? I tell you truth, sir, and it breaks my heart in the telling. She went of her own free will, and nothing could stop her. She must have planned it all with him yesterday when he was here: the cruel villain! I knew he didn't come after them pictures; but I never thought Miss Alma would have come to *this*. She went of her own will, sir—she did, indeed! Lord Vane's carriage came here between twelve and one this morning; not him in it, but his valet, and he asked straight for Miss Tressillian, and said he had a message for her, and went in to give it. I thought nothing of it, so many people have been coming and going lately for the pictures; and indeed, sir, I thought he was your servant, for the man looked like one you used to send here, till my boy, Tom, came in, and said he'd asked the coachman, and the coachman told him his master was the Duke of Tiara's son. The man wasn't there long before I heard Miss Alma run upstairs, and as I went across the passage I see her coming down them, with her little black hat on, and a cloak over her muslin dress; and a queer dread come over me, as it were, for I see her face

was flushed, and she'd tears in her eyes, and a
wild, excited look; and I asked her where she was
going. But she didn't seem to hear me; and she
brushed past me to where the man was standing.
" I am ready," she says to him, very excited like;
and then I caught hold of her—I couldn't help it,
sir—and I said, though I didn't know where or
why she was going, "Don't go, Miss Alma! don't
go, my darling." But she turned her face to me,
with her sweet smile—you know her pretty, im-
perious, impatient ways—" I must, nurse!" and I
got hold of her, and kept on saying, " Don't go,
Miss Alma, don't!—tell me *where* you're going,
at least—do!—my dear little lady!" But you
know, sir, if she's set her heart on a thing, it ain't
never easy to set her against it; and there was
tears in her eyes. She broke away with that
wilfulness she's had ever since she was a little
child: " I cannot stop, nurse—let me go!" and
she broke away, as I said, and went down the
garden path, sir, the man following after her, and
she entered Lord Vane's carriage, and the valet
got up in front, and they drove away, sir, down
the road; and that's the last I ever see of my
poor master's darling, Heaven bless her! and she'll
be led into sorrow, and ruin, and shame, and she'll
think it's all for love, poor child; and he'll break

her heart, and her high proud spirit, and then he'll leave her to beg for her bread ; for that bird's better notions of work than she; and a deal fit she is to cope with the world, that's so cold and cruel to them that go against it !' . . . . .

But long ere she ceased her garrulous grief, heedless of his presence or his absence in her absorbed sorrow for her lost darling, De Vigne had staggered from the chamber, literally blinded and stunned by the blow he had received. A sick and deadly faintness as after a vital wound stole over him, every shadow of colour faded from his face as on his marriage-day, leaving it a grey and ashy hue even to his very lips; his brain was dizzy with a fiery weight that seemed to press upon it; he felt his way, as if it were dark, into an adjoining room, and sank down upon its single sofa, all the strength of his vigorous manhood broken and cast down by his great agony. How great that agony was Heaven only knew.

He threw back, as a hideous nightmare, the thought that Alma could be false to him ; that a girl so young, so frank, so fond, could be so arch an actress ; that all those loving words, those sweet caresses, that earnest and impassioned affection lavished on him but a few short hours before, were all a lie. Yet the curse of evidence chimed

strangely in; he recalled her blush at his mention of Castleton's name; he remembered that
his ex-valet, Raymond, had entered Castleton's
service on being discharged from his; the mere
circumstance of her having left with anyone, for
anywhere, without an explanation, a word, or a
message to him—her lover, whom she had parted
with so passionately the night before—these alone
wrote out her condemnation, and shattered all
hope before his eyes.

He sat there in as mortal anguish as man ever
knew. If wrong there had been in his acts and
his thoughts it was fearfully and cruelly avenged,
and the punishment far outweighed the sin.
Across the midnight darkness of his mind gleamed
lightning flashes of fiery thoughts. Once he
started to his feet—in the delirium of jealousy he
swore to find Castleton wherever he had hid, and
make him yield her up, or fight for her till one or
the other fell. But pride was not all dead in him
—nor ever would be while he had life. Since she
had gone to another, let another keep her!

And now it was that the great faults of De
Vigne's nature—hasty doubt and passionate judgment—came out and rose up against him, marring
his life once more. That rank scepticism which
one betrayal had engrafted on a nature naturally

trusting and unsuspicious, never permitted him to pause, to weigh, to reflect; with the rapidity of vehement and jealous passion, from devoted faith in the woman he loved, he turned to hideous disbelief in her, and classed her recklessly and madly with the vilest and the falsest of her sex. Of no avail the thousand memories of Alma's childlike purity and truth, which one moment's thought would have summoned up in her defence; of no avail the fond and noble words spoken to him but the day before, which one moment's recollection would have brought to his mind to vouch for her innocence, and set before him in its vile treachery, the plot to which she had fallen victim;—of no avail! Passionate in every impulse, hasty in every judgment, too cruelly stung to remember in his madness any reason or any justice, he seized the very poison that was his death-draught, and grasped a lie as truth.

How long he sat there he never knew; time was a long blank to him; roll on as it might, it could only serve him in so far as it brought him nearer to his grave. His brain was on fire, his thoughts lost in one sharp, stinging agony that had entered into his life never to quit it; he sat there in dull stupor till her little dog, that had followed him up the stairs, and now crouched near him, awed as animals

always are at the sight of human suffering, crept up
and licked his hand, uttering a long, low whine, as
if mourning for the one lost to them both.   The
touch roused him: how often in happier days, before
the curse of love rose up between them, had he
smiled to see her playing like a child with her little
terrier !   The touch roused him, calling him back
to the life charged with such unutterable woe.
He lifted his head and looked around ; the clouds
had rolled away, and the evening sun, bursting out
in all its glory, shone with cruel mockery into the
little chamber which, as it chanced, was Alma's
apartment.   The lattice windows were open, and
the wind swept in, stirring the muslin curtains of
the little white bed where, night after night, her
blue eyes had closed in sleep, as pure and sweet
as a harebell folding itself to slumber.   As he
lifted his eyes and looked around the little chamber, his glance fell upon his own portrait, which
hung against the wall with the sunlight streaming
full upon it—the portrait which she had drawn
from childish memory of her friend ' Sir Folko.'
The sight of the picture told him that it was her
room into which he had staggered in his unconscious suffering, and recalled to him the early days
when she had first shown him that portrait, lavish-
ing on him her innocent gratitude, her playful

tenderness; the early days when their intercourse had been shadowless, and the curse of love had not entered their lives and risen up between them. As he gazed around him, at all the trifles that spoke to him like living things of the woman he had loved and lost, the bitter agony in his soul grew greater than he could bear; the fierce tension of his strained nerves gave way; with one cry to Heaven in his mortal anguish, he fell like a drunken man across the little couch, his brow resting on the pillow where her golden head had so often lain in childlike sleep, deep sobs heaving his breast, burning tears forcing themselves from his eyes, tears which seemed to wring his very life-blood from him in their fiery rain, yet tears which saved him in that horrible hour from madness.

* • * *

That night he wrote thus briefly to the Major:

'DEAR DUNBAR,—I desire to exchange with you if it can be effected. There is no time to be lost.

'Yours sincerely,
'GRANVILLE DE VIGNE.'

CHAPTER XII.

THE BRIDAL JEWELS GO TO THE MONT DE PIÉTÉ.

IN their salon in the Champs Elysées, that
crowded, gaudy, and much-bedizened room, sat
as they had sat twelve months before, old Fantyre
and the Trefusis, the old woman huddled up
among a pile of cushions, shawls, and furs, with
her feet on a *chaufferette*, older and uglier, with
her wig awry, and her little piercing black eyes
roving about like a monkey's as she drank her
accustomed *demie tasse*, which, as I before ob-
served, looked most suspiciously like cognac undefiled. The younger one, with her coarse, dashing, full-blown, highly-tinted beauty not shown
off to the best advantage, for it was quite early
morning, *madame n'était pas visible*, of course, in
common with all Parisiennes, whether Parisienne
by birth or by adoption; and not being visible,
the Trefusis had not thought it worth her while
to dress, but hastily enveloped in a peignoir

looked certainly, though she was a fine woman still, not exactly calculated to please taste, used to the sight, and the society, of delicate aristocrates.

'Well, my dear, ain't he killed yet?' demanded old Fantyre, in her liveliest treble.

' No,' said the Trefusis, running her eye through the Returns of the 25th October. 'Halkett, Nolan, Lord Fitzgibbon—lots of them—but—'

'Not the right one,' chuckled the old Fantyre, who, though she had her own private reasons for desiring De Vigne's demise, as his property was so ruled that a considerable portion must have have come to his wife whether he had willed it so or not, had still that exquisite pleasure in the Trefusis's mortification, which better people than the old Viscountess indulge in now and then at their friends' expense. 'Deuce take the man! Tiresome creature it is; shot and sabre carry off lots of pretty fellows out there. Why on earth can't they touch him? And that beautiful creature, Vivian Sabretasche, is *he* all right?'

'Slightly wounded—that's all.'

'How cross you are, my dear. If you must not wear widow's weeds, I can't help it, can I? They are not becoming, my dear—not at all; though if a woman knows how to manage 'em,

she may do a good deal under her crape. Men
ain't afraid of a widow as they are of an unmar-
ried woman, though Heaven knows they need be
if they knew all; the "dear departed" 's a capital
dodge to secure a new pigeon. Mark my words,
my dear, De Vigne won't die just because you
wish him !'

'Wish him!' reiterated the Trefusis. 'How
disagreeably you phrase things, Lady Fantyre.'

'Give 'em their right names, my dear? Yes,
I believe that *is* uncommon disagreeable for most
people,' chuckled the old woman. 'In my time,
you know, we weren't so particular; if we did
naughty things (and we did very many, my dear,
almost as many as people do now!), we weren't
ashamed to call 'em by their dictionary names.
Humbug's a new-fangled thing, as well as a new-
fangled word. They say we were coarse; I don't
know, I'm sure; I suppose we were; but I know
we didn't love things under the rose, and sneak
out of 'em in daylight, as you nineteenth-century
people do; our men, if they went to the casinoes
at night, didn't go to Bible meetings, and Mainten-
ance-of-Immaculate-Society boards, and Regene-
rated Magdalens' Refuges the next morning—
as they do now-a-days. However, if we were more
consistent, we weren't so " Christian," I sup-

pose! Lor' bless me, what a deal of cant there
is about in the world now; even you, whom I did
think was pretty well as unscrupulous as anybody
I ever met, won't allow you'd have liked to see De
Vigne among them Returns. I know when poor old
Fantyre died, Lady Rougepot says to me, " What
a relief, my dear!" and I'm sure *I* never thought
of differing from her for a minute! You've never
had but one checkmate in your life, Lucy—with
that little girl Trevelyan—Tressillian—what's her
name?'

'Little devil!' said the Trefusis, bitterly; she
had not grown the choicest in her expressions,
from constant contact with the Fantyre. 'I saw
her again the other day.'

'Here?'

'Yes; in the Rue Vivienne—in a fleuriste's
shop. I passed her quite close; she knew me
again. I could tell that by the scorn there was
in her eyes, and the sneer that came on her lips.
Little fool! with the marriage certificate before
her very eyes, she wouldn't believe the truth.'
'The scheme was so good, it deserved complete
success. I hate that little thing—such a child as
she looks to have put one down, and outgeneralled
one's plans.'

'Child!' chuckled old Fantyre; 'she wasn't so

much of a child but what she could give you one
of the best retorts I ever heard. " It was a pity
you didn't learn the semblance of a lady, to support
you in the assumption of your rôle ! " Vastly good,
vastly good ; how delighted Selwyn would have
been with that.'

' Little devil ! ' repeated the Trefusis again. ' I
hate the sight of that girl's great dark-blue eyes.
De Vigne shall never see her again if *I* can help
it, little, contemptuous, haughty creature ! '

' She's a lady, ain't she ? ' said the Fantyre,
drily.

' I'm sure I don't know. She is as proud as a
princess, though she's nothing but an artist after
all. Good gracious ! Who is that ? ' said the
Trefusis, as she heard a ring at the entrance,
giving a hurried dismayed glance at her *négligée*.
' It can't be Anatole nor De Brissac ; they never
come so early.'

' If they do, my dear, beauty unadorned, you
know—'

' Stuff ! ' said the Trefusis, angrily. ' Beauty
unadorned would get uncommonly few admirers
in these days. Perhaps it's nobody for us.'

As she spoke a servant entered, and brought
her a piece of paper with a few words on it, unfolded and unsealed.

'What's that, my dear?' asked Lady Fantyre, eagerly.

'Only my dressmaker,' said the Trefusis, with affected carelessness, but with an uneasy frown, which did not escape the quick old lady.

'Dressmaker!' chuckled the Fantyre, as she was left alone. 'If you've any secrets from me, my dear, we shall soon quarrel. I've no objection whatever to living with you as long as you have that poor fellow's three thousand a year, and we can make a tidy little income with you to attract the young men, and me to play whist and écarté with 'em; but if you begin to hold any cards I don't see, I shall throw up the game, though we have played it some time together.'

·While old Fantyre, who had this single virtue amongst all her vices, that she was candid about them, thus talked to herself over her cognac and coffee, the Trefusis had gone, demie-toilette and all, into the salle, where there awaited her a neat, slight, fair man, with a delicate *badine* and gold studs, who looked something between a valet, an actor, and a would-be-dandy—such as you may see by scores any day on the Boulevards, hanging about the Bads, or lounging in the parterre of the Odéon.

He smiled, a curious slight smile, as the Trefusis entered.

' *Vous voilà, Madame !* Not *en grande tenue* to-
day ; too early for your pigeons, I suppose ? I dare
say you and the old lady make a very good thing
out of it, though of course you only entertain immaculate society, for fear you should give the
Major a chance to bring you up before a certain
Law Court, eh ? '

' What did you come for so soon again ? ' demanded the Trefusis, abruptly, with as scant
courtesy as might be. ' I have only five minutes to
spare, you had better not waste it in idle talk.'

' What do I come for, ma belle ? Now, what
should I come for ? What do I ever come for,
pray ? ' returned her visitor, in nowise displeased,
but rather amused at her annoyance.

' Money ! ' retorted the Trefusis. ' You will
get none to-day.'

The man laughed.

' Now why always keep up this little farce ?
Money I wish for—money you will give me.
Why make the same amusing little denial of it
every time ? '

' It is no amusing little denial to-day, at all
events,' said the Trefusis, coldly. ' I have none
left. I cannot give you what I have not.'

He laughed, and played a tattoo with the cor-
nelian head of his cane.

'Very well, then I will go to the Major.'

'You cannot. He is in the Crimea.'

'To the Crimea I can go to-morrow, *belle amie*, in the service of a gentleman who has a fancy to visit it. But I am tired of playing the valet, though it is amusing enough sometimes; and, indeed, as you pay so very badly, I have been thinking of writing to De Vigne, he will give me anything I ask, for my information.'

The Trefusis's eyes grew fiercer, but she turned pale and wavered.

'A line of mine will tell the Major, you know, belle amie, and I don't fancy he will be inclined to be very gentle to his wife, *née* Lucy Davis, eh?' he went on, amused to watch the changes on her face. 'He will pay very highly, too—what are a few thousands to him?—he is as lavish as the winds; as proud as the devil, and hating Mme. sa femme as he does, he will give me, I have no doubt, anything I ask. It will be a much better investment for me; I won't trouble you any more, Lucy; I shall write to your husband at once.'

He rose, and took his hat; but the Trefusis interrupted him.

'Stay—wait a moment—how much do you want?'

'Fifty pounds now, and as much this day week?'

'Impossible! I have not half—'

'Glad to hear it, madame. The Major will be the much better paymaster. With his thousands I can get a life annuity, buy stock, take shares, do what I like, even—who knows?—become an eminently respectable member of society! *Adieu! ma belle;* when we next meet it may be in the Law Courts over the water.'

'You villain!' began the Trefusis savagely, with a fierce flash of her black eyes.

He laughed:

'Not at all; you have the monopoly of any villany there may be in the transaction. Adieu! what shall I say from you to the Major—any tender message?'

'Wait,' cried the Trefusis, hurriedly. 'I have five naps—I could let you have more to-morrow; and—you could take one of my bracelets—'

'*One!* No, thank you, the other plan will be best for me. I am tired of these instalments, and De Vigne—'

'But—my diamonds, then—the ceinture he was fool enough to give me—' She tried to speak coldly, but there was a trembling eagerness in her manner which belied her assumed calmness.

' Fool, indeed!—and to think he was a man of the world! Your diamonds!—*ma chère*, you must be in strange fear, indeed, to offer me them. They must be worth no end, or they would not be the Major's giving. Well, come—I am willing to spare you, if I can, for old acquaintance sake.'

When he left the house, he carried with him that diamond ceinture worthy of an Empress which De Vigne had bought, in his lover's madness, for his bride ten years before, and took it up to the Mont de Piété. Three thousand a year was not a bad income, but the Trefusis's dress, the Fantyre's wines, the *petits soupers*, and her numerous Paris amusements, ran away with it very fast; and though écarté, vingt-et-un, and whist added considerably to their resources, the Trefusis was very often hard up, as people who have lived on their wits all their lives not unfrequently are. One would fancy such sharpening upon the grindstone of want might teach them economy in prosperity; but I don't think it often does; *canaille* ever glory in the ostentation of money, and waste hundreds in grand dinners, to—grudge the pineapple. Besides, the Trefusis, too, had a drain on her exchequer, of which the world and even Argus-eyed old Fantyre was ignorant.

CHAPTER XIII.

IN THE CHERSONESUS.

ALADYN and Devno!—those green stretching meadows, those rich dense forests, catching the golden glow of the sunshine of the East—those sloping hill-sides, with the clematis, and acacia, and wild vine clinging to them, and the laughing waters of lake and stream sleeping at their base— who could believe that horrible pestilential vapour stole up from them, like a murderer in the dark, and breathing fever, ague, and dysentery into the tents of a slumbering Army, stabbed the sleepers while they lay, unconscious of the assassin's hand that was draining away their life and strength? Yet at the very names of Aladyn and Devno rise to memory days of futile longing and weary inaction, of negligence inconceivable, and ennui unutterable, of life spent for the lack of simplest common sense, and graves filled by a schoolboy greed for fruit—such fruit as in such a land was

poison, when backed by a mad draught of raki.
Days, when forbidden to seek another foe, English-
men and Frenchmen went down powerless and
spiritless before the cholera, which had its deadly
grip upon them ere they heard its stealthy step.
Days, when you could not stroll on the beach, without finding at your feet a corpse, hastily thrust into
the loosened sand, for dogs to gnaw aud vultures to
make their meal, or look across the harbour without seeing some dead body floating, upright and
horrible, in the face of the summer sun. Days,
when pestilence was abroad through the encamp-
ment from Monastir to Varna.

We went out to the Crimea gladly enough ;
most of us had a sort of indistinct panorama of
skirmishes and excitement, of breathless charges
and handsome Turkish women, of dangers, difficulties, and good tough struggles, pleasant as sport
but higher spiced ; of a dashing, brilliant campaign, where we should taste real life and give
hard hits, and win perhaps some honour, and
where we should say, ' *Si l'on meurt, eh bien, tant
pis !* ' in the gay words of the merry French
bivouac-song. We thought of what our governors
or grandsires had done in the Peninsula, and
longed to do the same—we did not guess that as
different as the bundles of linen, with wrinkled,

hideous features, that the Tartars called women, were to the lovely prisoners from the convents of flaming Badajoz, would be the weary, dreary, protracted waiting while the batteries strove to beat in the walls of Sebastopol, to the brilliant and rapid assault by which Ciudad Rodrigo was won! I do not like to write of the Crimea; so many painful memories come up with its very name; memories such as all who were there must have by the score. Nothing personal prompts my anger; I liked the campaign well enough myself, having one of the very few tents that stood the hurricane, not missing more than nine-tenths of my letters, enjoying the exceptional blessing of something like a coat, and being now and then the happy recipient of a turkey, or some coffee that was *not* ground beans.

I was rewarded as much as any man could expect to be. I have a medal (shared in common with Baltic sailors who never saw the foe, save when securely anchored off Cronstadt) and clasps, like the privates of the Line, though I am not aware that any infantry man was present at the Balaklava charge. I am perfectly content myself, being independent of that very precarious thing 'promotion for distinguished services.' But when I think of them all, my dead friends, whose bodies

lie thick where the sweet wild lavender is blowing
over the barren steppes of the Chersonese this
summer's day, I remember, wrathfully, how civi-
lians, by their own warm hearths, sat and dictated
measures by which whole regiments, starving with
cold, sickened and died; and how Indian officers,
used to the luxurious style of Eastern warfare and
travel, asserted those privations to be 'nothing,'
which they were not called to bear; and I fear—I
fear—that England may one day live to want such
sons of hers as she let suffer and rot on the barren
plains of the Crimea, in such misery as she would
shudder to entail on a pauper or a convict.

Few of us will ever forget our first bivouac on
the Chersonese soil—that pitiless drenching down-
pour of sheets of ink-black water! What a night
it was! De Vigne, ever reckless of weather, had
not even a blanket to wrap round him, and lay
in the puddles of which the morass-like earth was
full, with the rain pouring down upon him, while
Sabretasche, who had loved to surround himself
with all that could lull the senses and shut out the
harsher world, passed the night in a storm to
which we should not expose a dog, in discomfort
for which we should pity a beggar;—yet gave
away the only shelter he had, a Highland plaid, to
a young boy who had but lately joined, a little

fellow with a face as fair as a girl's, and who had
barely seen seventeen summers, who was shivering
and shuddering with incipient ague.

The stamp of their bitter fate was upon both
those men ; the wounds were too deadly and too re-
cent to be yet skinned over; healed they deemed
they never would be. How Violet and Sabretasche
parted Heaven only knew ; no human eyes had
pried in upon them in that darkest hour; they
had parted on the very day that should have been
their marriage day ; parted—whether ever to meet
again on earth who could tell? His trial was
known to all; even the men, who had admired
Violet's fair face when she had driven up to the
barracks, had caught some glimmering of it, and
there was not one who did not, in his own way,
reverence the Colonel's sorrow.

De Vigne was yet more altered than he, and
I saw with astonishment all the icy coldness
which had grown on him after his fatal marriage,
but which had of late been dissipated, now closing
round him again.   I could but guess at the cause,
when before the embarkation, I, knowing nothing,
had asked him if he had been to bid Alma good-
by; and he had turned on to me, his face white
as death, his eyes black as night:

  ' Never breathe that name to me again !'

I knew him too well to press questions upon him, and I was obliged to be content with my suspicions as to the solution. But I was pained to see the bitter ·gloom which had gathered round him again, too deeply for trouble, danger, excitement, or care of comment, to have any power to dissipate it. He had an impatient, irritable hauteur to his men quite foreign to him, for to his soldiers he was invariably considerate ; he was much more harsh and stern in his orders, for before he had abhorred anything like martinetism ; and there was a settled and iron gloom upon him with which, every now and then, it seemed as if the fiery nature in him were at war, struggling like the flames of a volcano, within its prison of ice. From the time he took Dunbar's place as Major of Ours, I never saw him *smile ;* but I did see him now and then, when he was sitting smoking in the door of his tent, or riding beside me home from a dog-hunt or a hurdle-race, look across to where the sea lay, with a passionate agony in his eyes. All he seemed to live for was headlong and reckless danger, if he could have had it. The thing that roused him the most was when St. Arnaud, Bosquet, Forey, and their staff .rode along the front of our columns before Alma, and we were told what the Marshal said to the 55th, 'English, I hope you will fight well to-day.'

'By Heaven!' swore De Vigne, fiercely, 'if I had been near that fellow, I would have told him we will fight as we fought at Waterloo!'

It was a bitter trial to him, as to us all, that the Cavalry could not do more on the 20th, when we sat in our saddles, seeing the serried columns of the Line dash through the hissing waters, red with blood and foaming with the storm of shot, and force their way through the vineyards of the Alma—that little tortuous stream where we tasted blood for the first time on Crimean soil, whose name, with all his self-command, made De Vigne wince, more than a Cossack lance thrust through his side would have done. To have to sit through that day like targets for the Russians' round shots, while their storm of balls tore through our lines, and ripped up our horses, was too quiet business for any of us.

We were weary of inaction; our Arm had had little or nothing to do; we were not allowed to push on the pursuit at Alma, nor the charge at Mackenzie's Farm; we were stung by certain individual sneers that we were 'too fine gentlemen for our work,' and we were longing to prove that if we were 'above our business of collecting supplies for the army,' we could, if we had the chance, send home to England such a tale as would show them how cheaply the "fine gentlemen" of the Light Cavalry held life when honour claimed it, and would cover our slanderers for ever in the shame of their own lives. And our time came at last, when we were roused by the notes of Boot and Saddle, and drawn up on the slopes behind the redoubts. The story of that day is well enough known in England. How brightly the sun shone that morning, dancing on the blue strip of sea, and flashing on the lines of steel gleaming and bristling below; on the solid masses of the Russians, with their glittering lances and sabres, and their gay accoutred skirmishers whirling before their line of march like swallows in the air; on the fierce-eyed Zouaves lying behind the earthworks; on our Light and Heavy brigades in front of our camp; on Sir Colin's Highlanders drawn up *two deep*; for the 93rd did not need to alter their line even to receive the magnificent charge of Muscovite cavalry! How brightly the sun shone,—and how breathlessly we waited in that dead silence, only broken by the clink and the ring of the horses' bits and the unsheathing of sabres, as the Russians came up the valley, those splendid masses of cavalry moving en echelon to the attack!

Breathless every man on the slopes and in the
valley ; French and English ; soldier and amateur; while the grand line of the Muscovite
Horse rode on to the 93rd, who quietly awaited
them, motionless and impenetrable as granite,
firm and invulnerable as their own Highland sea-
walls—awaited them, till their second volley, rolling out on the clear morning air, sent that splendid
body of horse flying, shivered like sea-foam breaking on a rock.   Then came the time for Scarlett
and his Heavies—and all the lookers-on gathered
up yonder on the heights, held their breath when
Greys and Enniskilleners, with the joyous cheer
of the one, the wild shout of the other ringing
through the air, rushed at the massive columns of
the Russians, charged them, shaking their serried
masses as a hurricane shakes woodland trees, and
closing with their second line as it came up to
retrieve the lost honour of the priest-blessed
lances, mingled pêle-mêle with them, reckless of
all odds, cutting their way inch by inch through
the dense squadrons closing round them—those
' beautiful grey horses' pushing their road with
that dash and daring which had once won them
Napoleon's admiration—till the 1st Royals, with
the 4th and 5th Dragoon Guards, dashed to the res-
cue, and sent the Russian columns flying over the

plain, like a routed herd of cattle without a leader.
How the lookers-on cheered, waving their caps in
their hands and shouting rapturous applause, till
the heights rang again, as the Brigadier and his
Heavies rode back from their assault!—and De
Vigne muttered, as he glanced down the line of
our light brigade :

'By Heaven! when *is* our turn to come?'

Our turn was near at hand, An hour after we
received the order to advance on the Russian
guns. With the blame, on whomsoever it may
lie of that rash order, I have nothing to do. That
vexatious question can never be settled, since he
on whose shoulders they place it, lies in the valley
of Balaklava, the first who fell, and cannot raise
his voice to reply, or give the lie, if it be a lie, to
his calumniators. If Louis Nolan were to blame,
his love for our Arm, and his jealousy over its
honour, his belief that Light Cavalry would do
the work of demigods, and his irritation that
hitherto we had not been given the opportunity
we might have had, must plead his excuse ; and I
think his brilliant courage, and the memory of
that joyous cheer which ended in the wild death-
cry which none who heard can ever forget, might
silence the angry jar and jangle of contention above
his grave, and set the seals of oblivion upon his error?

The order was given us to take the **Russian**
guns. For the first time since we had landed a
light of joy and pleasure came into the Colonel's
eyes ; and his old smile flashed over De Vigne's
face. We were so sick of inaction, of riding about
the Chersonese doing nothing, and letting other
men's names go home in the despatches !

At ten minutes past eleven we of the Light Brigade shook our bridles and dashed off with Cardigan,
in the morning sunlight towards the Russian battery. Lookers-on tell me they could hardly credit
that so few in numbers, entirely unsupported, were
going to charge an army in position ; and that they
gave us up for hopeless destruction as we swept
past them full gallop, the sunshine catching the
points of our sabres and flashing off our harness.
If they did not credit it, *we* did. We knew it
was against all maxims of war for Cavalry to act
without support, or infantry at hand. We knew
that in all probability few indeed, if any of us,
would ever come back from that rapid and deadly
ride. But the order was given. There were the
guns—and away we went, quickening from trot to
canter, and from canter to gallop, as we drew
nearer to them. On we went, spurring our horses
across the space that divided us from those grim
fiery mouths. On we went: Sabretasche's voice

cheering us on, and the delicate white hand that
Belgravian belles admired, pointing to the guns
before us; De Vigne sitting down in his saddle as
in bygone days, when he led the field across
Northampton pastures. On we went! All *I*
was conscious of was of a feverish exultation;
a wild, causeless delight; a fierce, tiger-like
longing to be at them, and upon them. The ring
of the horses' iron hoofs, the chink of the rattling
bits, the clashing of chains and sabres, the whistle
and screech of the bullets as they flew amongst us
from the redoubt, all made music in my ear.
God knows how it is, but in such hours as that
the last thing one thinks of is the death so near
at hand. Though men reeled from their saddles
and fell lifeless to the ground at every step, and
riderless chargers fled snorting and wounded from
our ranks; though the guns from the redoubt
poured on us as we swept past, and volleys of
rifles and musketry raked our ranks; though every
moment great gaps were made, till the fire broke
our first line, and the second had to fill it up;
though from the thirty guns before us poured a
deadly fire, whose murderous balls fell amongst
us as we rode, clearing scores of saddles, sweeping
down horses and men, and strewing the plain as
we passed with quivering human bodies, and

chargers rolling over and over in their death-agony,—on we rode, down into that fiery embrace of smoke and flame, that stretched out its arms and hissed its fell kisses at us from the Russian line. De Vigne spurred his horse into the dense smoke of the blazing batteries as Sabretasche led us in between the guns. Everyone was for himself then, as we dashed into the battery and sabred the gunners at their posts, while the oblique fire from the hills, and the direct fire of musketry, poured in upon us. Prodigies of valour were done there, never to be chronicled. Twice through the blinding smoke I saw De Vigne beside me—the Charmed Life, as they had called him in India—reckless of the storm of balls that fell about him, sitting in his saddle as firmly as if he were at a Pytchley meet. We had no breathing-time to think of others in that desperate struggle, but once I heard Pigott near me shout out, 'The Colonel's down!' Thank God it was not true; down he was, to be sure, for his horse was killed under him by a round shot; but he sprang up again in an instant, as collectedly as though he were pacing the Ring in Hyde Park, and vaulted on a riderless charger that was by him. That wild mêlée! I remember nothing distinctly in it, save the mad thirst for blood that

at such a time rises in one as savagely as in a
beast of prey. A shot struck my left arm, breaking the bone above my wrist; but I was conscious
of no pain as we broke through the column of
Russian infantry, sending them flying before us,
broken and scattered like thistle-down upon the
wind, and were returning from our charge, as
brilliantly as the Scots and Enniskilleners had
returned from theirs, when the flank fire from the
hill battery opened upon us—an enemy we could
not reach or silence—and a mass of Russian
Lancers were hurled upon our flank. Shewell
and his 8th cut through them—we stayed for an
encounter, hemmed in on every side, our little
handful shrouded by the dense squadrons of their
troops. It was hot work, work that strewed the
plain with the English Light Brigade, as a harvest-
field is strewn with wheat-ears ere the sheaves are
gathered. But we should have broken through
them still, no matter what the odds, for there were
deeds of individual daring done in that desperate
struggle, which would make the chillest blood
glow, and the most lethargic listener kindle into
admiration. We should have cut through them,
coûte que coûte, but that horrible volley of grape
and canister, on which all Europe has cried shame,
poured on friend and foe from the gunners who

had fled before our charge, the balls singing with
their murderous hiss through the air, and falling
on the striving mass of human life, where English
and Russian fought together, carrying death and
destruction with its coward fire into the ranks of
both, and stamping the Church-blessed troops of
the Czar with ineffaceable infamy.

It was with bitter hearts and deadly thoughts
that we the remnant of the Six Hundred, rode
back, leaving the flower of the Light Brigade dead .
or dying before those murderous Russian guns ;—
and it was all done, all over, in five-and-twenty
minutes—less than a fast up-wind fox-hunt would
have taken at home !

De Vigne was unhurt. The Charmed Life
must still have had his spell about him, for if any
man in the Cavalry had risked danger and courted
death that day he had done so ; but he rode out
of the lines at Balaklava without even a scratch.
Sabretasche had been hit by a ball which had
only grazed his shoulder; the *raffiné* man of
fashion would have laughed at a much more
deadly wound. We were not too 'fine gentlemen' for *that* work ! Days afterwards he
looked back to the plain where so many of his
Dashers had fallen, torn and mangled in the
bloody jaws of those grim batteries, the daring

spirits quenched, the vigorous lives spent, the gallant forms food for the worms, and he turned to De Vigne with a mournful smile, ' *Cui bono?* '

True indeed—*cui bono?* that waste of heroic human life. There was a bitter significance in his favourite sarcasm, which the potentates, who for their own private ends had drenched the Cherso-nese in blood, would have found it hard to answer. *Cui bono* indeed! Their bones lie whitening there in the valley of Balaklava; fresh fancies amuse and agitate the nations; the Light Cavalry Charge is coldly criticized and pronounced tomfoolery, and their names are only remembered in the hearts of some few women whose lives were deso-lation when they fell.

Winter in the Crimea—the Crimea of 1854-55. The very words are enough to bring up again to me-mory that sharp, stinging wind, of whose concentred cold none can imagine in the faintest degree, save those who have weathered a winter in tents on the barren steppes before Sebastopol. Writing those very words is enough to bring up before one, the bleak, chill, dark stretch of ground, with its hor-rible roads turned to water-courses, or frozen like miles of broken glass; the slopes, vast morasses of mud and quagmire, or trackless wastes of snow; the hurricane, wild as a tropical tornado, whirling the tents in mid-air, and turning men and horses roofless into the terrible winter night; the long hours of darkness, of storm, of blinding snow, of howling wind, of pouring ink-black rain, in which the men, in the trenches, and the covering parties and pickets, watched with eyes that must never close, and senses that might never weary; the days when under those pitiless skies officers and men shared alike the common fate, worse clad than a beggar, worse cared for than a cab-horse; —all rise up before one as by incantation, at those mere words, Winter in the Crimea.

My left arm turned out so tedious and tiresome that I was obliged to go down to Balaklava for a short time. The day before I went up again to the front, a transport came into harbour with a reinforcement of the —th from England. I watched them land: their fresh healthy faces, their neat uniforms, their general trim, and all-over-like-going look, contrast enough to the men in the trenches at the front; and as I was looking at them disembark I saw a face I knew well—the face fair and delicate as a girl, with his long light curls and his blue eyes, and his lithe slight figure, of our little Curly of Frestonhills. Twelve months before, Curly had changed from his cap-taincy in the Coldstreams to the Lieutenant-

Colonelcy of the —th, and had been savage enough at having done so when the Household Brigades went out to the Crimea; but now his turn had come. We met as old friends did meet out there, and had a long haver of the things that had been done in England since we left, and the things we had done ourselves in the Chersonese. Knowing nothing of those fierce words which had passed between Curly and De Vigne, I was surprised at the silence with which Curly listened to my details of the heroic pluck with which our Frestonhills hero had cut his way through the Russian squadrons on the morning of the 25th; knowing nothing, either of the love which had entered into them both for the same woman, I set my foot in it unawares by asking him if he had seen the Little Tressillian before he left? Curly, though Heaven knows life had seasoned him as it seasons us all, busied himself with poking up his pipe, while the muscles of his lips twitched, as he answered simply, 'No!'

'No! What, didn't you even go to bid her good-by?'

'For Heaven's sake, Arthur, hold your tongue!' said Curly, more sharply than I had ever heard him speak. 'It is grossest brutality to jest on such a subject.'

'Brutality to ask after the Little Tressillian?'
I repeated, in sheer amazement. 'My dear fellow,
what on earth do you mean? What has happened
to Alma? Is she dead?'

'Would to Heaven she were, rather than what
they say she is: another added to Vane Castleton's list of victims!'

The anguish in his voice was unmistakable. I
stared at him in amazement. The Little Tressillian gone over to Vane Castleton! That girl
whose face was truth, and innocence, and candour
in itself! I stared at him in mute bewilderment.
The bursting of Whistling Dick between us at
that moment would not have astonished me
more.

'Alma—Vane Castleton! My dear Curly,
there must be some mistake.'

'God knows!' he answered between his teeth.
'I do not credit it, yet there are the facts: She
has left St. Crucis; her nurse saw her leave in
Castleton's brougham, and she has never returned.
She must have been deluded away; she never
could have gone willingly. He may have lured
her with a false marriage. God knows! I should
have found him out to know the truth, and shot
him dead if he had beguiled her away against her
will, but I never heard of it until the day before we

sailed. I could not leave my regiment at the eleventh hour.'

' Do you care so much for her, then ? '

' I loved her very dearly,' said Curly, simply, with his pipe betweeu his lips. ' Don't talk of it again, Arthur, please; she cared nothing for me, but *I* will never believe her face told a lie.'

He was silent; and since the loss of Alma had stung him so keenly and so deeply, that not even the elasticity of his gay, light, affectionate nature, could rebound or recover from it, it was easy to understand how it had overwhelmed De Vigne, if, as I doubted not, the love that Sabretasche had predicted had come between himself and the Little Tressillian.

The fierce words that had passed between them were not forgotten. De Vigne was not a man to forgive in a moment. Curly, with reasons of his own for believing that, true or untrue, this story of Alma's flight with Vane Castleton, the heart of the woman he loved was De Vigne's, and De Vigne's alone; sought no reconciliation. Perhaps he harboured a suspicion that it had been to him, and not to Castleton, Alma had flown, for he knew De Vigne would have left the woman he most tenderly loved, at any call to arms. They seldom met—De Vigne being in Lord Lucan's

camp, and Curly in that of the Light Division—
and they avoided each other by mutual consent.
The love of woman had come between them, and
stretched like a great gulf between De Vigne and
the young fellow he had liked ever since he was a
little fair-haired, bright-eyed boy.

Curly came just in time for that grey wintry
dawn, when the bells of Sebastopol rang through
the dark, foggy air, and the dense masses of troops,
for whom mass had been said, stole through the
falling rain up the heights of the valley of Inkermann.

Curly was in time for Inkermann, and for the
winter work in the trenches, where he, so late the
Adonis of the Guards, the 'best style' in the Park,
the darling of Belgravian boudoirs, who at home
never began his day till two o'clock, had to turn
into the trenches in rain, which made the traverses
like Dutch dykes, or in blinding snow blown into
his eyes; to come back to a tent without fire, to
food either semi-raw or else burnt black as a
cinder; and to sleep rudely, roused by a hurricane
that whirled away his sole frail shelter, and turned
him out into the bitter black Crimean night. That
winter showed us campaigning with the gloss off;
no brilliant succession of battles, the space between each filled up with the capture of fallen

cities, and balls and love-making in friendly ones,
such as make the history of the war among the
green sierras of Spain so favourite a theme for
fiction and romance; but nothing save an eternal
cannonading from the dawn of one day to the
dawn of another; nothing but months dragging
away one after another, seeing horses and men
dying off by scores.

The weary inactivity of the siege, which weighed
down even the lightest hearts before Sebastopol, was
but one long torture to De Vigne, who longed for
danger and excitement as the sole anodyne to a
passion which pursued him as the Furies pursued
Orestes; while Sabretasche, the most luxurious
of voluptuaries, bore uncomplainingly the mise-
ries of that Crimean winter. The wild Chersonese hurricane turned him out at night, shelter-
less, to the full fury of the storm; his food
was such as at home he would have forbidden to
be given to his Newfoundland* dog; his servant had to fight with another for some scanty
brushwood to light his fire; loathsome centi-
pedes crawled over his very bed; he had to
wade through mud, and rain, and filth, over paths
marked out by the sick and dying fallen by the
roadside, with the carrion birds whirling aloft over
the spot where the corpses lay. Yet I never heard

him utter a complaint, except, indeed, when he
turned to me with a smile :

'How horrible it is, Arthur, not to be able to
wash one's hands!'

One night, just before we were ordered into
Balaklava, a friend of his who was staying on board
one of the vessels in the harbour was dining with
him—De Vigne, a French colonel of cavalry,
whom Sabretasche had known in Paris, a man of
the —th Lancers, and myself, making up the
party. All of us thought of the Colonel's charming dinners in Park Lane as we sat down to this,
the best money could procure, and miraculously
luxurious for the Crimea—a turkey, some preserved beef, and a little jam, with some brandy
and whisky, for which his man had paid a price
you would not believe, if I recorded it parole
d'honneur.

'I am equally glad to see you, Carlton,' said
Sabretasche, ' but I'm afraid I can't entertain you
quite so well as I did in Park Lane. *Il faut
manger pour vivre*, else I fancy you would hardly
be inclined to touch much of anything we can
give you in the Crimea.'

'The deuce, Sabretasche! we have what we
care for;—our Amphitryon,' said Carlton. 'I
wonder when we shall have you back among us?

I say, you're quite a hero, De Vigne, in England. Lady Puffdoff and scores of your old loves are gone mad about you, and have been working their snowy fingers to the bone over all sorts of wool things for you and the rest of the Dashers, that are now tumbling about in the holds, and will rot in Balaklava harbour, I suppose, till the hot weather comes.'

'Hero! Bosh!' said De Vigne, with his most contemptuous sneer. 'If the people at home would just believe the men are dying away here, more than three thousand sick in camp, and would provide for them with just a little common practical sense, they'd do us more service than by writing ballads about us, and showering epithets on us that they'll forget in twelve months' time, when they are running after some new hobby.'

(De Vigne spoke prophetically!)

'But you like campaigning, though you rough it, old fellow?' asked Carlton.

'By George! I should say so! If I were a medical man, and had to deal with hypochondriacs, frenzied poets, nervous *littérateurs*, or worn-out public men, I would send them all off to active service. Boot and Saddle would soon have all the nonsense out of them, and send them back much healthier and better fellows. Campaigning is the only thing to put a dash of cayenne pepper into the soup of life.'

'Our cayenne gets rather damped here,' smiled Sabretasche. 'I confess I miss my "Times," my reading-chair, my periodicals, my papers, my club—the "sweet shady side of Pall Mall;"— above all, Society. All these are great *agrémens* of life.'

'But confess, Colonel, you're less fastidious and less dandified,' asked De Vigne.

'I never was a dandy. I dress well, of course; any man of good taste does by instinct. As for fastidiousness, I manage with a shirt a week in the Crimea, because I can't have more; but I shall have two per diem again as soon as ever I go back. I let my beard grow here because I have no time to have it shaved; but I shall have it very gladly cut to a decent length as soon as I rejoice in a decent valet!'

'Nonsense! What are shirts or beards, compared with the *verve*, the excitement, the reality of active service?'

'Certainly nothing! If our days here were all twenty-fifths of October, they would be delightful,' said Sabretasche, with that sad smile which, when he exerted himself to be cheerful, showed how painful and unreal the effort was. 'All I say is, that I *do* prefer an Auxerre carpet to this extremely perilous mud; that I do like much better to have hot water and almond soap, to being only able to wash my hands at very distant intervals; and it would be ridiculous to pretend that I don't think a dinner at the Star and Garter more palatable than this tough turkey; nor my usual toilette more agreeable than these ragged and nondescript garments?'

'And yet one has never heard a word of complaint from that fellow from our first bivouac till now!' said De Vigne to Carlton.

'*Cui bono?*' smiled Sabretasche. 'It all comes in the fortune of war. Besides, there is not a murmur heard out here; the Dashers will hardly set the example! Come, Carlton, you have not told us half the news.'

Carlton told us plenty of news; of marriages and deaths; intrigues of the boudoir and the cabinet; of who had won the Grand Military, and who was favourite for the Cesarewitch; of how Dunbar had married Ela Ashburnham, and Jack Mortimer's wife run away with his groom; of how Fitzturf had been outlawed for seventy-thousand, and Monteith made a pot of money at the October meetings; of all the odds and ends of the chat, *on dits*, scandals, and gossip he had brought from the lobby, the clubs, and the draw-ing-rooms.

'I say, De Vigne,' said he, at the last, 'do you remember that bewitching Little Tressillian, who was at a ball in Lowndes Square, and whom all the men went so mad about? You knew her very well, though, didn't you?'

Carlton had never heard much of the intimacy between De Vigne and Alma, and never guessed on what ground he trod; by the feeble lamplight I could see De Vigne's face grow crimson with the blood that leapt into it.

'What of her?'

Carlton never noticed the chill stern tone of those brief words, hissed rather than spoken be-tween his set teeth.

'What of her? Only that people say she le-vanted with that cursed fool, Castleton. I pity her if she did! I fancy it's true, too, because as I came through Paris—where I know he is—on my way here, I saw her in a carriage in the Champs Elysées that was waiting at a door, a very dashing carriage, too. I didn't know her enough to speak to her, but I recognized her in a second—it's a face you can't forget. I should have thought she'd been a cut above that, wouldn't you? But, women are all alike.'

De Vigne sat quite still without moving a muscle, but I saw in his face the death-like pallor I had seen there on his marriage-day. Happily for him, at that moment an orderly came to the door with a despatch from head-quarters to Sabretasche, and De Vigne, rising, bid us good night, and went out into the storm of pitiless, drenching, driving rain to seek his own tent.

The next morning a mail came in: there were some letters from Violet, by the flush that rose on the Colonel's impassive face as he received his epistles, and there were more than a dozen for De Vigne, some from men who really liked him, some from Leila Puffdoff, and women who liked to write to one of the most distinguished men of the famous Light Brigade. He read them *pour s'amuser*. The last he took up, struck him keener than a sabre's thrust—it was in Alma's handwriting. Twenty-four hours before he would have seized it, hoping against hope for an explanation of that mystery which had robbed him so strangely and suddenly of her. But now, sceptical of all good, credulous of all evil, he never for a moment doubted, or dreamed of doubting, Carlton's story. Circumstantial evidence damned her, and with that insane haste which had cost him so much all his life long, without waiting or pausing, allowing her no

justice, no hearing, he tore her letter open, then
flung it from him, with an oath, as he saw its
heading, ' No. —, Champs Elysées, Paris.'   It was
confirmation only too strong of Carlton's tale for
him to doubt it.

' He has deserted her, and she turns to me to be-
fool me a second time !' was his madman's thought
as he flung her letter from him ; then resealed without reading it, and directed it back to her before his
purpose should fail him. So, in our madness, we fling
our better fate, happiness away ! One letter still re-
mained unread, indeed unnoticed, which De Vigne
never saw until he took it up to light his pipe late
that night; then he opened it mechanically, glanced
to the last line, and found the signature was that
of the valet whom he had discharged for reading
Alma's note in Wilton Crescent : ' A begging-
letter, of course,' he thought, too heart-sick with
his own thoughts to pay more heed to it, as he
struck a match, held it in the flame, and lighted
his meerchaum with it.

So we throw aside, as valueless cards, the honours life deals us in its uncertain whist !

END OF VOL. II.

LONDON : PRINTED BY W. CLOWES AND SONS, STAMFORD STREET,
AND CHARING CROSS.

www.ingramcontent.com/pod-product-compliance
Lightning Source LLC
Chambersburg PA
CBHW060542030726
47498CB00004B/1287